BIRTH
OF THE
BACCHAE

IMMORTAL RELICS: BOOK 1

STEPHANIE MIRRO

TANNHAUSER PRESS

Visit stephaniemirro.com for more information.

Cover design by TS95Studios

Published by Tannhauser Press
tannhauserpress.com

ISBN: 978-1-945994-45-6
First Edition: June 2019

10 9 8 7 6 5 4 3 2 1

ALSO BY STEPHANIE MIRRO

IMMORTAL RELICS
Her Majesty's Fury

COLLECTIONS
The Outsiders: An Hourlings Anthology

For Lincoln and Tenley.
It's never too late to follow your dreams.

CHAPTER 1

Serafina

Blood soaked through the dirt. At least, that's what it looked like at first. Sera's pulse quickened as she carefully swept dirt off the item buried beneath the soil. A dark crimson pendant attached to a chain appeared before her. She used her soft-bristle brush to clear the area around the necklace until she was certain it was on its own.

Oh my god...

Sera stared at the artifact, holding her breath as if she might blow it away. Her heart pounded like a drum.

Despite Chad's warning not to waste her time, she had picked the zone she was digging in with a sense of purpose, knowing the other sites around the ancient Roman temple's altar would have long since been looted. She'd expected to find common pottery shards along the temple's sidewall, where niches were often found in excavations. But a silver necklace with what appeared to be a ruby a little bigger than a quarter? Never in a million years.

Knowing she shouldn't touch it with her bare hands but unable to resist, Sera ran a fingertip along the chain to the gemstone. It drew her in like a mythical Siren calling from her treacherous shore.

Serafina...

"Holy shit!" Nora's voice over her shoulder sliced through the enchantment, making her jump. Nora knelt next to Sera, green eyes wide as she stared at the artifact. "Is that a necklace?"

"Okay, good. You see it, too," Sera said, still not quite trusting her vision.

Blonde curls bounced as Nora laughed. "It's not a ghost. Of course I see it." She turned around, still on her knees. "Hey, Chad! Come see what Sera found."

Sera's heart sank at the thought of sharing her find with Chad and the rest of the crew. Eventually, he would see it, of course. It wasn't like she could just pocket it and walk away, but she wanted more time alone with it first, to study the amulet—yes, that was the right word for it. *Amulet.* Certainty settled over her, like the word had been implanted in her mind. She knew, beyond a shadow of a doubt, that protection was its purpose. Of what, she hadn't a clue.

"Did you find some shards like we—" Chad stopped short, his jaw dropping as he caught sight of the amulet. He recovered quickly as other members of the team wandered over. Word of the amulet spread like wildfire, and Sera found herself surrounded by the entire crew within moments.

As excited chatter buzzed in her ears, Sera's breath grew shallow and her vision hazy. The amulet swam before her eyes as she attempted to calm herself. An intense desire screamed at her to grab the artifact and run far away as fast as possible. It *wanted* her to take it. To have it. The irresistible force drew her hand toward the amulet and—

"Hey, girl, you okay? Your skin is pastier than normal." Nora's face appeared in front of her. "Everyone step back. Sera needs some space."

A breeze swept back strands of her hair as the crew complied. Sera closed her eyes and filled her lungs with the Italian air, her heart slowing its racing cadence.

"Let's get her into some shade before she passes out. It's not every day the team makes the discovery of a lifetime," Chad said.

The *team?* Sera's eyes snapped open at his choice of words. He raised an eyebrow, almost daring her to correct him. But of course, she wouldn't. She would avoid the confrontation, as usual.

"Josh, you and Lauren start recording the location of the necklace," he said.

She did a double take. He was assigning *undergrads* to a find of this magnitude?

"I feel better now. I'll work on the amulet," she said shakily as Nora helped her to her feet.

Chad's eyebrows pulled together. "The what?"

"It's an amulet. It's here to protect the temple." She did her best not to cringe from his glare as she explained.

"It sure did a piss-poor job." Nora snorted.

"Let's not get ahead of ourselves. You're going to rest." He turned around. "Back to work, everyone. We'll have time to gawk at the pretty necklace later."

Sera frowned as he casually dismissed her and walked away. World-renowned archaeologist Dr. Charles Lambert—Chad, as he preferred to be called by students—made significant advancements in remote sensing technology in the last decade, sending his career skyrocketing. The college's archaeology department had been using his new methodology last year when they discovered the buried temple in Campania, Italy.

After requesting to lead their excavation this summer, Chad had agreed to return to the university as a visiting scholar for the next school year, much to the excitement of the entire archaeology department. At just under forty, the man was beginning to show signs of his age with salt-and-pepper hair and reading glasses. According to Sera's best friend Nora, he also happened to be the star of almost every female student's romantic fantasies. His bachelor status only added fuel to the flame.

For the most part, Sera found him to be charming, witty, and good-looking. But as she remembered some of his more suggestive comments and inappropriate touches over the summer, her nose scrunched up. She had a feeling he was single for other, less attractive reasons than just not having found the right woman. Much to her annoyance, trying to be polite and not rock the boat somehow meant he didn't get the hint she wasn't interested.

Even now she caught a glimpse of his true, petty colors as he referenced taking credit for the find away from her. More than once that summer, he'd hinted that he could use his celebrity-like status in the archaeological world to make or break their careers after graduate school. Most of the students thought his influence was awesome, practically lining up for autographs. Not Sera. In fact, it wouldn't be a total surprise if she bruised his ego by ignoring his directions about where to dig and then making a career-altering discovery. After today, it looked like he might try to break her career.

Even though Nora often said Sera and her boyfriend Hiro were made for each other, she thought Sera was crazy for not being absolutely gaga over Chad.

If only she knew the full truth about his behavior.

"I'm totally taking advantage of your fainting spell to take a break myself," Nora said as she sat in the sparse grass beneath a pine tree. The parasol-shaped trees littered the rolling hills around the site.

It wasn't unusual to still be friends with the same people from elementary school. But it was far less common to share similar interests all the way through college. Serafina and Eleanor had formed a lifelong bond the moment they met in their Li'l Archaeologists summer program, despite being opposites in just about every way. Nora was the light to her dark—blonde and outgoing next to brunette and reserved.

Sitting next to her, Sera scoffed. "I didn't faint."

"I wouldn't have blamed you. Did you see the size of that ruby? It was a ruby, right?"

Josh and Lauren's animated conversation as they took measurements and recorded data sparked a fire in the pit of Sera's stomach. It wasn't like her to be so possessive over a find, but she couldn't help the jealousy that burned inside, especially because she couldn't hear what they were saying about the amulet. Chad walked over to the pretty blonde undergrad and said something that made her laugh as she placed a hand on the man's arm. Rolling her eyes, Sera dropped her gaze.

"That or some kind of glass bead or lesser gemstone made to look like a ruby. It's hard to tell while it's still in the dirt." Sera gulped half of her water bottle, choking on the last bit as it went down the wrong tube.

Nora gave her a few hard pats on the shoulder to help clear her airway. Sera waved her away as she coughed. It was hardly the first time she needed rescuing while doing something as simple as drinking water. Being the opposite of graceful came with risks.

"Didn't Chad tell you not to dig in that area? I'll bet he's kicking himself so hard right now." Nora laughed, leaning against the tree.

Unease roiled in her belly as she glanced over at the man, still chatting with Lauren. "Not too hard, hopefully. He might not give me credit for the find if I've gone and hurt his feelings."

"He wouldn't do that." Nora shook her head, brushing loose dirt off her pants as she stood. "I know you have something weird against him, but he's really a good guy."

Sera kept her mouth shut as Nora returned to her tools on the exposed temple floor, the only part of the ancient structure left besides the wall built into the side of the hill. Sera had tried to tell her about the interactions, but her best friend had the man up on a pedestal. It wasn't completely out of the ordinary for Sera's imagination to get the best of her, and Nora had brushed off the comments as if that were the case.

Because she normally enjoyed attention from most of the male population, it infuriated and motivated Nora that Chad didn't seem to notice her interest. Sera had already mentioned her boyfriend to the guy more than once and pointed out her friend's hard work and dazzling personality. He just didn't seem to get it. Or more likely, he just didn't care.

Over the summer, she had reluctantly come to the conclusion that women who didn't fawn over him excited Chad—but also angered him. Shivers ran up her spine as she remembered his clenched jaw when she brushed him off the last time. She hadn't disclosed everything to Nora yet because she didn't want to admit her thoughts out loud and make them a reality. Besides, the summer was almost over and she wouldn't have to see him again for at least a few weeks. No sense in stirring up trouble.

What would I even say, anyway? Hey, Chad keeps flirting with me and it's annoying? Yeah, like that would go over well. Nora would kill to have the man's attention on her.

A breeze swept through and rustled the tall grasses surrounding the excavation site on the Campanian hillside. The sweet smell of lavender, prolific in the nearby village, mixed with the musty scent she loved from the overturned dirt. Mounds of earth removed from the buried temple sat not far from the site, waiting to be replaced when the summer ended.

It was moments like these that reminded Sera how happy she was to be following in her mother's footsteps. If only her mother had lived to see it.

A half hour later, she joined Josh and Lauren to provide oversight as they carefully removed the amulet from the ground and prepared it for transportation. The amulet would be stored in a box and cushioned with foam for the drive back to the hotel, where it would be locked up in the safe.

"This is the last of it for today." Chad's voice echoed across the valley. The shadows grew long as the team wrapped up, the sun beginning its final descent toward the hills.

After placing the amulet's box inside the van, Sera straightened, wincing when her back resisted. It had been a long day. A tug pulled at her heart as she watched the van pull away. They didn't have a lab set up at the hotel for proper cleaning of the amulet, but she hoped to spend more time studying it before the Italian government came knocking at their door. Fat chance.

An image of the bright red gem flashed through her mind. Sera thought she'd gone crazy when the glint of metal in the dirt caught her eye. It seemed improbable, even impossible, something so valuable had simply been left behind when almost nothing else could be found in the temple, not even the columns that had once stood as tall as giants. She must've gotten lucky. Goosebumps ran up her arms.

"You ready?" Nora asked.

Her sudden appearance made Sera jump. "Shit, Nor!"

"That never gets old."

Never for Nora, anyway. Her petite five-foot frame made it easy to slink around and stay out of peripheral vision, and she knew it, too. Nora loved to see how long she could glean information or stand there without anyone noticing.

Grabbing their packs, faded from summers in the sun, the two women followed the van toward the village. Crickets started their evening song as the sun's glow washed over the village rooftops. Locals nodded at them as they passed on the cobblestone streets, shops and restaurants now open for the evening following the afternoon siesta. The smell of freshly baked bread and browning meats wafted out the door of Sera's favorite pizza place, setting her stomach growling.

It was a short walk to the old-world hotel, but entirely uphill. Both women collapsed onto the white steps leading up to the building's front porch. Sera tucked her bag under her head and closed her eyes, relaxing in the few moments of peace before they needed to go inside.

"Something about this summer feels different," Nora said.

Sera cracked one eye to peek at Nora. She was sitting up, gazing back down the valley toward their dig site. "Different how?"

"Final somehow. Like it's closing out a chapter in our lives."

Groaning as her sore muscles resisted, Sera pulled herself back to sitting. "I mean, it kind of is. We'll be moving on to a new site next summer. Another fresh crop of grad students will take over here. I'm sure they'll be excited to see if there were any other valuables left behind."

Nora nodded, but her expression remained thoughtful and distant. "Or pissed they weren't here this year." She winked as she used Sera's shoulder to push up to her feet. "I'll meet you upstairs. I get first dibs on the shower."

Leaning back onto one of the columns that supported the Romanesque hotel, Sera stretched out her legs in front of her, still ivory-skinned despite her best efforts with the

Italian sun. Something felt different that summer, for sure, but she attributed it to making such a rare discovery. If anything, her chapter was just beginning.

Taking one last look over the rolling hills and picturesque landscape, she got to her feet and followed her friend inside.

* * *

Later that evening, ancient-looking sconces lit the dining hall, their warm glow illuminating local artists' paintings of the village and surrounding countryside hanging on the walls. The room was just large enough to hold their entire crew, including the handful of Italian workers.

Dinner in Italy is an event. Not the typical microwaveable meal, cell phone in hand, kind of dinner Sera was used to back home in America. In Italy, dinner is a time to gather together to enjoy food, family, and wine, sometimes lasting long into the night. Tonight was such a night, although the amulet was all anyone could talk about. Plates half-filled with pasta sat forgotten as hurried voices spoke with excitement about the rare find.

Sera found herself bombarded by questions from just about everyone, particularly the undergraduate students, as if she had all of the answers already.

"How did you know to dig along the wall?" Lauren brushed some of her dark blonde hair behind her ears as she leaned forward onto the table.

"Past excavations have shown that the walls often had niches for things like candles, incense, and amphoras. Looters usually focus on areas they think are most important, like the altars." She avoided looking at Chad, the so-called expert, who had specifically directed the team to focus on the area around the altar despite her recommendations otherwise.

After downing the rest of her third glass of wine, Sera excused herself from the table before any more questions could be directed her way. She wished she'd followed through with her original plan to skip dinner and work on her dig notes instead.

Halfway up the stairs, she lost her balance on the top step and crashed to the floor. The world spun around as she pulled herself to her feet, giggling. Thankfully, no one was around to see her inebriated state. Although, to be fair, it wasn't much different from her everyday, awkward self.

Three glasses of wine wasn't normal for Sera. Hell, wine itself wasn't her thing. She preferred a wine cooler or some other fruity mix to the full-bodied drink she'd had tonight. But she hadn't gotten a chance to see the amulet again, and drowning her sorrows the fastest way seemed like a good idea. The wine turned out to be quite tasty, too.

After climbing into bed, Sera's imagination ran wild in the dark. Just how old was this amulet? Would it make her famous? Who did it belong to? Why was it left behind when all the other valuables were long gone?

This research paper is going to write itself… Mom would have been so proud.

Wine-fueled sleep came quickly, but the night ahead was restless.

* * *

"Are you scared, Tavia?" Liviana asked.

As she finished lacing up the back of her older sister's white dress, Liviana paused, her hand resting at the top, her heart filled with warmth and pride. It was a special dress, sewn with care and reserved just for that night. She and her sister had sewn it together, giggling over the needles and threads as they wondered what the night would have in store for Octavia. Neither of them had been invited to the Bacchanalia festivities before, and those who returned never spoke about it. Nor about those who didn't return at all.

"Not at all. I'm excited to finally learn what all this secretive nonsense is about." Octavia double-checked her hair in the hand mirror, securing an errant strand back into her braid.

Liviana gasped at the disrespectful comment. "Tavia! It's not nonsense."

Octavia rolled her eyes. "Someday you'll learn that adults make a big deal out of a lot of little things." She tapped Liviana on the nose before leaving their bedroom.

Liviana followed her sister out to the open-air atrium of their villa, where they met with their parents. The lamps had already been lit as the day turned to dusk.

"It's time, Octavia." Father glanced out the open roof at the red sky. "Let us hope that Bacchus shows you favor."

Wiping away her streaming tears with a handkerchief, Mother held their baby brother in the other arm.

"Come now, Agathe, this is no time for weeping." Father's tone held a softness despite his frown.

"I know. But may Bacchus grant us favor and let you return." Mother tenderly touched Octavia's face.

After kissing Mother's hand, Octavia pulled a cloak around her own shoulders. She picked up the lantern by the door and followed Father outside, casting one last smile over her shoulder. In the distance, flickering lights from the temple sconces illuminated the hill on which the ancient building sat.

Liviana's heart clenched as the door shut behind her sister.

* * *

The next day, Sera wiped the sweat from her brow with the back of her dirt-stained hand as the group gathered beside the dig site. The summer had reached its end, and the team spent the day making last-minute notes and preparing the site for next year. Despite the lack of digging, it was an equally exhausting day as any other as they ran from task to task.

Looks like rain tonight, Sera thought, eyeing the grey clouds brewing on the horizon. *Angry rain.* She shivered. The details were fuzzy, but that damn dream about the two girls had left her with a sense of foreboding that hadn't left her all day.

"All right, attention here please." Chad's voice interrupted the chatter. "This was an amazing year. I'm impressed with your work this summer. The Italian government should be pleased—we've made some incredible finds, especially the artifact Serafina discovered. I'm sure we're all eagerly awaiting that report."

He grinned in Sera's direction, receiving only a groan in return. Everyone laughed, understanding the feeling all too well. Or at least in part. Chad would be the first to review her report, and there was no way to know what information he would change. Her nostrils flared at the idea of needing to suck up to him later if he tried to take more credit than he deserved for the find.

"I want to thank you all for your hard work and dedication to this dig." Chad paused as a boom of thunder sounded in the distance. "Go get cleaned up and ready for dinner before the rain starts. We'll meet in the dining hall in one hour." He clapped his hands to release the team.

The group gave a half-hearted cheer, exhaustion starting to settle in as they rested in the shade.

"Doesn't he look so hot right now?" Nora nodded toward Chad, who was directing the Italian workers to use mounds of earth to backfill the temple their team had just spent all summer digging out.

Sera drained her water bottle and licked her lips to catch the last drops, tasting salty sweat and dirt. Always dirt. At least she didn't choke that time.

"I'll admit he's a good-looking man, Nor," Sera agreed, somewhat relieved Chad had acknowledged it was her find. For now.

* * *

That evening, the dining tables had been pushed together to make one long one, and wine flowed in abundance. The rain beat a steady rhythm against the windows of the hotel as the crew ate and drank. From time to time, thunder joined the rain's chorus with a resounding clash, as if the gods battled for attention.

Most of the team had already left the table, retiring to the library or heading upstairs for much-needed rest. Staying behind to finish yet another glass of wine, Sera and Nora were too excited about the start of their beach trip the next day to consider sleep. Chad and Claudio, the owner of the hotel, smoked cigars to celebrate the end of a successful summer. The strong tobacco scent drifted under Sera's nose each time one of the men took a drag.

"I've been reaching out to peers of mine regarding the necklace. I'm getting the sense from them it's a once in a lifetime type of find. Or even once in a few lifetimes. This could really launch your career, Serafina." Chad swirled the wine around in his glass before lifting it to his lips again. His eyes remained fixed on her.

"Honestly, I just can't wait to see it fully cleaned. From what I could make out yesterday, both the chain and the stone had intricate design details." Her stomach clenched from the unwanted attention, and she looked down at her own glass.

The red hue of the wine reminded Sera of the amulet— a deep burgundy that undulated when she turned it as if there was liquid inside. She'd only gotten another brief look when they packed the amulet away, but the shifting color told her it might not be a ruby like some of the others thought.

An odd sensation floated through Sera's mind, like a fuzzy image tickling the outer reaches of her memory.

2484…

The code to the hotel's safe. Her gaze clouded over as she tried to remember how she knew it. She must have seen Chad enter the numbers when they unpacked the van. That was the only explanation. Maybe after everyone went to sleep, she could slip down and—

The sound of glass shattering made Sera jump. Someone in the kitchen muttered a curse, followed by clinking shards. Taking a deep breath, she took a sip of wine, pushing her previous thoughts away. The dream still had her on edge. She wouldn't risk her scholarship money on getting another glimpse of the amulet.

"Leave it to the girls to worry about how 'pretty' the necklace is." Chad smirked, wisps of smoke curling around his lips.

Almost forgetting their conversation, Sera's cheeks flushed in embarrassment.

"Don't be such an ass, *Dr. Lambert,*" Nora said with a slur.

Sera's head snapped to the side to look at her friend. If she was brazen before alcohol's assistance, she became even more so after a few drinks. It was time to get her up to bed before she could embarrass herself or, worse, try to get herself into bed with Chad.

He waved his hand in dismissal, giving Sera a wink. "Oh, it'll be pretty all right, much like the girl who dug it up."

Claudio chuckled and raised his cigar like a toast in agreement.

"And that's our cue." Sera got to her feet, pulling her resistant friend along with her. She had no intention of letting Chad continue his commentary.

"Buona sera," the hotelier called out as the two women left the room. Chad said something under his breath to the man, and they both burst out laughing.

"Why, I never!" Nora tried unsuccessfully to pull her arm away to charge back into the dining room.

"Let it go, Nor. They're acting like chauvinist pigs. We're better than that." Sera continued to drag her up the stairs. She opened the door to their room and pushed Nora inside.

"It's *so* annoying that he's still *so* hot even when he's being a prick," Nora whined as she threw herself onto her bed.

Sera kicked off her flats and tucked them under her bed. "I don't find anyone attractive when they act like that."

Afraid she may have offended her friend when she didn't respond, Sera turned back around to find Nora's eyes closed. Soft snores purred beneath the tousled blonde curls covering her face.

Sera shook her head wistfully at the idea of falling asleep with such little effort.

Opening the door to the balcony and walking under the awning, Sera watched the rain fall like a sheet across the rolling hills whenever lightning lit up the sky. The musky smell of the wet countryside filled the air. Rain always reminded Sera of her mother, and she missed her more when it rained. Unlike her friends' mothers, who kept them inside during a storm, Sera's mother would grab her by the hand and dance with her in the mud-filled puddles. They would raise their arms to the sky and make up silly chants as they welcomed sweet relief on stifling summer days.

Normally, Sera would bask in the energy that came with the battering rain, the rolling thunder, and the crackling lightning. But tonight was different—tonight it felt ominous. Like a raging storm was looming on the horizon of her life. She shivered and closed the door, drawing the curtains to shut it out.

CHAPTER 2

Serafina

*T*he stars were just beginning to fade when her sister finally returned home. Liviana sat up in bed when Octavia stumbled in, but she barely recognized her in the predawn light.

Having come loose, Octavia's immaculately braided hair flew in all directions, and mud caked the hem of her once-white dress. Only one shoe appeared to make it back. Her cloak trailed behind her in one hand until she let it drop onto the floor of their bedroom.

"Tavia," Liviana whispered, fearful that her sister was injured. "What happened?"

Octavia smiled dreamily despite her ragged appearance. "I can't wait for you to find out next year." Climbing into their shared bed, she wrapped her arms around Liviana's waist, warm breath tickling her neck. "You smell delicious."

"You smell absolutely horrid," Liviana said, catching a trace of a wet, earthy smell. That and some other primal scent she couldn't identify. She was confused but relieved at her sister's return. Light snores were her only reply.

Sleep eluded Liviana as she tried to imagine what had caused her sister to return in such a state. She couldn't wait to hear the story.

Liviana snuck out an hour later, finally giving up on falling asleep, and let her sister get some much-needed rest. It wasn't until early afternoon that Octavia finally emerged from their room.

"Gods, I have such a headache." Putting both hands to her head, her elbows thumped on the kitchen table as she sat.

Liviana placed a cup of wine, which she had watered down a little more than usual, in front of her sister.

"Are you going to tell me what happened?" she asked, taking a seat.

"Don't be absurd. I'm sworn to secrecy," Octavia said haughtily, reaching for the cup. Pausing mid-reach, a puzzled look came over her face. She lifted her head and sniffed the air like a cat. Her eyes grew wide as Father came in with a slab of the venison they'd be preparing for dinner that night.

Confused at the odd behavior, Liviana's eyebrows pulled together.

Knocking over her chair in a rush, Octavia stumbled her way over to the raw meat. She grabbed a chunk of the animal flesh with her bare hands and shoved it into her mouth without hesitation. Blood dripped down her face and arms.

"Octavia, what are—" Father started to yell, but he was cut off by their mother's scream.

"No! No, tell me it's not true," Mother cried out as she ran over to her eldest daughter. She cupped Octavia's blood-stained face in her *hands and searched Octavia's eyes, ignoring the blood that now dripped down her arms.*

"He's chosen you."

Red lips curled up in response. Octavia wiped her mouth with the back of her hand, leaving behind a crimson streak as Mother dropped her trembling hands and backed away.

"Why have you returned?" Mother asked.

"You know I don't like to follow the rules."

"How did you get in?"

Octavia gazed at her bloody hand. "The change hasn't solidified yet."

The change? Liviana frowned, wanting to know more.

"So be it then." Mother turned to leave the house, a hand covering her mouth as she shook her head. A moment later her wailing echoed from the yard.

"Gather what things you can and return to the temple. You shouldn't have come back here." Father's voice was strained.

He looked to Liviana. "Come with me, Livy."

"But—"

"Don't argue, Liviana. We're not safe here." He took her arm and dragged her forcefully to the door.

Liviana looked over her shoulder. Octavia was slowly licking the blood off her fingers, oblivious to their departure.

* * *

"It's just so weird, Nor." Sera scrunched up her nose as she put the sparkly blue dress back on the rack and continued to flip through hangers. "I know I've dreamt about this Liviana girl before. But now the dreams feel so real, like flashbacks to a previous life. Ancient Roman times or something."

She wasn't in the mood for shopping, and she really didn't like sparkles. After school started back up two months ago—and through some unknown miracle—the Italian government had approved the university's request to bring the amulet back to American soil for the initial research phase. It wasn't completely unheard of, especially considering Chad's connections, but their chances of success with such a valuable find seemed impossible. "Magic must have been involved," became the joke around the department.

As a doctoral candidate and the one who had discovered it, Sera had been given the honors of deep cleaning, recording, and researching the amulet once it arrived on campus. To celebrate the finding, the university, Smithsonian, and Italian embassy put together a special exhibit of Roman antiquities featuring the Bacchic amulet. A gala at the National Portrait Gallery would introduce the exhibit, and Sera had been selected to present her research. It was a dream come true. And terrifying.

Then the realization had hit that the gala—which was now only two nights away and just before Halloween— brought her even closer to the Bacchic amulet's return to Italy at the start of the new year. The thought of the amulet being so far away weighed on her heart and made shopping difficult to focus on. She spent every waking moment thinking about the damn thing, and it'd even invaded her dreams.

An image of the impeccably carved, pinecone-shaped gemstone seared through her mind as if she still looked through a microscope. The vial of blood had been artfully hidden within its depths but gave the entire stone a reddish hue like a ruby. Even the silver chain with its filigree grape leaves was a work of wonder. Flawless.

"It's just a dream, babe. You're probably stressed about talking at the gala." Nora's voice drifted out from behind the changing curtain. "Okay, what do you think about this one?" She emerged before Sera could point out the dreams started in Italy, long before the gala was planned.

Nora wore a black gown with a plunging neckline, snug in all the right places. It contrasted rather elegantly with her blonde bob and fair skin. Her inner Marilyn Monroe, a lifelong idol, shone through. She put her hands on her hips as she turned around to look at the back of the dress in the mirror.

They had taken the Metro to the Tysons Corner mall to partake in a day of bargain shopping. At least, that's what Nora had called it. It wasn't quite as "bargain" as Sera hoped for, nor would the majority of Americans consider a hundred dollars or more on a dress bargain shopping. But it was better than the multitude of designer stores D.C.—the District, as it is now commonly named—had to offer, and Nora simply didn't "do" thrift stores.

"I think you're going to get a lot of attention. But, it's you." Wishing she had the confidence to wear something so dramatic, Sera held in a sigh. No one liked a pity party.

"I know, right?" Nora smiled at her own reflection.

As they paid for their selected gowns, Sera's grumbling stomach announced it was lunchtime. She had chosen a deep blue, non-sparkly gown in the end, a color Nora swore up and down complemented her grey eyes and dark hair best.

"Mall food is the work of the devil, but your tummy's right. I'm famished," Nora said as she took the garment bag from the cashier.

Sera eyeballed her own bag with pursed lips. "I don't know about this dress. The price was a bit higher than I wanted to spend. Should we look somewhere else?" The idea of spending money on something she'd likely only wear once almost made her sick to her stomach. Growing up in a house where bills could go unpaid for weeks, if not months, had that effect. Maybe she could wear it again to a wedding.

"Nonsense. It's beautiful, and you're worth it." Nora took her by the hand and led them out of the store before she could argue. "I think Dr. Davis is out to get me," she said about one of their professors, then raised an eyebrow at Sera. "What's wrong?"

"I don't know, I just feel…weird." She stopped walking, trying to identify the feeling that had come over her. Her hands had gone clammy, her heart had leaped into her throat, and she had that impending doom sensation something terrible was sneaking up on her from behind.

Instead of turning around, Sera looked across the open courtyard where two men stood behind the railing on the other side. Something about them didn't sit quite right with her, but she couldn't put a finger on it. One wore a black jacket and leaned on the railing, sporting a round belly and chubby cheeks. Blond curls rivaled Nora's. The other stood poised at a height several inches taller than his companion, but hard muscles could easily be seen under the dark brown skin of his arms. They were staring at Sera and Nora with open interest.

"Do you see those two guys? I think they're watching us." Super obviously, too. The hairs on the back of her neck stood on end, making her skin prickle.

A sinister sneer crossed the blond one's face as he commented to the other.

Nora turned to look, a smile perking up her face when she saw them. "Oh yes, I sure do see that incredibly handsome man and his friend." She purred like a cat. "Let's go say hello." Grabbing Sera's arm before she could protest, Nora led them toward the upper-level bridge that connected to the other side of the mall.

Halfway across, Sera let out a yelp as strong arms wrapped around her from behind, causing her to drop and spill her purse contents across the floor.

"It's me." Hiro's voice laughed in her ear.

Spinning around to face him, she pushed him away, placing a hand over her thumping heart. "Holy shit, Hiro!"

Despite the fear coursing through her veins, she couldn't help the flutter that whirled through her stomach in her boyfriend's presence. His natural olive-toned skin complemented his black hair and dark brown eyes beautifully. After pushing his glasses back up his nose, he flashed white teeth as he grinned. He was such a nerd, but he was *her* nerd.

"Aww, don't be mad." Pulling her back into his chest, he kissed the top of her head. "Nora told me where you guys would be, and I couldn't resist seeing you today."

Sera inhaled his familiar scent as she hugged him, her heartbeat returning to its normal pace as she practically melted into the safety of his arms. Hiro was the type of boyfriend who made every moment special. Maybe it was due to his experience working as a resident in the hospital's oncology ward, seeing firsthand how precious life was. Or maybe he was just wired that way.

When they missed their second anniversary thanks to her summer dig, he'd sent a care package of some of her favorite things. Sometimes she thought she didn't deserve him because she usually prioritized her research above him, but she didn't plan on letting him go anytime soon.

"I think I got everything." Standing back up, Nora adjusted her off-the-shoulder shirt before handing over the dropped purse. "Let's go get some men."

"I already have a man, thank you very much." Interlacing her fingers with Hiro's, she looked over to where the men had stood before and breathed a sigh of relief. They were gone. "Sorry to burst your bubble, but it looks like they left. Guess they're not into clumsy girls."

Nora stuck out her bottom lip in a pout. "Well, *I'm* certainly not clumsy."

They continued on to the food court, returning to the topic of dreams. Nora mentioned visiting a psychic friend of her mom's, and Sera soon forgot about the two mystery men altogether.

* * *

Solomon

"The amulet! It has been found!" Lorenzo exclaimed in his thick Italian accent as he ended the call on his cell phone.

Solomon wondered if his maker had to practice to keep the inflection after all these years. The Immortal certainly fit the Italian stereotype, from his slicked-back hair down to his leather loafers. Not that Lorenzo cared.

"Where?" The leather chair groaned as he leaned forward. They had been looking for the elusive relic for the past two decades.

Lorenzo smirked. "A temple near Salerno. Ironically, the temple where Danae had once been a priestess. The god thinks he is so clever." He wagged a finger as he rose from his chair and walked to the mansion's library window, looking out over the moonlit gardens below. "It is here in the District."

The two Immortals had met in the library to discuss a handful of bureaucratic issues keeping Lorenzo awake at night. That was how Lorenzo had phrased it in his attempt at humor anyway. Immortals didn't need much rest and never at night. The library was one of Solomon's favorite rooms in the sprawling hilltop complex as it contained rows of manuscripts mortal historians thought lost.

A breeze swept through the window causing Solomon's nostrils to flare from the musty, aged scent of his maker hidden deep beneath several layers of cologne. The old man would need to feed again soon.

"I want you," Lorenzo pointed at him, "and Alexander to follow someone for me. For Danae."

"Of course. Who?"

"A graduate student at some university here in the District. She found the amulet. Danae believes the god may have chosen this girl already. We must know for sure." Lorenzo's calculating blue gaze burned with eagerness.

Solomon raised an eyebrow. It didn't make sense to him that they wait to find out. "Why don't we just bring the girl here?"

"No. Danae says we play by her rules on this one." Lorenzo shook his head, then raised a hand to smooth his hair back into place. "The god cannot know we are coming for him. Danae is already working with the Italians to purchase the amulet. With our powers waning, any disturbance could cause unnecessary obstacles."

Apprehension settled over him. While he hadn't been privy to this particular conversation, as Lorenzo's right-hand man, most conversations with Danae had him lingering somewhere nearby. And though his maker's trust might be implicit, Solomon had a feeling that Danae, one of the highest-ranking members of the Council and rumored to be the oldest Immortal still breathing, had secrets she didn't share with anyone.

"And the Council thinks the amulet is the key to restoring our powers?" Solomon asked, leaning back into the chair.

Lorenzo nodded. "It is crucial to our survival we obtain the amulet before it disappears again." The sharp snapping of fingers accentuated his last few words.

Solomon frowned, not quite sure how to take the last comment. Their powers had lessened significantly over the last two decades, but he didn't think it would affect their lives.

"Survival?"

"The girl, Serafina Finch, is giving a presentation on the amulet in a few days," Lorenzo said without acknowledging the question. He turned back to the window. "See if she gives you any indication that she knows more than she should."

Lorenzo raised a hand in dismissal, oversized rings gleaming in the moonlight.

Confusion swept through his mind as Solomon ran a hand over his closely cropped hair. He pushed himself to his feet and headed for the door. Growing up as a slave in the South over two centuries ago, he'd learned the hard way what questioning his masters could mean. Lorenzo may not own him per se, but Solomon had no desire to deal with his maker's wrath when he could avoid it.

As he passed the vast bookshelves, he knew he'd have to spend some time in the mansion's library later, seeking answers within the ancient texts.

"One more thing, Solomon." The accented voice stopped him as he reached for the handle. "Do not give Alexander any more information than is necessary. He will not fully understand, not yet."

"As you wish," he replied, having no intention of disobeying. Alexander caused enough trouble with the little knowledge he did have.

* * *

Like ants on the hunt for crumbs, people strolled from store to store beneath the domed glass ceiling of the Tysons Corner mall. Shrieks of laughter pierced Solomon's ears as children ran from their parents into the open storefront of a bookstore, where a popular costumed character opened her arms for hugs. The tantalizing smells of hops and sizzling meat drifted up from the brewery on the bottom floor, making his fangs ache to extend in anticipation.

"Who actually shops at a mall these days?" Alexander asked as he leaned his arms against the second-floor railing overlooking the courtyard, his belly hanging over his designer jeans.

Solomon didn't bother to respond. Sometimes it just wasn't worth getting into a debate with a kid like Alexander, someone who still acted like the entitled frat boy he'd been when he underwent the Immortal change. Instead, he focused his attention on the dark-haired girl they were tracking as she and her friend exited a store, bags in hand. She stopped with a confused look on her face a few feet from the store, then turned to look directly at him.

"Lorenzo didn't say anything about needing the blonde one, right? I'd like to suck her body dry." Alexander stared at the two women, licking his lips. The kid stiffened next to him, his eyes flashing red and his nostrils flaring. He still found it difficult to be among mortal crowds without thinking of humans as food.

Putting out a hand to stop him, Solomon waited for the younger Immortal to regain control. He'd known it would be risky taking his protégé, despite making sure he had eaten before they left the mansion. The kid did try to be a better Immortal from time to time.

"We're not here for lunch. Let's go." Unnerved at her apparent ability to sense them watching, he walked away from the rail, unable to resist rubbing the scar running from his hairline through his left eyebrow. A human habit he never seemed to be able to shake.

Alexander groaned but followed.

"She sensed us watching," Solomon said as they walked out of the mall and toward the black Maserati.

Even with sunglasses in place, he squinted against the harsh glare of daylight. His upper lip curled as the smell of old cigarette smoke and rotting garbage stung his nostrils from the nearby mall garbage cans. As much as he enjoyed his enhanced Immortal senses, he wouldn't mind losing some of the heightened vision and smell.

"Maybe she's a witch." Alexander laughed at his suggestion, clearly considering it a good joke. He backed the sedan out of the parking spot and sped out of the lot.

Solomon wasn't quite so sure it was funny. Witches still existed, of course. Mostly the powerful ones, although they were few and far between in this day and age. Witchcraft was a dying art. But Alexander had never had the pleasure, if it could be called that, of encountering a witch face-to-face.

"Why did we just spend our morning at a mall? What's Lorenzo's agenda?" Alexander asked, his fleshy, infantile face suiting his clueless nature.

Solomon shrugged as he looked out the window. "Lorenzo doesn't have to give a reason. He just wants her whereabouts known at all times."

The kid made a noise of annoyance in response.

Solomon thought back over the last few weeks they'd been watching the girl. As far as he could tell, she hadn't been chosen by the god. And yet she had shown an uncanny ability to sense their presence.

Was Alexander right without knowing it? Was she a witch?

CHAPTER 3

Serafina

Between Hiro's residency schedule and Sera's daily lectures and late-night study sessions, finding time to spend with him that didn't involve research or quick couch cuddles could be an onerous task. They'd managed to make it out to their favorite steak restaurant that night for a belated anniversary and pre-gala celebration dinner.

Salad, steak, and French fries drizzled in a secret, house-made sauce made up the entire menu, other than dessert and wine. Votive candles on every table lit the room, and jazz music drifted out of the speakers, providing a soothing ambiance after a hectic month.

Hiro raised his wineglass for a toast, smiling over the rim. "To my lovely lady on her fantastic achievements. I can't wait to see you present at the gala tomorrow night."

"To my sweet boyfriend, who loves me even when I miss out on our life events because I'm busy digging in the dirt." Their glasses clinked together.

"Ugh, we're so sweet, we're going to give each other diabetes." She swirled the wine in her glass before taking a sip, inhaling the soft scent of black cherries from her Merlot.

They'd eaten at the restaurant several times before, which many would consider almost sacrilegious in a city filled with world-renowned chefs and rotating menus. But Sera and Hiro remained creatures of habit. Not to mention she'd had a bad experience at a restaurant that surprised her by serving octopus, a creature she'd feared ever since her mother had read her bedtime stories of the Kraken. Seafood was usually out of the question.

"I would not wish any companion in the world but you," he said.

Sera let out a surprised laugh, her stomach fluttering. "Since when do you quote Shakespeare?"

"What? A man can't be romantic?" Shaking his head, he tsk-tsked. "I still can't believe you drink wine now."

"It grew on me this summer. You know it's pretty much all they drink with dinner over there." Sera shrugged.

He chuckled as he set down his glass. "Did you tell your dad about the amulet yet?"

She sighed, her shoulders slumping forward. "I tried. It's hard to talk to him about my work because of my mom. He never wanted me to follow in her footsteps."

Love of archaeology ran in her blood. When Sera was in third grade, her mother had been exploring a newly discovered cave with colleagues after they received word it may contain evidence of prehistoric cave drawings.

At least, that's what her mother had told Sera's father. No one knew where the information came from or what caused the cave entrance to collapse, but when rescuers finally removed enough of the debris to enter, there was no trace of her mother or anyone else. Finding out what her mom had been searching for, and perhaps even continuing her work, would be the ultimate moment of success.

Hiro reached across the table to take her free hand in his, giving it a gentle squeeze. "It may be hard, but I'm sure he's proud of your achievements, even if it comes with sadness."

"I'm sure you're right, but he blames himself for her death. Like he could have somehow stopped the cave from collapsing had he been there. And he thinks something like that will happen to me." She stared at her wineglass, the movement of the dark liquid reminding her of the amulet once again.

Despite Chad's disparaging remarks about her "uneducated fantasy," and the questioning, sometimes downright nasty, looks she received from the other faculty members, she just *knew* the fluid inside the pinecone was blood. But unlike the location at the dig site, Sera couldn't explain how she knew this time. Maybe her dreams made her think outside the scholarly box. Regardless, the liquid molecules inside confirmed the amulet was filled with blood—and human. Chad's face, when her theory had proven correct, was priceless.

The same colleagues, who had scorned her theory until she proved it to be true, now questioned the authenticity of the amulet itself. They just couldn't believe blood would survive over the centuries—the millennia—and rightfully so. It should have dried up. The old joke about magic being involved had become a cruel taunt as some claimed she had been the one to place the amulet in the dirt, trying to become famous. But they still couldn't explain away the age of the artifact, which couldn't be denied. The fierce competition in academics sucked.

"Hey," Hiro said, drawing her attention back to the present. "You're the most incredible woman I've ever met. You're the kindest person I know, humble almost to a fault, and a complete nerd, which is a huge turn-on." He said the last with a big grin on his face.

Sera laughed and batted her eyelashes. "You mean it's not my stunning looks that keep you comin' round?"

"That's just the icing on the cake." Hiro winked.

Feeling her cheeks flush, Sera smiled back at him and wondered for the umpteenth time how in the world she got so lucky to find a man like Hiro. Not many guys still opened doors for people, hailed taxis for little old ladies, or sent their moms and girlfriends flowers just because he was thinking of them, but he did all those things and more.

The first time she met Hiro, at a bar of all places in a world where she could get a date or a lay with a quick swipe on her phone, she'd thought he'd looked just okay, nothing to call Nora about. But the more time she spent with him, the more his looks improved in her eyes. Sera didn't find much else sexier than a man as intelligent and caring as Hiro.

They continued to talk and laugh over dinner until the restaurant closed. Taking her hand in his as they walked down the street to the Metro, Hiro squeezed it in rhythm with his heartbeat, a gesture he had done since he told her he loved her and hadn't failed to do since.

* * *

The following evening, Hiro opened the door of the taxi for Sera. She took his offered hand so she could exit the vehicle as gracefully as possible in her gown and heels. It wouldn't be a great start to the night if her inner klutz kicked in, causing her to trip and break a heel or fall.

The ground-level spotlights of the National Portrait Gallery lit up the Greek Revival–style architecture, giving the building an even more ancient and imposing look as dusk slid into night. It was the perfect venue to announce the special exhibit—and it also meant higher ticket prices for that evening's event. The exhibit would open to the public the next day at the National Museum of Natural History.

Man, they really went all out, Sera thought with a gasp as they entered the building.

A statue of a satyr appeared to leap toward her on the left, while statues of disheveled women dancing in various stages of undress had been placed throughout the lobby. As they walked through the marble forest toward the interior courtyard, she pointed out a few especially revealing ones to Hiro with a giggle.

He leaned close and whispered in her ear, "I'd like to see you in that pose later."

Laughing, she squeezed his hand and leaned into him.

This night is going to be unforgettable.

As they entered the Kogod Courtyard, Sera gazed upward, her mouth dropping open. Multihued lights added a new dimension to the famed glass canopy ceiling. The wavy glass and steel structure appeared to float over the courtyard, letting in natural light during the day but protecting visitors from the elements. Sanguine velvet couches and chaise lounges were scattered throughout one half of the courtyard, along with a handful of cocktail tables, two pop-up bars with long lines, and an empty dance floor.

In the other half of the room, a handful of people sat at round dining tables draped in red and set with gold dinnerware, close to buffet tables filled with a variety of appetizers and salads. A third pop-up bar was placed nearby. Alcohol and deep pockets went hand in hand.

At the far end of the courtyard, on the other side of the dining tables, stood the stage and the display case holding the amulet. It was the only artifact in attendance, the rest already waiting in their temporary homes at the museum, but two guards stood on either side of the stage to warn off any admirers getting too close.

Sera couldn't see the amulet from where they entered, but the pull she always felt in its presence strengthened. It was there waiting for her. She longed to be at its side.

Nora found them a few moments later. "Isn't this just grand?" she asked, waving her arm around emphatically. Before either of them could respond, she grabbed Hiro's face and kissed each of his cheeks. "Hi, handsome."

"Well, hello to you, too," he said, adjusting his glasses, which had been knocked off-kilter. He was used to Nora's exuberant personality by now, but in the first few months of getting to know her, he had blushed in her presence at least once every time.

"Are you drunk already?" Sera asked somewhat rhetorically, smelling the alcohol on her friend's breath from a few feet away. No judgment on her end, though—she'd already had a glass of wine to help calm her nerves.

Nora gave a dismissive shrug. "Sol and I did a little pre-gaming."

"Sol?"

"My date for this evening. I found him on one of those dating apps. He's at the bar." Nora pointed to a tall, dark-skinned man standing at one of the bars ordering drinks, his back to them.

"There you are. Ms. Finch, I'd like to introduce you to the museum director, Dr. Josiah Cumberland," Chad interrupted as he approached, indicating the far older man on his left.

As much as she hated to admit it, Chad looked fairly dapper, though a little too extravagant, in his black tailcoat, white vest, and bow tie. Most of the men, Hiro included, wore tuxedos.

Despite the flaws she saw in the man, her heart warmed to him a bit when she had learned he convinced the Smithsonian into donating a majority of the gala's profits to his scholarship fund for disadvantaged teens. Maybe she really should cut him some slack like Nora suggested.

"It's a pleasure, Ms. Finch." Dr. Cumberland shook her hand eagerly, his wire-framed spectacles slipping down his thin nose in the movement. He pushed his lenses back into place and gestured her toward the small stage. "You're our first speaker of the evening. If you'll follow me?"

Sera nodded to Dr. Cumberland and gave an excited grin to Hiro and Nora. Following the director around the perimeter of the tables, she stood next to the stage where he indicated she wait. The amulet glittered inside the display case next to the podium, catching her eye.

As Dr. Cumberland welcomed the audience to the gala, Sera glanced at the amulet. The connection she felt to it intensified to an almost palpable feeling. She wanted nothing more than to rush over, snatch it from the case, and hang it around her neck. It *belonged* on her neck.

Just as she started to raise an arm toward the amulet, Dr. Cumberland's voice called her name to introduce her and broke the trance. He ushered her onto the stage.

"Thank you, Dr. Cumberland, for that warm welcome, and, uh, thank you all for attending tonight's unveiling," Sera began shakily as she tried to refocus on the task at hand. "It is an honor to be here with you to celebrate the achievements of the Smithsonian, the university, and my peers."

As the lights in the courtyard dimmed, the start of her presentation flashed onto the large white screen, which had descended from a metal post behind her. She placed her phone with the Notes app open on the podium in front of her.

"It is with great pride that I introduce to you the Bacchic Amulet, found in the recently discovered Temple of Bacchus in the Campania province of Italy." Sera scrolled to the next page of her notes as the audience applauded.

"The temple had been used in the *Bacchanalia*," she explained, "a mystery rite devoted to Bacchus in which the revelers danced maniacally—screaming, whirling, and stamping their feet—to the sound of beating drums. Celebrants tossed around a staff topped with a pinecone to promote fertility—pinecones being semi-phallic and all. Wine flowed in abundance as partygoers tried to achieve a state of intoxicated ecstasy to experience a glimpse of the afterlife. The festivities also included feats of godlike strength such as uprooting trees, tearing apart a bull with bare hands, and eating its raw flesh. But because participants were sworn to secrecy, very few details have been validated."

Sera did her best to avoid looking at the amulet throughout her presentation, but she could feel its presence thrumming beside her in the case. A gentle hum resonated in her mind. No one else seemed to notice the sound as all eyes focused on the screen behind her. Why the hell was it affecting her this way? She *did* have wine on an empty stomach earlier. As her heart beat in tune with the amulet's hum, she was thankful she had her speech all but memorized.

"One of the more interesting facets of the amulet is the pinecone-shaped gemstone, the pinecone being a symbol of Bacchus, of course. At first, we believed it to be a ruby based on its red hue. On closer inspection, however, we discovered a vial of blood hidden inside." She paused for a moment while gasps and murmurs rippled through the audience, before continuing to point out the other features of the amulet and temple, which indicated their connection to Bacchus, the Roman god of frenzies, festivities, and wine.

"At this point," Sera said at the end of her speech, perspiration beginning to form on her forehead as she fought the overwhelming urge to run to the amulet, "we still don't have an answer as to how the amulet survived intact and without damage these few millennia, but we are incredibly grateful that it did. Please enjoy your evening. Thank you."

Applause echoed through the hall as she stepped back from the podium, the next speaker approaching the stairs leading up to the stage.

As Sera turned to exit the platform, the amulet demanded her full attention in the darkened courtyard. She could no longer resist it. The blood within the pinecone pulsated with life despite the lack of light. She heard—no, *felt*—the faintest of whispers drift its way through her mind, as light as a feather, calling to her, wanting her. Mesmerized, her fingers reached out toward the case.

A heavy hand landed on her arm, jarring her from the daze. Blurred vision landed on Chad's face.

"I'd like to have a quick word with you before you mingle with our guests." He pulled her toward glass doors off of the courtyard, the whispers forgotten as she fought to keep her balance. Red wine sloshed in his glass when he opened one of the doors and nodded her inside the empty stairwell.

"I wanted to see the rest of the presentation, Chad. Why—"

"Call me Dr. Lambert," he cut her off as he drained his glass and set it down on the stairs.

Resisting the urge to roll her eyes, she said, "Okay, Dr. Lambert—"

Chad pushed her back against the wall and smashed his lips against hers, stubble scratching her chin, his hands groping her body through her gown. The taste of wine danced across her tongue, making her sick as she stood frozen, unable to fully process what was happening.

Footsteps echoed in the stairwell, and Chad pulled himself away, tripping as he did so. A door's squeaking hinges on the floor above them indicated it opened, and the footsteps departed, the door clicking shut.

"I don't know what the *hell* you are thinking," Sera hissed at him as she recovered her wits and wiped her mouth with the back of her shaking hand, "but if Hiro finds out—"

"He'll do what?" Chad glared at her as he regained his balance, using the stair rail to right himself. "Call the police? Kick my ass?"

He snickered as she failed to find words. "If you even think about telling anyone about us, I'll end your career before it starts."

She stumbled back toward the wall as he took a threatening step toward her. A satisfied smirk crossed his face as he straightened his coat and left the stairwell.

Collapsing onto the steps, Sera tried to stop the tears threatening to spill down her face. She couldn't believe what had just happened. What had almost happened. And of course he had chosen that moment when all eyes would be on the next presenter. No one would even realize she had been pulled away.

About us? She had always avoided Chad's advances, always told him she wasn't interested in him that way and that she had a boyfriend whom she had no interest in leaving or cheating on. There was no way she hadn't been clear enough. Pressing her hands to her face, her cheeks felt hot to the touch and wet where tears had slipped out despite her efforts to contain them.

Sera shook her head, trying to clear her thoughts before she could completely lose control of her emotions.

He is clearly drunk and not in his right mind, she told herself, trying to justify his actions. The last thing she needed was Chad trying to sabotage her academic career. Archaeology was her life. *The amulet obviously excites us all.*

The small mirror she kept in her clutch confirmed she looked as frazzled as she felt. She stood, straightening her gown and hair, and took a deep breath. Pushing open the doors and slipping back into the courtyard, Sera hoped to forget that unfortunate part of the evening with the help of copious amounts of wine.

The remaining speakers had finished their presentations and the lights had returned to normal while she and Chad were in the stairwell. She spotted Hiro, Nora, and Nora's date aiming for an open table. She headed their way, giving quick nods and forced smiles to seated gala attendees who thanked her for the presentation. It was lucky timing that dinner had just been served or else she was sure she'd be inundated with questions about the amulet. She choked back a sigh of relief when she finally reached Hiro's side.

"Sera, where'd you disappear to? I want to introduce you to Solomon," Nora said, reaching for her hand.

She looked up at Nora's date and froze. He was one of the men Sera had seen watching them at the mall the week before. Her breath caught in her throat as he took her hand in his and kissed the back of it.

His lips felt like ice.

"My friends call me Sol. It's a pleasure to meet you, Serafina," Solomon said, his amber-colored eyes almost glowing next to his mahogany complexion.

"Likewise," she managed to get out at last. Her thoughts were racing faster than she could keep up. Was his appearance just a coincidence, or did he somehow track Nora down online?

"I was just filling Sol in on the grittier details of the dig. He doesn't believe I can get down and dirty," Nora said with a wink, wrapping her hands around Solomon's well-developed arm, noticeable even through his tuxedo jacket.

Nora raised an eyebrow at her, but Sera found it difficult to form words. How did her friend not see he was the same man watching them? A man that good-looking was hard to forget.

"I think I need to go home," Sera said, feeling woozy, her forehead perspiring. The events of the evening were catching up to her, and she almost lost her balance—or her lunch—as a sense of vertigo washed over her and the room spun. She wasn't even sure when she last ate.

Hiro wrapped his arms around her, his eyebrows pulling together as he supported her. "You're white as a sheet. Let's get you out of here." He directed her toward the exit.

"But the night just started," Nora protested behind her.

She looked back to her friend, whose mouth hung open in disbelief. "I'll text you tomorrow, Nor."

"It was nice to *finally* meet you." Solomon's voice followed her.

Sera's head spun the entire cab ride home, the mystery man's drawn-out words haunting her.

CHAPTER 4

Solomon

*F*ear. Solomon's nostrils flared as Serafina and Hiro left the Kogod Courtyard. He smelled fear and revulsion drifting behind her, but not just from seeing him. How odd.

"She looked like she just saw a ghost. Poor thing," Nora said, turning back toward Solomon, her arm still entwined with his. Eyes the color of a green Anjou pear looked up at him through thick eyelashes. "More time for us to get to know each other, I guess."

"I'll go get us more drinks."

Before she could object or offer to join him, he headed to the bar near the stage. She was an attractive woman, and he planned to take full advantage of his need to get close to her for information. More wine would make both of those objectives a reality, but he also wanted to get an uninterrupted view of the amulet.

The line to the bar wrapped around the perimeter of the tables and ended close to the stage and display case. Two guards eyed the crowd with indifference, hands resting casually on their holstered guns. That's what an untrained eye would see, anyway. But to Solomon, their hawklike gaze took in the room carefully. He noted how each guard stood with his back to the curtained backdrop, the wall of the courtyard directly behind it. The only guards in uniform stood on the stage and at the entrance to the gallery, but he had counted at least six more in evening dress, mingling with the crowd, although their constantly shifting eyes and avoidance of drink gave them away.

Being so close to the amulet, Solomon could almost feel victory in his hands. If—and it was a big *if*—he could conjure up enough power to disperse attention away from him, then he could simply waltz up to the case and deliver the relic to Danae.

It was too big of an if.

Up until the last few years, he could have easily exerted his *influence* without a second thought. But now he found himself standing next to the stage, unable to sway that many people at once without causing a scene. Instead, he looked over at the display case while the line inched forward. His six-foot-two frame allowed him to see the amulet from where he stood.

What's your endgame, old man? Solomon pushed his thoughts toward the amulet, wanting the god to hear him.

"I almost got to fuck the girl who found it," a voice slurred beside him.

Solomon looked down to see the archaeologist who led the excavation—Chuck? Chad. The smell of Serafina's fear drifted under his nose, clinging to the man's tailcoat.

Solomon frowned down at him. "Pardon?"

Swirling his glass, filled with just a mouthful of red wine, Chad raised it to his lips and drained it.

"The girl who found it, *Serafina*." Chad drew out her name. "She wants me. They all do. But she's playing hard to get." He looked up at Solomon, one eye squinting. "You look like a man with fine tastes. Ever sleep with a grad student? You should. They're not all needy like the undergrads. And they've learned some new tricks. This one time, I—"

"You've made an error in judgment speaking to me, sir."

Solomon urged the little bit of *influence* he did have toward Chad, filling the drunken man with terror. His face paled as he looked into Solomon's eyes, which flashed red momentarily in his reflection in the man's pupils. The astringent scent of urine filled the area around them as Chad backed away, bumping into several chairs as he fled.

Having seen more than his fair share of women brutalized by barbaric men over the years, he wasn't about to listen to this imbecile of a man brag about his forced conquests.

Dizziness swept over him, and he reached out to the back of a chair for support. Using even a little bit of *influence* came with consequences these days, but the last thing he needed was interference getting the amulet. Whatever the man did to Serafina that night, he would think twice before attempting it again.

Besides, if anyone was going to terrorize the girl, it would be Solomon.

A crimson flash caught his eye, and he looked back toward the amulet as the red light faded. He smiled beneath narrowed eyes. So, the god had heard him after all.

* * *

Solomon left Nora—naked, sated, and asleep—back at her place just after midnight to answer Lorenzo's summons. It was a Friday night, which meant Lorenzo could be found in the VIP section of In The Flesh, the District's only strip club with both male and female dancers.

The bouncer nodded Solomon in, ignoring cries of protest from those waiting in line. Music reverberated through his body as Solomon entered the dimly lit room, each beat of the deep bass felt down to his bones. The club was almost always at capacity on weekends due to its unique entertainment draw, as well as the elite social status of the members of the VIP section. Tonight was no exception. Solomon found himself having to move people out of his way more often than normal; his height and brooding demeanor were usually sufficient to part the sea of bodies.

Strobe lights flashing out of disco balls lit the room, hanging over raised walkways on which the dancers moved and gyrated. The main stage held several couches where two or more dancers of either gender pressed their gleaming bodies against each other, acting out erotic scenes.

Tables and C-shaped booths surrounded the walkways and stage on all sides, not a single one empty, which explained the line at the door. As he smelled the sweat glistening on patrons' foreheads, both from the heat of the room and excitement over the show, his fangs threatened to extend. He clenched his jaw as he resisted. It had been too long since his last feed, especially after the night spent with Nora. The woman was insatiable.

When he caught sight of Solomon, another bouncer unclipped the red velvet rope barricading the stairs up to the second floor, which was reserved for VIPs. The second floor was set up like a balcony in a theater, opening up to look down on the stage and walkways below.

Lorenzo sat in his usual booth in the corner overlooking the stage, his arms draped over two of the most popular dancers. They wore nothing but strips of cloth to cover their private parts. A curtained room behind the booth provided the privacy needed whenever the desire to feed came upon him.

Alexander leaned casually against the back of the booth, watching a curvaceous blonde woman perform gravity-defying moves on a pole below.

Looking up when he approached, Alexander asked, "Where have you been?"

"You called?" He directed his question to Lorenzo. The kid would pout if he knew Solomon had taken the blonde friend to the gala then back to her place. Both men had found her scent especially alluring, hinting at a fine meal within her blood.

Lorenzo removed his arms from around the two dancers. They slipped out of the booth, relief crossing each of their faces. The Immortals' powers may have been fading faster than any of them had realized if even their maker couldn't hold the dancers' interest at such close range.

"Sit, sit." Lorenzo waved his hand at the chair across from him. "Danae believes the girl will have the amulet before we do."

Feeling the accusation in his words, Solomon frowned as he took a seat, his back to the stage below. "I don't believe she's capable of a theft of that magnitude. It's under close watch in a museum."

"The how is not important." He glanced at Alexander out of the corner of his eye, but the kid was once again focused on the antics below. Leaning back in the booth, Lorenzo popped an olive into his mouth, sucking on it a moment before spitting out the pit. "But I would like to meet this girl, this finder of the amulet. Scare her a little. I have decided to throw a dinner party, and I need you to deliver the invitation."

Lorenzo slid an envelope across the table. Not questioning the antiquated methods, Solomon picked up the envelope and placed it in his blazer pocket. His maker preferred the old way of doing most things.

"I know what you are thinking, 'Lorenzo is so old,'" he mimicked in a high-pitched voice, then laughed.

At least he found himself humorous.

"Hand deliver it to *encourage* her attendance. You make certain she accepts the invite." His eyes locked hard onto Solomon's.

First, he'd been burdened with babysitting Alexander for all eternity, now he would be playing fetch. Solomon missed the days when he actually got to feel like an

Immortal, when his tasks included murder and mayhem. It's not that he *enjoyed* killing humans and other Immortals, not always anyway, but it beat the mundane life of the last twenty years.

If only Alexander's previous babysitter hadn't gone and gotten himself killed. Then he'd only be dealing with the human girl.

"Anything else?"

Lorenzo licked his lips and raised his hand, beckoning to the two dancers who waited outside of earshot. They sauntered back over, hips swaying to the beat of the music.

"Sì. You work too hard with no fun." Taking the young man's hand, he drew him down into the booth.

Relief washed over Solomon as his maker missed the grimace that crossed the dancer's face. He would be none too pleased to see his *influence* fail in front of others.

The brunette woman slid her arms around Solomon's shoulders from behind, running her hands down his chest. He didn't protest—he had worked up an appetite.

The dancer took Solomon's hand and pulled him to his feet, winking at him before leading him into the back room. She closed the curtain behind them before pushing him onto a couch, straddling and grinding against him. Gripping her hips with his hands, he rolled her over onto her back on the couch with a speed and dexterity no ordinary human could make.

Her eyes widened in surprise, but the look quickly turned to fear when his fangs extended. She opened her mouth to scream, but Solomon was at her throat and feeding before she could make a sound, the quick-acting sedative in his saliva lulling her to sleep.

As much as he wanted to drain her in his hunger, Solomon knew when to stop. Sealing the wound with his saliva, he scowled as two small pink marks remained. He left the woman sleeping on the couch, his satisfaction over eating marred by the revelation of yet another ability vanishing. It's a good thing he hadn't fed from Nora yet.

What would they lose next?

CHAPTER 5

Serafina

Biting her lower lip in frustration, Sera glared at the laptop in front of her. She'd spent the last two hours at the university library researching dreams, particularly reoccurring dreams, trying to decipher what hers might mean.

She was meeting up with Nora later to tell her about the encounter with Chad at the gala the night before, but she needed something to keep her distracted until their coffee date. Vomit threatened to rise every time she thought about that stairwell. Her usual TV shows weren't cutting it, and staying in her apartment made her antsy. Telling Hiro about the incident wasn't an option because his damn sense of honor would require him to confront Chad, and possibly reconfigure his face. She also had to tell Nora she recognized Solomon from the mall. It was all starting to pile up.

So much drama, she thought with a quick shake of her head.

Unfortunately, the internet was not being very helpful in decrypting her dreams. All she knew so far was Liviana's classic Roman villa and style of dress meant the dreams were set sometime in ancient Italy and involved the Bacchic mysteries. Sera let out a small groan and sank back into the cushion of her chair, ignoring the distracted library students who cast scowls in her direction. Visiting Nora's psychic friend might end up being her best option.

Sera shivered as a feeling of apprehension slithered up her spine. Looking up from her computer and around the open study area, she could tell that something in the atmosphere had *shifted*, though no other students sitting at nearby tables seemed to be responding to whatever it was. The library was as well lit as any other day, but the shadows between the rows of shelves grew even darker and longer, reaching toward her as if wanting to devour her.

She cast a glance out the window to see if any clouds had moved in front of the sun, but it was a beautiful blue, cloudless day. Her heart started to pound as an unknown fear crept into her mind, as if someone snuck up behind her with a butcher's knife raised to plunge into her back. It would have been next to impossible to sneak up on someone to commit murder with so many students around. But then again, she never knew. She allowed herself a moment to breathe before swiveling in the squeaking chair to look behind her.

Nothing except a few startled faces from other students as she faced them.

Sera almost laughed in relief at her ridiculousness. Spinning back around, she nearly jumped out of her seat—two men stood in front of the desk.

"Jesus! Scare a girl half to death." She held a hand over her racing heart. It was only then that she recognized them.

"You're Solomon." Her hands gripped the table in front of her as she prepared to run. First the mall, then the gala, now here? He had to be following her.

"My apologies for scaring you, Serafina. We come in peace, I assure you," Solomon said in a soothing tone, raising his hands in mock surrender. A smile flashed across his lips. "This is my colleague, Alexander." He indicated the light-haired, pudgy young man on his left, who simply glanced at her before thumbing through a travel book on the desk.

"What do you want?" She could hardly hear over the thumping of her pulse.

"Our employer is one of the most prominent collectors of antiquities here in America. He has been following your team's work over the summer and is especially interested in learning more from you about the amulet." He reached into his blazer pocket and pulled out an envelope, placing it on the table in front of her.

"He's hosting a private dinner event for collectors next week and would be delighted if you could attend."

Her fear dissolved into astonishment. "Did you seriously take my best friend out on a date just to invite me to an event?"

Alexander's jaw clenched as he glared at his friend.

"Ah, yes and no. My employer sent me to the gala to confirm the amulet's authenticity. Your friend happened to be looking for a date, as well. Coincidence." Solomon said the last with a shrug.

"Authenticity?"

"We'll see you at the dinner." He nodded at his silent companion. The two turned and walked away before Sera could open her mouth to ask another question.

She blinked in their direction, then stared down at the envelope in front of her, her mind reeling. Turning the envelope over revealed a wax seal impressed with the letter "V" fastening the flap. Breaking the seal, she pulled out the letter inside.

The lettering on the paper was written in gold ink and dried with soft sand, as if it had been written by a calligrapher from centuries ago. *How fancy*, she thought. It took a moment for her eyes to adjust to the script, but when they did, Sera realized she was reading a formal dinner invitation, exactly as Solomon had stated. There was no way she was going, not with all that had occurred since the day at the mall. But this elaborate invitation and the two strange men who had delivered it had certainly caught her attention.

Sera had time to kill before she met up with Nora, but she couldn't sit still any longer, not after that encounter. Packing up her laptop, she left the library, lost in thought even as she descended the Metro escalator and boarded the train.

The Metro car rocked to and fro as it sped down the tunnel, nearly as fast as her racing mind. She had hoped finding the amulet would launch her career, but she never imagined the oddities that had occurred since then.

When the train doors opened again, her feet carried her onto the platform on autopilot. It wasn't until she looked up at the doors of the museum that she realized where she was going.

It seems I can't get enough of this thing, Sera thought with a rueful smile. *I've only been studying it for months now.*

She followed a couple through the doors, down the main corridor, and made her way over to the display case in the Ancient Romans hall. Lights inside the case focused on the amulet, allowing the viewer to see the elaborate details of the silver chain and pinecone-shaped gemstone. She found herself leaning closer and closer to the case until her nose almost touched it. The glass fogged up with each breath.

The gentle whispering sound from the night before returned, fluttering through her mind like a butterfly but staying to the fringes so she couldn't quite make out what it said. She stared at the amulet, being drawn into its depths. If only she could pick it up, then—

"Excuse me, miss?" a voice interrupted her reverie.

"Sorry. Yes?" Sera stepped back from the case, blushing. She must have looked absurd the way she had been staring.

"We're closing now," the security guard said and indicated the door. Sera blinked and looked at her watch. It was almost time to meet Nora. How had she been standing there for an hour and a half? The kink in her neck confirmed it had been far longer than she intended.

"I guess I lost track of time," Sera said.

The security guard only nodded, an annoyed expression flashing across his face. He scratched his belly, the buttons on his shirt threatening to pop loose from the strain of holding the mass in, before walking away.

Feeling foggy, like she had just woken from a dream, Sera retraced her steps back to the Metro to meet Nora at their favorite diner.

* * *

Solomon

"You took the blonde out on a date? I called dibs on her, man. I want to rip her pretty little throat out," Alexander snapped in the library when they were out of Serafina's range of hearing.

Solomon rolled his eyes behind his sunglasses as he pushed the door to the library open. He loathed being out during daylight hours, particularly sunny days—the glare of the light hurt his heightened eyesight. Tasked with tracking a human meant being in the sun more often than not. For the briefest of moments, he envied Alexander's more humanlike senses, which hadn't developed as strongly after his change due to their waning powers.

"You're not her type." He had zero intention of telling the kid that he slept with Nora the night before, or that he was going to meet her later for coffee.

"I don't want to date her, I—"

"Yes, and that's the problem," Solomon snapped, his fangs extending in his anger. "She needs to think you do, and you're only focused on feeding from her. Or worse.

When this is over, and the amulet is in Danae's hands, you can do whatever you want with her."

Alexander grumbled but didn't argue. They got back into the Maserati parked in front of the library to wait for the girl's next move.

The kid could be so dense, or maybe it was his sadistic nature that clouded his judgment. Sure, he didn't have centuries of experience under his belt as Solomon did, but common sense—well, that was the issue. If Alexander had been born with any common sense, his luxurious upbringing as the son of an intended Immortal had scrubbed it out of him. Alexander's father would have made a far greater Immortal, though he did a disservice to his son raising him the way he did. Such a shame the man had passed before the change.

A few minutes later, Serafina emerged from the building. She took off on foot in the direction of the Metro, her gait purposeful, but her eyes deep in thought.

Solomon opened his door and climbed out. "She's on the move. Let's go."

The younger Immortal didn't look up from his phone.

"Alex, hurry up," he leaned back in to say.

"She's easy to follow. I'll wait here." Waving a hand in dismissal, Alexander continued to scroll.

"Get out of the car. *Now*." The sound of metal groaning alerted him to the fact that he was about to dent the car door with his hand. He closed the door and took a deep breath. Dealing with Alexander was worse than pulling teeth, and he knew from experience.

"You seriously need my help?" Alexander asked as he pulled himself out of the car.

They followed the path the girl had taken toward the Metro, her usual floral scent tinged with something new. Bitter.

"Needing your help is not the phrase I would use. Lorenzo has seen fit to join us together for all eternity, so you will obey his command." Solomon took the Metro escalator steps down two at a time to catch up to the girl before she slipped out of sight in the tunnel.

Metro on the weekends was hit or miss—it was either packed to the brim due to twenty-minute waits and delayed thanks to track work, or empty. Today, it was the former, only the crowded platforms were filled with zombies, superheroes, and scantily costumed women of various professions.

Halloween happened to be Solomon's least favorite holiday because it had become the anniversary of his second birth, the start of his Immortal life. Having lived as a tobacco farmer's slave in the South, a farmer who had enjoyed using his whip far more often than necessary, it had been easy for his mortal self to accept the idea of immortality as a free man. Lorenzo had promised him adventure and luxury beyond his wildest dreams in his employ. But some two hundred years and change later, he had a very different idea of what an immortal lifetime actually meant. It hadn't been all that bad until Alexander had become his sidekick.

Solomon caught sight of Serafina's dark ponytail as she boarded a train. He slipped through the closing doors at the opposite end of the train car, the crowd keeping him well hidden. Not that it would have mattered—even from where he stood, he could see she wasn't really aware of her surroundings. She held onto one of the hand straps hanging from the ceiling, balancing against the rocking of the train car with the other passengers.

When she exited at the Smithsonian stop, he knew where she was headed. Solomon glanced around the platform as he rode the escalator up, but he didn't see Alexander's blond head. Before stepping off the moving stairs, he sent a quick text to let him know she was visiting the amulet. Again. Their time was running out. He didn't know how yet, but he knew the god would make his move soon.

* * *

Serafina

The Morning Grind had been Sera and Nora's meeting point since they moved to the District for graduate school. It was far enough away from the university that they didn't have to worry about running into anyone they knew, yet close enough to each of their apartments that it wasn't inconvenient for late-night chats—the diner was one of the few places in the city open twenty-four hours.

"Wait a second, *the* Lorenzo Vicari?" Nora snatched the envelope from Sera's hand. Her red-lipped mouth dropped open as she read the invitation.

"Who is Lorenzo Vicari?" Sera asked, raising an eyebrow. She took a sip of her black coffee, letting the full-bodied brew simmer over her tongue before swallowing.

It was Halloween night, which meant Nora had arrived at the diner in her 1920s flapper costume, ready to party in layers of shimmering silver fringe, while Sera had forgotten about the holiday altogether while preparing for the gala, working on her thesis, and keeping up with grading. Not to mention trying to squeeze in time with Hiro. The only creature she could pass for that night would be an exhausted grad student. At least she pulled it off well.

Despite the late hour, they had managed to find an open table near the bar top, although the guy behind Sera kept bumping his chair into hers every time he leaned back. She didn't complain. There wasn't anywhere for him to go. It was packed thanks to the holiday party crowd, caffeinating before pulling all-nighters. The hissing of the espresso machine and clanking dishware kept their conversation as private as it could be in a public space. That and the fact that everyone else was on a cell phone or laptop.

"How do you even live, Sera? Lorenzo is one of the most notorious socialites here in the District. I've been trying for years, *years*, to get into one of his epic parties." Nora looked like she was almost in tears.

"I don't think this is going to be an 'epic party,' and I'm not going. It's on a Sunday." She tried to calm her friend down with logic. "Anyway, he said it was a private dinner event, not a party."

"Who's 'he'? You didn't tell me who gave this to you." Nora tapped the invitation a little too emphatically.

Biting her lip, Sera wasn't sure how to tell her best friend that her date hadn't been a real date.

"Solomon," Nora said, her eyes drifting to the diner's door.

Sera blinked. "What? How did—"

"My date at the gala, Sol, is coming over," Nora said with a smile, straightening in her seat. "I think he's really into me. Try not to run away this time."

"Hey, beautiful." Solomon took Nora's hand as he walked up and kissed the back of it before grabbing an empty chair from the table next to theirs. Ignoring the sound of protest from the other table's occupant, his deep golden eyes casually drifted to Sera after he sat in the chair. "Hi, Serafina."

"You don't mind him joining us, do you?" Nora asked, her eyes fixed on Solomon.

"Uh, no, of course not. I was about to say I had to go anyway," she managed to stutter out. There was no way she could tell Nora about her library encounter with him sitting there. The man had been practically stalking them for his employer. Nora would die of embarrassment at being used. That or murder him right then and there.

"But we need to talk about visiting my mom's friend. About your dreams," Nora protested, irritation written across her face.

"Let's text later, okay?" Grabbing her bag, Sera tripped over a chair and almost fell out the door. She still hadn't told Nora about the incident with Chad either, thanks to the excitement of the invitation, and both issues were weighing on her mind.

How do I tell her that Chad is actually a monster? That he tried to force himself on me when all Nora wants is his attention on her? And then follow that up with, "Oh, and hey, your new beau may just be using you to get to me."

She shook her head in frustration.

Sera took a deep breath as she stepped outside, inhaling the crisp evening air. Even if she let the Chad thing go, she needed to tell her friend about Solomon, no matter how difficult it was, before Nora fell head over heels for his dazzling smile.

If it wasn't too late already.

* * *

As she lay in bed later that evening, Sera's thoughts ricocheted like a wayward Ping-Pong ball. If Solomon wasn't being true with his intentions, then she needed to let her best friend know as soon as possible. But maybe she was creating drama where there wasn't any. It's not like he had threatened any kind of violence. What did she even know about the guy anyway?

After a few hours of tossing and turning, exhaustion won over and she drifted to sleep.

Liviana awoke in the dark. She lay still, trying to determine what had woken her from her slumber. Was it raining? A tapping sounded on the window shutters. Gripping the sheets, she held her breath, hoping whomever or whatever it was would pass.

Tap tap tap.

"Livy, it's me," her sister's familiar voice whispered through the wood.

She exhaled forcefully and climbed out of bed, nearly falling as her feet tangled in the blankets. Her breath came out in puffs in the chilly pre-dawn air as she peeked through a hole in the shutter.

There was her sister. But also, not her sister.

"Livy, open the window and let me in," Octavia whispered, her eyes and hair wild and untamed. She wore a dress suited for summer

even though it had been several months since she left home, and winter's cruel bite snapped at their doorstep.

"Tavia, where have you been?" Liviana reached up to unlatch the shutters and pushed it open. Her sister was standing on part of their red-tiled roof to reach the second-floor window. "And how did you get up here?"

"Never mind that. Invite me in. I'm hungry," Octavia whispered more urgently this time, her nails dug into the wooden window frame. Her eyes fixated on Liviana's.

Drawn into those eyes, like a deep, dark pit, the world fell away around Liviana.

"Tavia, come—" she started to say, but their baby brother woke up crying in their parents' room, shattering the mesmerizing hold her sister had on her. It was then that Liviana saw her fangs and eyes that had transformed to a fiery red.

Octavia snarled and tried to reach through the window, but yelped as her hand met an unseen resistance.

Stumbling as she pulled back from the window, Liviana crashed to the floor.

Silence.

She stood slowly, legs shaking beneath her. A cold wind brushed the curtains back from the window.

Octavia was gone.

CHAPTER 6

Solomon

"She doesn't like me, does she?" Solomon asked after Serafina retreated from the coffee shop. Not that he cared one way or another what the human girl thought about him, but he needed to know if she had told Nora about his library visit yet. Chances are she hadn't, not with the way the blonde was leaning into him.

Nora shook her head. "Nonsense. She doesn't even know you. I think she's still frazzled after presenting at the gala last night."

"She seemed rather ill after," he agreed. "Is she better today?"

"I guess so. She didn't mention anything about last night."

Solomon nodded, relieved. It seemed he was in the clear. Taking Nora's hand, he stroked her palm, smiling as he gazed into her green eyes. A soft pink blush appeared on her cheeks as she smiled back. What a pity her charm and beauty would be wasted on Alexander after all was said and done.

"Tell me more," he said. He didn't bother to exert any *influence*—she was under his control from natural instincts. Alexander may have pouted at him after the library for his alleged theft of the blonde meal, but he simply couldn't risk the kid screwing up such an important task. Besides, she obviously preferred tall, dark and handsome to an overweight man-child.

Even if he wanted to control her mind, which he rarely had a need to do in the past, he found doing so more difficult as time went on. They needed to get the amulet back before the ability vanished completely—that would be a devastating loss.

"Oh, she was invited to Lorenzo Vicari's house for some dinner event. She said she wasn't going to go, but she'd be an idiot not to. And she better take me." Nora pursed her lips.

Well, that would certainly put a kink into things. Although, he had a feeling Serafina would be taking muscle with her rather than her flirtatious best friend. From what he'd seen, the girl was far too practical.

"You don't think she'll take her boyfriend? What was his name again?"

"Hiro?" Nora scoffed. "Don't get me wrong, he's great, but he doesn't know the social scene the way I do."

"Social scene? Didn't you say it was an event for collectors?"

Her eyebrows pulled together. "Did I mention that? Maybe Sera isn't the only one with a frazzled brain. Or maybe you just have that effect on me."

Solomon cursed himself silently for his slipup, but she looked away demurely—or at least feigning demure. He knew from experience she was far more adventurous than modest.

He took Nora's chin in his hand and turned her face back toward his. Leaning down, he kissed her, feeling her body melt into his. This task was going to be easy. She would help convince her friend to attend the dinner, if only because she thought Serafina would invite her as well. He'd have to rely on the brunette's more rational brain to take her boyfriend instead. This charade wouldn't last much longer.

Over the next few days, Solomon and Nora flirted nonstop via text. Each day he dropped gentle hints to make sure she would encourage Serafina to attend the dinner. By mid-week, he was confident the girl would make it.

* * *

Serafina

"How do you know this lady again?" Sera asked the next day, scrunching up her nose at the idea of seeing a psychic. Not that she had anything personal against psychics, but the popular reality show *Midnight Mediums* made it all seem terribly ridiculous. The hosts even wore colorful turbans and gazed into crystal balls as part of their acts.

To be fair, it had been her idea to go that day after running out of other ideas. The dreams were getting even more disturbing, and it was difficult to focus on anything other than the young girl or the amulet. But she needed to clear her mind to nail down her thesis if she had any hope of making it in the archaeology world.

Passing a purple bike chained to the front yard's iron fence, the two women walked up the steps to the door. A neon OPEN sign glowed in the window of the green Victorian-style brick row house. The entire street was a rainbow of color as each house and each door had been painted a different hue.

Nora rang the doorbell. "She's like an aunt to me. My mom has known her since they were little. I swear she's the real deal. Try to have fun, if nothing else, okay?"

Fun? Sera wasn't sure she could have fun. She'd hoped to talk to her about Chad and Solomon before arriving at the house, but her friend had spent the majority of the drive over talking about how wonderful her date was without taking a breath.

Perhaps she'd been wrong all along. Chad had avoided her since the gala, so he must have *finally* gotten the hint, and Solomon might have been telling the truth when he said their meeting was a coincidence. She couldn't remember the last time Nora had been so excited about a guy she was dating.

Maybe she should give him the benefit of the doubt. He hadn't actually done anything wrong, and he'd have to tell Nora about working for Vicari eventually. If Sera interfered now, she could ruin the man's image for Nora. And if he turned out to be a decent guy, Nora would end up being mad at *her*. Oi.

The Solomon gush-fest also meant Sera hadn't told her that she'd decided not to accept Vicari's dinner invitation. Nora would be livid, and that was almost enough to make her change her mind and go anyway. But Hiro's argument about the danger of two women going to a private dinner at an unknown man's house spoke to her logical side more, especially after the incident at the gala. She'd wanted to ask Hiro to go in Nora's place, with his martial arts background and all, but one of his patients was going downhill fast, and there was no way she would take him away from the man's bedside. His patients were family.

"She must do well for herself living on Capitol Hill," Sera said, trying to get into the spirit.

"No clue, but she's also lived here for a long time, before the neighborhood gentrified," Nora said.

The door opened just then, and a middle-aged woman with short grey hair and a friendly smile greeted them.

"Eleanor, what a pleasant surprise. And you brought a friend. Please come in." She stepped back from the doorway to let them pass.

They followed the woman down a narrow hall to a sitting room filled with books. Lots and lots of books. The smell of old paper was intoxicating.

Sera's jaw went slack. "I have complete library envy right now." She gingerly touched a stack of books lying on the floor, the wall-to-wall shelves too full to hold any more.

The woman chuckled as she sat down in a purple wingback chair worn with age and use. She motioned for them to take a seat across from her in similar chairs.

"Thank you so much for seeing us, Renee. Mom sends her hello and a hug." Nora hugged the woman tight before sitting. She pointed to Sera. "This is my best friend, Serafina Finch. We're hoping you can help us understand some dreams she keeps having."

Renee smiled. "You know you're always welcome here." She tilted her head to the side as she turned her gaze on Sera. "Finch… Was your mother Rachel Finch?"

Caught off guard, Sera's mouth popped open again. "Uh, yes. Did you know her?"

"Not exactly." Renee's expression turned sympathetic. "I only had the pleasure of meeting her once. I'm so sorry for your loss."

"Thank you." *What an odd coincidence.*

"Well, let's get right into it, shall we? Tell me about your dreams."

Shaking off the strange moment, Sera told her about the nightly encounters with the young girl, Liviana, and her sister, Octavia. "The sense of foreboding when I wake up is just so strong, it's hard to shake for a few hours." A shiver ran up her spine from the memories.

"You are the one who found that amulet, yes?" Renee asked, though her eyes looked unfocused as she stared at a picture on the wall. She chewed on the end of her lavender-framed glasses, which hung from crystal strands around her neck.

Sera glanced at Nora, wondering if she had spoken to the woman before their visit. Based on Renee's reaction when they arrived, she didn't think so. Her friend's shrug confirmed it.

"Yes."

"And the dreams started after you found it," Renee said in a matter-of-fact tone, her eyes moving to meet hers again.

Light goosebumps ran up her arms as she nodded—she hadn't mentioned when the dreams started, not even to Nora.

"What happens when you're around the amulet?"

"I feel drawn to it, like I need to pick it up. Almost as if…it wants me to," Sera said, her palms sweating.

Nora's eyebrows pulled together. "You didn't tell me that."

"There are a few things I need to discuss with you," she said, wiping her palms on her jeans.

A cell phone ring sliced through the tension. Nora dug around in her purse and pulled out her phone, rolling her eyes when she saw who was calling.

"It's my brother. I'll be right back." She stood and left the room.

Sera's gaze lingered on the door, dreading the conversation they still needed to have about Vicari's dinner.

"Do you hear anything when you're near it?" Renee asked, drawing her attention back to the amulet and her dreams.

Not really wanting to admit she had been hearing whispers calling out to her, Sera gave a quick nod. Her pulse quickened, and she swallowed, her mouth turning to cotton. This whole psychic thing might actually be legit.

Sera jumped as Nora's angry voice rose in pitch from the hallway. She charged back into the room a moment later.

"I have to go. My brother got into some trouble at school, *again*, and he needs a lift home. He doesn't have his Metro card or wallet on him because he's an idiot."

Nora's brother was what some call a "blessing" due to the fact that he was born eight years after her. Up until then, she'd been a very happy only child.

"I might kill him." She threw the phone into her purse.

"I'll help. You know I love a good murder." Sera leaped to her feet. As much as she wanted to figure out the reason behind her dreams, discussing it with this woman, who seemed to know about her intimate connection with the amulet, made her skin crawl. Add in the fact that she knew Sera's mother and she was sufficiently creeped out for the day. And it had been her idea.

"Sorry for the short visit." Nora cast an apologetic look Renee's way.

"Not a problem. I've heard many a tale about your brother's behavior these days," Renee said with a chuckle as she stood.

Sera followed Nora out of the room, a little annoyed but mostly relieved to be leaving before she had to tell her about the plan to skip the dinner. Having a neutral third party present sounded like a good plan, but telling the tiny yet fierce blonde while she fumed about her brother seemed like a recipe for disaster.

"Come back soon." Renee grabbed Sera's hand before she could follow Nora out the front door and gave it a hard squeeze.

"*Soon.*"

CHAPTER 7

Solomon

The night before the collectors' dinner, Lorenzo requested Solomon and Alexander's presence in the formal hall he used for Council meetings. The hall was a replica of a medieval throne room he had visited during some king's reign. Solomon couldn't remember who. His maker had been doing research to test a theory that royalty tasted better than common blood, but he concluded the premise was false. Some blood certainly tasted better than others, he had said, but it wasn't based on societal status.

When they arrived, Lorenzo was finishing his meal. Pushing the girl off his lap, her limp body fell to the floor with a thud. He wiped a trickle of blood from the side of his mouth with his silk pocket square.

Solomon's fangs extended as he caught the metallic scent, but he suppressed his predatory instincts to act. The kid shifted next to him but also remained in place. It had taken twenty years, but he was finally learning.

"Remove this," Lorenzo said with a wave of his hand.

A servant rushed up to drag the comatose girl out by her arms, while another cleaned up the crimson trail left in their wake.

"My boys." Lorenzo opened his hands toward them without moving from his seat upon the dais. They took a knee in front of him—it was expected in that hall, regardless of the day. "What news do you bring me?"

"She'll come." Solomon had no reason to believe she wouldn't, Nora had been talking about going all week. His fangs retracted as the smell of blood dissipated.

"Splendid news! Simply splendid." Lorenzo clapped his hands.

Alexander glanced at Solomon. "Are you going to tell him the rest?"

"Oh, come now, you know I don't like surprises." Despite the humor in his tone, their maker's blue eyes narrowed.

"I didn't want to say until I was certain," Solomon said as he cast a sideways glare toward his cohort, "but I believe the god will make a move soon. The girl's been visiting the amulet more frequently, and her scent is changing."

Lorenzo leaned back in the throne and rapped the arm with his fingers, his eyes not leaving Solomon's. "I will see for myself when she comes. If he disappears, your jobs will become exceptionally more difficult, and the Council will not be pleased. Capisci?"

"Yes," Solomon said.

Alexander remained silent. Lorenzo waved his hand, dismissing the two men, not concerned with or not noticing the other's silence. The kid got away with too much, with or without their familial connection.

"'The Council will not be pleased,'" Alexander repeated with a huff after they left the hall. "Like we have any control over whether or not the girl gets chosen. Maybe they should hurry up the stupid deal instead or let us take it by force."

"The deal will take as long as it takes. Our job is to watch the girl. End of discussion." Solomon wasn't about to partake in any blasphemous conversation with him. Eavesdropping was a common and welcome practice in the mansion. Lorenzo heard everything whether present or not.

Leaving the younger Immortal in the hallway, he returned to his own room to get changed for a date with Nora. He pulled on a maroon woolen sweater over a white collared shirt. The slim-fit jeans he already wore during the day received many a compliment from swooning ladies, so he left those on, along with brown leather, wingtip oxfords. The modern world was definitely his shining era.

Even though he had succeeded in his task to get Serafina to attend the dinner, Solomon continued to see dating the blonde as a means of collecting information. She had a sharp wit he found lacking in many women her age, and more than once he found himself forgetting his mission all together. Although he had to admit, he was also enjoying her talents behind closed doors and even sometimes in public.

* * *

Serafina

The morning of Vicari's dinner, Sera had finally worked up the courage to tell Nora she wasn't going. By phone. To say her best friend was angry was a serious understatement. Sera had cringed, her heart clenching with guilt, as Nora screeched through the phone until the line finally went quiet. It was completely her fault for letting her friend think they were going for so long. She deserved Nora's wrath.

"Are you sure you want to stay in?" Hiro asked, accepting the glass of wine she had poured for him. "We've got time if you want to go."

Shaking her head, Sera sank down into the couch beside him, curling up under his outstretched arm before taking a few sips of her wine.

They were relaxing at her place that night. She'd been lucky to find the junior one-bedroom apartment within her price range, even though the neighborhood was a bit sketchy. Living off graduate student stipends and assistantships meant she couldn't afford much else.

Picture frames lined the hallway to her bedroom on either side, filled with the faces of her family, friends, and dig mates. Framed copies of ancient murals and maps hung above the couch, and replicas and collectibles filled almost every flat surface. She was obsessed with her job and not ashamed to show it.

"You know I'm a homebody through and through." Being there with him was her idea of heaven.

The deciding factor in not going had been Hiro's phone call to her that morning. His patient had passed away overnight despite the months of radiation and chemotherapy trying to save his life. Cancer is a hateful bitch. One of his fellow residents swapped shifts with him to allow him a day to grieve the loss. Hiro may have offered to take Sera to the dinner since his night was free, but the pain in his eyes and weakness of his voice spoke volumes.

"Is Nora still giving you the silent treatment?" Hiro asked.

She sighed. "Yes. I haven't even gotten the chance to tell her about Chad."

"Chad?"

Oh, shit. Her heart sank as she realized her mistake. Well, she couldn't keep it from him now.

"Okay, don't be mad, but I didn't tell you guys something that happened at the gala." Sitting up to face him, she told him everything—well, almost everything—from the remarks that started in the summer to the encounter in the stairwell. His body visibly tensed as she talked, and his olive-toned face turned a darker shade as it reddened.

When she finished, he set down his wineglass and stood, pacing the floor of her living room, fists clenched tight. "What the hell!"

"I'm sorry, really. I just didn't want him to ruin my career if I said anything. Think about it, Hiro. Men in his position get away with this kind of thing all the time," she said.

"I'll kill him." He glared at her, although she knew he saw Chad's face in his mind.

"And I'm sure you could. Easily." Grabbing his hand as he got close in his next lap, she drew him back down to the couch. "But then you'd go to jail, and I'd be all alone. No Nora, no you. What would I do with myself?"

As she stroked his cheek with her hand, his shoulders slumped forward.

He sighed. "Fine. No killing."

"I love that you would murder for me."

"But if he even so much as looks at you wrong again, I'll make sure he knows what it feels like to be in your shoes." His anger was tangible as he clenched his fists again.

Sera tilted her head to the side. "Protected by the most amazing boyfriend?"

The look of disbelief that crossed his face made her laugh.

"This is not a joking matter, Sera," he said, though his lips quirked upward.

"Let me help get your mind off things." After draining the last of the wine from her glass, she grabbed his hand as she jumped off the couch and pulled him toward her bedroom. Walking backward down the hallway, she yanked his shirt off over his head.

He drew her toward him as they entered her room, his hands caressing her cheeks before moving down to the top of her leggings. Their lips met hungrily, as if starved from the short time apart.

* * *

Hushed but urgent whispers drifted up from the living area below. Liviana crept toward the stairs, avoiding the creaky floorboards she knew would give her away. She knew every inch of their small villa by heart.

"We've already lost one daughter, I can't lose another," Mother cried into her hands.

Father wrapped his arms around her and kissed the top of her head.

"We don't have a choice, Agathe. It is Bacchus's will that she attend. Whether he chooses her or not..." He let the statement drift off, not needing to explain to his wife what would happen.

Liviana gripped the stair rails, her knuckles turning white. She had no idea what had happened to Octavia or what would happen to her at the mystery rite. It was her sacred duty to attend since she received an invitation, but her blood ran cold as she remembered the last time she had seen her sister at her window over half a year ago. Would her sister be there tonight? Was her sister even alive?

The city of Salernum wasn't too far away. Maybe she should have run away and tried her hand at some sort of trade. Mother always said she was far more adept with a needle than Octavia had been.

"Livy, it's time to go," Father called up the stairs, interrupting her thoughts.

She took a deep breath. No, I can do this, she thought. Bacchus wouldn't choose someone like me. Octavia was strong and beautiful; it made sense that he chose her.

Liviana took the stairs slowly, trying to delay their departure as long as possible. Mother stood at the bottom waiting. As soon as she was in reach, Mother grabbed her, pulling her into a tight hug.

"I love you, more than you could ever possibly know," Mother whispered in her ear. She gave Liviana a final kiss on the forehead then released her.

Father draped a cloak around her shoulders. Nights could get chilly in their mountains, even in the middle of summer. He looked

Liviana in the eyes with lips pressed together in a thin line, then nodded at her before turning and walking out the door.

Moving over to where he sat, Liviana picked up her little brother. His chubby little arms wrapped around her neck as a single tear slid down her cheek. She nuzzled his neck, not knowing if she'd ever have the chance to do so again. When she set him down, he knocked over his wooden block tower in glee, clapping his hands. She smiled sadly at his innocence, unaware he once had two sisters who loved him, and after tonight may have none.

She turned and followed her father out the door in silence, grief streaming down her face.

CHAPTER 8

Solomon

The final guest left the mansion's drawing room as dawn's pale light crept over the horizon. Despite receiving Nora's text an hour before dinner that Serafina wouldn't attend, Solomon had kept the information to himself. It would be better for him if Lorenzo had a distraction once he learned the girl wasn't going to show.

"How *dare* she disrespect me?" Lorenzo hissed, spittle flying as he paced the floor in front of the couch. "We are too close to fail now. The deal with the Italians is almost complete. He cannot escape us." He shook his fist in the air.

Lorenzo often made rash decisions, letting his impulses and heightened emotions drive his direction in life. So, even though Danae had been explicit with her instructions that the amulet had to be obtained her way, to keep the god from up and disappearing again, Solomon was a bit surprised his maker hadn't tried to push the effort more.

The ancient Immortal needed a meal before he did something reckless. Solomon gave a quick nod to Alexander.

"The lady awaits you, sir." The kid grinned and indicated a brunette woman from the party who had caught Lorenzo's eye. Two guards restrained her, a gag in her mouth and eyes wild with fear. The distraction worked.

"Ah, yes. Take her out to the labyrinth. I will enjoy a good hunt," Lorenzo said, his tongue flicking the fangs that now extended into full view.

The woman began to shriek behind her gag and kicked her legs out, trying with little success to stop the men from dragging her out of the room through the French doors. Abandoned heels were the only sign she had once been in the room with them.

Lorenzo removed his jacket and made a show of stretching his arms overhead and to the sides. As if he needed to. "All right, boys, my breakfast awaits." He followed the woman out of the drawing room.

"He certainly has a type," Alexander said, making motions at his chest to imitate a well-endowed woman. "Speaking of, I still call dibs on the best friend."

"Do whatever you like, *after* we obtain the amulet," he firmly reminded his impulsive partner, watching the scene outside.

The guards pushed the terrified woman through the labyrinth entrance, seven-foot hedges forming an arch through which only more greenery could be seen. The equally tall iron gate slammed shut behind her, sealing her fate.

He could hear Lorenzo counting down in Italian. She must have heard it as well because her eyes grew wide and she bolted from view. On a normal night, Lorenzo wouldn't kill the woman, he knew better than that when she had been seen with him earlier in the night. But tonight had not been a normal night. They would need to stage a cover-up later.

Solomon turned on his heel and headed for the front door. "Come on, let him hunt in peace."

A shrill scream pierced the air. It would be the first of many—Lorenzo loved to play with his food.

* * *

The museum security guard yawned as he leaned back, putting his boots up on the desk. His twelve-hour shift was only halfway through that night, and he would need some coffee soon to get through the rest of it. He rubbed his face with his hands as he thought about the fight he had with his girlfriend that morning, a fight which had kept him from getting any meaningful rest before his shift. She could be such a stubborn bitch sometimes.

A flash of light on one of the cameras caught his attention. Quickly dropping his feet, he leaned forward. Even though he didn't see any more movement, he grabbed his flashlight and went to investigate. He should wait for his partner to get back from her rounds, but he didn't want to miss out on any action. A walk would help wake him up at any rate.

Always on with the help of batteries in case of a power outage, floor lights gently illuminated the rooms of the museum. The guard used his flashlight to check dark corners, the red lens keeping his eyesight adjusted to the dark. He rattled door handles to ensure they were locked, then made his way down the hall. The flash of light had come from the display case holding the Bacchic Amulet.

It was still there.

The guard sighed in relief, glad he didn't have to worry about any security breaches on his watch. Talk about a paperwork nightmare. He scratched his portly belly as he leaned on the display case, gazing at the necklace. It was a pretty little thing.

As he stared, smoky tendrils of crimson light wafted up from the stone and wrapped themselves around his head. In any other situation, he would have been scared to see such a thing, but comforting thoughts soothed his nerves. His eyes glazed over as he imagined his girlfriend's reaction when he presented the amulet to her as a gift, apologizing for his earlier behavior. She would be ecstatic and proud of her man. He envisioned getting down on one knee to propose, and her glee when she said "Yes!"

The guard's feet guided him back to the control room, where he disabled the cameras and alarms. He was too busy imagining how the amulet was going to change his life to notice what his hands were doing as they lifted the amulet out of the display case and tucked it away in his pocket. As he pushed open the doors of the museum, the last thing he noticed was the chill in the early morning air.

I wonder if we'll have snow this winter, he thought as the stars began to fade.

Then he blacked out.

* * *

Catching Alexander's questioning glance, Solomon shook his head, indicating he wait before saying anything else. Their maker hadn't said a word since the kid had broken the news in the mansion's private bowling alley, large enough to hold six lanes.

Focused on the lineup at the end of the lane, Lorenzo gripped the bowling ball in both hands before walking forward and releasing.

The crash of the ball hitting the pins filled the air, almost painful to Solomon's ears. He still didn't understand why the Immortal loved to bowl, the sound alone drove *him* crazy, but it had always been a favorite pastime of Lorenzo's. If it wasn't for the awful racket, he'd think it was a meditative kind of thing.

A strike. Indentations left in the polyurethane ball when it returned provided a sign of Lorenzo's rising fury despite the outward calm. Their maker wouldn't hold it together for long. Good thing Solomon wasn't doing the talking.

"What do you mean, 'the amulet is gone'?" Lorenzo asked quietly as he picked up the ball again. He stepped forward onto the lane, lined up his approach, and released.

"It's all over the news this morning," Alexander explained further. "The security guard on duty is their primary suspect because he's missing, too."

Another crash, another strike.

"And I am finding out about this after it reached the news, why?" Lorenzo reached for the ball again.

Alexander shrugged. Because the two shared a common lineage from Lorenzo's human family centuries before, he rarely showed the respect their maker demanded of the rest of his staff thanks to his special, childlike status within Lorenzo's eyes. Their maker often said he saw himself in Alexander and wanted to be a father figure to him. Especially because it had been his blood that changed Alexander. The problem being, of course, that Lorenzo wasn't much of a father figure to begin with.

It infuriated Solomon to no end, but it was also why Alexander was the one sharing the news.

"I dunno. Your special phone never rang," he said.

This time when the ball crashed into the pins, it resulted in a split. That was a very bad sign.

Lorenzo turned slowly to look at the kid, his eyes narrowed. "You don't *know*?" He stalked toward Alexander. Although having at least half a foot of height on their maker, he had the decency to recoil before the older Immortal's red-eyed glare.

"If you expect to see the night, you will find out. And *presto*," Lorenzo hissed as he jabbed his finger into Alexander's chest.

A servant entered the bowling alley, holding up a cell phone. "Sir? Mistress Danae for you."

Lorenzo jabbed Alexander one more time, the force of which caused the kid to stumble back. "I need answers. Now!" He snatched the phone from the servant's hand as he left the bowling alley.

Solomon smirked as he followed Lorenzo out, then headed in the opposite direction toward the back door. The kid's footsteps joined his a moment later. It was about time

Alexander got a taste of what the rest of the Immortals in Lorenzo's employ had lived with for years.

Alexander drove them to the museum, not once opening his mouth to speak. The silence of his company was a welcome change to his usual chatter or humming.

Police cars and news vans blocked the streets surrounding the museum. An invaluable, ancient antiquity and the guard on duty gone missing drew a lot of attention.

They parked the Maserati in a neighboring museum's loading dock and walked over to the crime scene. Crowds of reporters, news cameras, and onlookers pressed against the wooden barricades, trying to get a better look to spread any gossip. Cell phones filled the air, the users snapping pictures, hoping to take the next viral video du jour.

"Think we can get in?" Alexander asked, the silence broken at last. It had been good while it lasted.

"We don't need to get in. Use your senses." The scent was strong.

The kid surveyed the crowd for a few moments. "I don't see anything."

Solomon sighed. "Your senses consist of more than just sight. What do you smell?"

Alexander tilted his head up slightly and inhaled, his nostrils flaring out. A look of confusion passed over his face as his eyebrows furrowed.

"A whole lot of B.O. How does that help me?" he asked.

The crack of a tooth alerted Solomon to relax his jaw before he broke it altogether. He silently cursed his fate for being chosen to partner with such an ignorant being, and he certainly didn't want to babysit when his anger was trying to get the best of him. Alexander may not have developed the same keen sense of smell, but it still should have been better than a human's. Was this really going to be his life for the rest of eternity?

"Try again," Solomon said, trying to be patient. "You should be able to pick out notes of cherries and chocolate. What does it remind you of?"

Alexander took another sniff of the air. "Wine?"

"Exactly. The god's scent. We'll follow it from here." He led the way, tracking the scent past a bitter smell. To be fair, Solomon found the crowd's body odor to be overpowering as well. He should be teaching Alexander how to follow the trail, but his patience only stretched so far.

The wine-like aroma led them a mile through the city to the front of a row house on Capitol Hill. The dark green building stood amongst a rainbow of houses, all of which were painted various colors. Flowers filled the window boxes, including the upstairs. A purple bike leaned against the fence inside the yard, chained to the wrought iron. It was all very charming.

Solomon's eyebrows pulled together as he recognized the house in front of him. Serafina's scent floated on the calm air. She must have the amulet. But how did the girl know the witch? Unless the girl was a witch herself, like Alexander had joked about. If there were any other signs, he had missed them.

He would need to see what information he could get out of Nora. A witch chosen by Bacchus would make for a truly formidable foe.

CHAPTER 9

Serafina

Sera woke tangled in sheets and hair with an alarm blaring in her ear. Rubbing her eyes, she tried to bring clarity to the blur. She couldn't remember the dream, but the ominous feeling lingered.

Ugh, I hate that feeling.

Cobwebs spread through her mind after the wine and sex the night before. Or maybe it was the dream that made it difficult to clear her thoughts. She couldn't tell. Either way, she wasn't going to make it to her Latin seminar that morning. At least it wasn't a day she taught her own classes.

She hit the off button to cease the incessant beep and rolled under a pile of pillows. The ring of her phone woke her again an hour later.

"What," she said into the phone, not even opening her eyes to see who had called.

"Babe, haven't you seen the news?" Hiro's voice asked on the other end. Confused he wasn't sleeping next to her, she felt around the bed. A hazy memory drifted to the surface—he had to be at work early that morning.

"I'm asleep," she replied, hoping he would call her back later.

"The amulet was stolen," Hiro said.

Pillows flew off in all directions as Sera shot up in bed. She juggled her phone to keep from dropping it. "What did you just say?"

"It's gone. So's the security guard," he explained.

Missing? I'll never see it again... Her heart clenched at the thought. *How could a museum-protected antique simply go missing?*

"Lorenzo," she breathed, her mind reeling with the news.

"What? Why would you think it was Lorenzo?"

"I gotta go. Love you." Click.

She needed to call Nora and warn her that Solomon was nothing but trouble. There was no way she would let her friend get involved in anything illegal or dangerous. She touched Nora's contact image on her phone.

"Now is not the time to give me the silent treatment, Nor," she grumbled as the call went to voicemail.

Still tangled in her sheets, Sera grunted as she fell out of bed. Getting back up, she threw on the closest warm clothes she could find, grabbed her bag and a hair tie, and started to head for the coatrack by the door. Her phone rang as she reached for her boots.

"Nora, listen—"

"It's Dr. Lambert," Chad's voice said on the other end.

Sera's heart dropped to the bottom of her stomach. She had been able to avoid him since the gala. Maybe he was avoiding her, too. She could only hope to be that lucky.

"What do you want?" Acid rose in her throat, burning her esophagus. So much for thinking she'd gotten over it.

"I'm sure you've heard the news. There's an emergency faculty meeting happening in one hour."

"I'm not on campus."

"I expect you to fix that," he said and ended the call.

Her nostrils flared in anger at his comment, but it was quickly doused as she remembered Hiro's call.

Good, that means Nora will be there, too, she thought as she pulled on her boots and scarf, falling into the wall in her haste. Rubbing the now-sore spot on her forehead, she locked her apartment door, took the flight of stairs two steps at a time down to the lobby, and headed for the Metro. The wind whipped her scarf into her face and made her eyes water as she walked.

Yuck, and now I have to see Chad again. What a mess!

* * *

The large break room used for the weekly faculty meeting buzzed with chatter as graduate students and professors hurried in. Several rows of chairs faced the front of the rectangular room, which had space for a projection screen and whiteboard. A small kitchenette on the opposite end provided snacks and drinks. It seemed like the entire graduate department—professors and students alike—

decided to attend a meeting for what felt like the first time in forever.

Sera found a free spot to lean against the wall. The meeting hadn't started yet, so she had a moment to catch her breath and try to spot her friend in the rows of chairs. Unfortunately, catching her breath meant she also caught a whiff of the wet cardboard smell that permeated the room, courtesy of the freshly brewed pot of what the department head considered coffee. Her nose crinkled, unable to escape the invasive smell.

When Chad walked in, cocky as ever, she almost forgot where she was. Clenching her fists, Sera's heart began to race, her cheeks flushing in anger. She really thought she'd gotten past the encounter at the gala, mostly anyway. Just a blip in the history of her career. But seeing him again in person brought back all the mixed feelings. Her annoyance rose as another female graduate student got up so that Chad, their so-called "guest of honor" for the year, could have a seat.

What an ass.

The room quieted when the dean, Dr. Walter Shipley, walked in with an unknown man and woman wearing police badges. Sera took a deep breath to relax so she could hear the dean over the blood pounding in her ears.

"As you all have heard by now, the Bacchic Amulet has been reported missing from the museum's antiquities vault, as is the security guard on duty. That's the only information I have right now," Dr. Shipley said, raising his hands to quiet the room as everyone started asking questions at once.

"These two detectives," he indicated the man and woman wearing badges, "will be conducting interviews with our entire staff due to our closeness with the missing artifact. I encourage you all to cooperate to the best of your ability."

Excited and angry voices erupted around the room.

"Is anyone here a suspect?" a male voice asked near the front.

"No. As of right now, this is just standard protocol for the investigation," said a woman as she stepped forward. "I'm Detective Julia Dixon, and this is my partner, Theodore Pratt. We'll try to keep our presence in your lives as quick and quiet as possible. Please don't hesitate to call us with any information you have, no matter how small."

Dr. Shipley called the meeting to an end with an open invitation to come to the front with any questions. As people turned to gossip with their neighbors, a curly blonde head caught Sera's attention across the room. She stood up on her tiptoes to try to see Nora better, but because the meeting had ended and people stood up, her view was blocked completely.

Sera pulled out her phone and sent a text: "We need to talk."

Nora: "Busy."

Letting out an exasperated sigh, Sera dove into the crowd, trying to make her way over to where Nora had been. By the time she squeezed through, her friend was gone.

She tapped Josh on the shoulder. "Hey, did you see where Nora went?"

He shook his head before returning to his conversation with a professor. Sera rubbed her face with her hands.

"Long night?" Chad's voice infiltrated her thoughts.

She turned to glare at him. "I'm not sure why you think that's any of your business," she spat back at him.

A few people turned their heads her way.

"I think it's time for you to head home, Ms. Finch. You look exhausted," he said a bit too loud. Then quietly to her, "And before you embarrass yourself with wild accusations."

Her cheeks burned as he walked away, and she noticed those around her staring for the first time. Releasing her clenched fists, she headed out the nearby door.

A few deep breaths of the outside air helped calm her racing pulse. Now what was she going to do? She certainly wasn't going to any more classes that day, Hiro was at work, Nora was ignoring her, and she didn't want to be alone after seeing Chad. She wiped away a tear before it could slide down her cheek.

Her racing thoughts landed on the psychic. *Renee. If nothing else, maybe I can get these dreams figured out.* Wrapping her scarf tighter around her neck, she started to walk the mile to Renee's house, the chilly fall air clearing her mind with every step.

* * *

Knocking on the door, Sera hoped the woman was home in the middle of the day for clients. Having left her apartment without any gloves in her rush, she breathed warm air onto her frozen hands.

A moment later, Renee gave her a knowing smile as she opened the door. "Somehow, I knew you wouldn't be far behind. Come in out of the cold."

Sera's eyebrows pulled together, puzzled, before catching sight of her best friend's bag hanging in the foyer. Relief washed over her like a warm blanket.

"Nora, listen—" she started to say as she walked into the library and caught sight of her friend sitting in one of the purple chairs, but Nora held up a hand.

"I know I'm being petty, Sera, but everything seems to be happening for you right now, and I'm feeling left out. And maybe jealous," Nora said with a sigh.

Sera blinked, taken aback by her friend's candor.

"Renee has been listening to me complain over the last week, and she's helped me put my thoughts into words. She's basically my therapist." Nora shrugged.

"I would never leave you out. I just didn't know how to tell you…" She trailed off as she dropped her bag and sank down into an empty chair.

Nora's forehead creased as she frowned. "Tell me what?"

Renee brought in hot cups of tea from the kitchen, handing one to each of them.

Holding the warm cup to thaw her numb hands, Sera took a deep breath. "Sol works for Vicari. He's the one that brought me the invitation. He's also one of the guys we saw watching us at the mall before the gala. He was following us."

Nora's lips tightened as she clenched her jaw.

"That's not all," Sera said before either woman could speak. She recounted the incident with Chad at the gala, with a few more details than she'd told Hiro.

"That bastard!" Nora yelled when she finished, nearly spilling tea as she slammed her cup down on the side table. "He's *not* going to get away with this."

Sera shook her head. "I can't rock the boat, Nor. My career could be in jeopardy."

"He *assaulted* you, Serafina," Nora practically growled back at her. "Sol, I get. But *why* did you not tell me about Chad before?"

Sera bit her lip as she realized at that moment how ridiculous her reason was for procrastinating. "Everyone else seems to love the guy. Honestly, I thought I was making it into a big deal when it wasn't."

Nora's mouth hung open as she stared at Sera. Then she shook her head and took Sera's hands in her own. "You are the smartest book nerd I know. But girl, you are as dense as a bag of bricks when it comes to life."

They stared at each other for another moment before breaking into laughter. Another huge sense of relief washed over Sera as Nora pulled her into a tight hug. A few tears squeezed out and slid down her cheeks.

"I don't like keeping my mouth shut on this, but I'll do what you want. Don't you ever keep something like that from me again. Does Hiro know about Chad?" Nora asked as she leaned back into her chair, wiping away moisture from her own eyes.

Sera grimaced as she rubbed her face. "Most of it. I left out some of the details. You know his sense of honor wouldn't let him leave it alone."

A quick smirk pulled at Nora's lips before her expression darkened again. "I can't believe Solomon was using me. He better hope he doesn't cross paths with me again."

Renee cleared her throat. "If I may interrupt, you mentioned the name Vicari. Is that Lorenzo Vicari?"

"Yeah, he invited me to a dinner event for antiquities collectors," Sera explained.

"Lorenzo is a very powerful and a very dangerous man," Renee said. "You both need to stay far, far away from him."

"Solomon said his boss was interested in learning more about the amulet, then it went missing that night. Do you think he had someone steal it?"

"I do not believe the amulet is in Lorenzo's possession." Renee sipped from her tea.

"Why do you say that?"

"Let's call it a psychic's intuition," she said with a wink.

Sera smiled back at her humor. "It's hard to believe a theft like this could happen in this day and age."

Nora kicked her feet up onto the ottoman. "I feel like we're in a 1950s film noir."

"So, Sera, have you had any more dreams?" Renee asked.

Hesitating for a moment, she nodded. "They're getting more vivid, too. I could barely remember the first dream at all when I woke up. But now, it's like I've just watched a movie playing in my head." Liviana's face flashed in her mind like the girl was sitting in the room with them.

Renee watched her thoughtfully. "Someone, or even possibly something, is trying to tell you a story."

"Some*thing*?" Sera gulped. That would certainly explain the whispers she'd been hearing.

"I just mean a spirit of some sort. Not a living human as you are," Renee explained, seeming to choose her words carefully.

"How do I find out who or what it is? And why they're telling it to me? Do you have a crystal ball?" Maybe *Midnight*

Mediums wasn't too far off. Did the woman have a turban, too?

Renee chuckled. "No crystal balls. You'll have to let the dreams run their course to the end. The spirit world works in mysterious ways."

"You're giving me goosebumps." Nora rubbed her arms to emphasize her point. "Speaking of the spirit world, did you hear that Dr. Brown is publishing her theories on the Bacchic mysteries?"

As the women sat and talked, Sera relaxed into the chair, feeling like a weight had been lifted off her shoulders. She hated having something to hide from Nora. All was right in the world again. Well, almost. She would still have to see Chad from time to time, but only until the end of the school year.

* * *

Later that evening, Sera left Hiro a video message, apologizing for hanging up on him and letting him know that Nora was speaking to her again. Hiro's residency program left him unavailable for a good twenty-four or more hours every few days, so catching up on their days via quick video chats had become a regular habit. She didn't talk about Lorenzo—accusing someone of stealing an ancient artifact didn't seem appropriate over the phone.

Emotionally drained from the day's events and wanting to find out what would happen to the girl in her dreams, she drank a glass of wine and fell asleep quickly.

* * *

Liviana kept her eyes on her feet as she followed her father through their small village toward the hilltop temple, thankful for her cloak as a cool breeze tugged at the hood. Fifty-six, fifty-seven, fifty-eight... *she was counting the cobblestones in the road, trying to keep her mind off the night ahead of her.*

A new pair of feet appeared in her periphery. She glanced to her left and recognized one of her friends, Horatia. The corners of Liviana's lips lifted in a nervous smile, then it was back to her feet and counting again.

She nearly fell backward as she bumped into her father when he stopped unexpectedly. She lifted her head to see why. They had reached the foot of the sacred hill. It had come too fast. This was where he would leave her, to ascend the stone steps to the temple above and to face her fate on her own. She winced slightly as his hands gripped her shoulders.

"Livy, my daughter, I pray that Bacchus returns you to us." His eyes searched her face as if for an answer before pulling her close into a hug, something she couldn't remember him doing in any recent memories.

Fear that her movement would break the moment's spell kept her as still as a statue. When he finally let her go, wet spots on his cheeks glistened in the full moon's light.

"Father, please..." she said, reaching out for him.

He shook his head and backed away. "Remember that the invitation to participate in the rite is an honor. We have been blessed to have two daughters selected. Make us proud."

Warm tears slid down her cheeks as he walked away.

Small fingers intertwined with her own. She glanced down at the joined hands, then up to see Horatia's warm smile.

"Don't be afraid, Livy. You'll be back home before you know it."

Liviana's throat clenched. Looking up the steps toward the temple, she didn't have the heart to tell her friend that they may never return home.

At least, not as they once were.

CHAPTER 10

Serafina

After teaching her last class for the day, Sera packed up her bag to head home. It had been a productive Tuesday despite the pall that hung over the department, and she was relieved at being on good terms with her best friend once again after their talk the night before. But she also couldn't stop thinking about the girl who haunted her dreams. What was going to happen to Liviana?

Sera shook her head, trying to shake the apprehension she always felt when thinking of the girl's fate. The sharp tap of multiple footsteps approached her door. When she looked up, the two detectives from the faculty meeting stood in the doorway.

"Ms. Finch, may we have a few minutes of your time?" the redheaded woman asked. Sera couldn't remember her name thanks to her unfortunate run-in with Chad.

"Of course. I'm happy to help any way I can. Well, not happy, you know what I mean." She set her bag back down on the desk and motioned to some seats to distract from her stumbling speech.

The woman smiled warmly at Sera as they all sat down. "You don't need to be nervous. We're just doing our job, trying to find any connecting dots. I'm Detective Julia Dixon and this is my partner, Detective Theo Pratt." She indicated the man next to her.

He looked young, his light brown skin not wrinkled in the slightest, like he had just joined the police force. It didn't seem likely he was a detective already. Julia looked to be in her forties, at least. Maybe he was in training.

"Pleasure to meet you, Ms. Finch," Theo said with a nod. His voice was deeper than she expected from such a youthful face, but it suited his stern demeanor.

"You both can call me Sera."

"Okay, Sera, talk to me about the amulet." Julia took out a notepad and asked a series of questions about other students and faculty, the dig, and the gala.

It went better than Sera expected, only mild perspiration when they spoke about the gala.

"Anything else you can think of?" Julia asked as she closed her notepad.

Theo hadn't taken any notes or asked any questions. Instead, he observed the classroom, her bag, and Sera for the length of their conversation.

Thinking of Lorenzo, she hesitated. But he didn't seem like the kind of guy she'd want to be responsible for dragging into a police investigation, even if he was guilty. Besides, there was no proof, only coincidence. She shook her head.

The two detectives glanced at each other.

Crap.

"Okay, well, thank you for your time," Julia said as they all stood. She handed Sera a business card. "Please let us know immediately if anything else comes up. We'll be checking weeks' worth of museum security footage, so a distraction would be welcome." She gave a sheepish smile and shook Sera's hand.

As the detectives left the classroom, Sera let out a long breath, like she had been holding it since they walked in. She scrunched up her nose, suddenly frustrated she hadn't told them about Lorenzo. But it wouldn't make sense to them. His boss was going the legal route to obtain the amulet— why would he steal it? Money obviously wasn't a concern. She rubbed her face and walked over to her desk to pick up her bag.

"Ms. Finch—" Chad began to say from the doorway.

"I don't know what is wrong with—" she spat back at him, stopping when she caught sight of Dr. Shipley next to him. Her cheeks grew hot as the dean raised an eyebrow.

"We stopped to check on you after we saw the detectives leave your room," Dr. Shipley said. "Did the interview go well?"

Seriously? It's like you're asking if my job interview went well, instead of being questioned by the police!

"About as expected. I didn't have anything to tell them that they wouldn't have already known."

Silence stretched between them like a gulf. They obviously expected her to have more to say.

She slung her bag over her shoulder to break the awkward tension. "Was there anything else?"

"No, enjoy your night."

Sera nodded as she left the room. Taking the short flight of steps outside at a quick pace, she tried to put the two encounters far behind her so she could enjoy her evening curled up on the couch watching her favorite show.

I think I'll open up that bottle of Merlot, she thought.

Just as she reached the bottom step, Sera tripped on a loose stone and dropped the cell phone she was digging out of her bag. She cursed her clumsiness, as well as the new pain in her big toe, and bent to pick up her phone. Hopefully, she hadn't broken either of them. She froze as she touched the screen, her skin prickling as a sense of dread coursed through her veins. The shadows around her darkened.

She was being watched.

How she knew, she had no idea, but every muscle in her body tensed, ready to fight or flee. Sera resisted the urge to panic as she snatched the dropped phone and stood back up, looking around as casually as she could. The lighting in the courtyard wasn't great, but it was enough to see the main walkway leading to the Metro station. No one else was around. But with night having arrived, there were plenty of places for someone to be hiding.

The feeling of being watched pressed down upon her like a thick fog as she walked toward the Metro. All of the hairs on the back of her neck stood on end, and goosebumps rose on her skin with every step. Running the last few feet to the entrance and down the empty escalator, she didn't stop until she could see the Metro's station manager in the control booth.

Leaning on the turnstile, breathing hard, Sera looked back up the escalator toward the night sky. No one, or no *thing*, had followed her except a couple of rowdy teens. It must have been a completely irrational moment of fear. The conversations with the detectives and then the dean and Chad had set her on edge, and after all that had occurred lately, it made sense to be a little jumpy. Not to mention the conversation with Renee.

Is a ghost stalking me? she thought with a nervous giggle.

A train thundered into the tunnel. Sera hurried through the turnstile, the gate nearly bruising her hip as it got stuck. As usual. Finally freeing herself, she rushed down the stairs, making it inside the train car just before the doors closed. She blew the hair out of her face in relief. It would have been twenty minutes until the next train.

Sinking down into an empty seat next to an elderly woman, she found comfort being close to someone who could be her grandmother. She was safe.

Sera pulled out a book to distract her wild imagination and calm her racing heart. By the time she reached her stop, her body had relaxed its near panic. She followed a father and his young daughter up the escalator, then turned in the opposite direction of the pair to begin the half-mile walk uphill to her apartment.

A black car not using headlights screeched to a halt just outside the crosswalk Sera used to get to her building, causing her to pull up sharp to avoid getting hit.

"Hey, watch where you're going!" She raised her hand to thump the hood of the Maserati, its windows tinted the same black as the exterior. To hell with any damage she might cause to the expensive vehicle. Surprised at her reaction, she stopped herself before she touched it. Where had that come from?

The front doors of the sedan opened, and Alexander and Solomon stepped out.

Sera gesticulated wildly at them. "You've got to be kidding me. You could have hit me!"

"Mr. Vicari would like to speak with you," Solomon said calmly as he opened the back door.

She couldn't hold back her incredulous laugh. "Are you serious? You expect me to just get in the car with you? No, thanks." She backed away, trying to fish her keys out of her bag with one hand while she did so. Glancing down into her bag to find her missing keys, she bumped into someone.

"How did you…" She blinked at Alexander, who blocked her path. She had only looked down for a second, and he didn't exactly come across as the stealthy type.

"You can get in the car by yourself, or I can pick you up and throw you in," Alexander said with a wink. "Which would be a lot more fun."

Sera's eyes darted around the street—she was virtually alone with them on the sidewalk. The only people loitering outside a corner market would be too far away to do anything to help. There had to be someone closer in one of the apartment buildings, even if she couldn't see anyone. She opened her mouth to scream, but Alexander's warning look cut her off short.

"I wouldn't." His eyes narrowed and were no longer playful.

She turned to look at Solomon, who still stood by the Maserati's back door. He tilted his head toward the car, indicating she get in.

"Hiro's upstairs right now waiting for me. If I don't come up, he's going to call the police." Sera stalled as she frantically tried to come up with a plan.

He shook his head. "No, he's not. He's having dinner with some friends tonight. Get in."

Fear trickled into her belly as she gaped at him. Of course working for a man like Lorenzo meant they were powerful men, but with Alexander moving so swiftly, and now with them seeming to know everything about her and her boyfriend, it made her wonder what they could do to *her* if she didn't cooperate. Even if she managed to catch someone's attention, would they be able to help her?

Alexander took a step toward her, and she threw her hands up in surrender, sliding into the backseat.

Solomon grabbed the phone she tried to slip out of her back pocket. "I'll return your device after your talk with Lorenzo."

She made a sound of protest as he shut the door. They got into the front, Alexander behind the wheel, and pulled the car into the street.

"Do you enjoy abducting women as part of your job?" Sera asked with as much condescension as she could muster. Feeling around the seat with her hands in the darkness, she tried to find something she could use as a weapon if it came to it. Nothing. She licked her dry lips, her heart racing.

Alexander snickered.

"I'm sure you'll be returned safe and sound," Solomon said without turning around.

"It doesn't sound like you're sure." She gripped the edge of the seat.

He shrugged.

"Why were you still dating Nora? I thought you only took her out so you could see the amulet?" she asked, needing to keep talking to avoid full hysteria.

When she mentioned Nora, Alexander's knuckles turned white in the dim light of the console as he gripped the steering wheel. Shadows deepened on his barely visible jawline as it tensed.

"She intrigues me. However, she has not returned my messages today," Solomon replied. "You wouldn't happen to know anything about that, would you?"

"I don't control what Nora does. But if you're asking if I told her you work for Vicari, then yes."

Silence filled the car.

Sera looked out the window, tracking their progress when familiar landmarks flashed by. Moonlight reflected off the water of the Potomac River as they drove up Rock Creek Parkway under the Kennedy Center. Just as she opened her mouth to ask another question, Solomon turned up the volume on the stereo, effectively drowning her out.

Kicking into hyperdrive as they drove, her imagination came up with all sorts of scenarios for what was about to happen. Maybe they'd murder her because Lorenzo had approached her previously before stealing the amulet. Or perhaps trafficking was more his style. What could he possibly want to speak to her about now? She wiped her sweating palms on her jeans.

She lost track of turns and time until they pulled off onto a road Sera hadn't seen before. A massive steel gate swung wide, opening before them. Nodding at the gate guard, Alexander drove the car up the winding single lane through the woods to the back of a sprawling, Mediterranean-style complex sitting on top of a hill.

Sera's heart was in her throat as she climbed out of the car. They were still in the District, but it wasn't the bustling city part Sera was familiar with. The lack of neighboring homes felt ominous, as if they had left the city altogether.

The two men ushered Sera through a door and across a hall into an office, large enough to hold a conference table surrounded by eight chairs in one corner, a desk with two chairs in another, and a couch beneath the window. A shorter than average man in a white suit, his black hair slicked back, was there waiting.

"Mr. Vicari, I'd like to introduce you to Serafina Finch," Solomon said.

Her eyes widened when the man turned his head toward her—his pupils were the brightest blue she had ever seen.

Lorenzo threw his hands up into the air in welcome. "Ciao, bella! What a pleasure to finally meet you," he said in a thick Italian accent. He glanced at her hands, which shook as she clutched her bag to her chest. "I hope they did not frighten you too much. I told them to play nice," he said with a flash of his white teeth. He wagged a finger at Solomon.

"Come and sit." Lorenzo patted the seat of the couch next to him as he sat.

She did as she was told, afraid to risk angering him and not trusting herself to speak. She swallowed hard.

"I will cut to the chase, as you Americans say. Let me see it." He leaned back casually, but she could see the eager gleam in his eyes.

Sera looked over at the other two men, then back to him in confusion. "See what?"

"The amulet."

Dumbfounded, she blinked at him. "Wait, you think *I* have the amulet?"

Lorenzo narrowed his eyes and leaned forward. An aging, musty scent wafted off of the older man, along with a thick layer of cologne.

"Do not play games with me, girl. You will not like losing." His face contorted with a snarl and his eyes flashed red, as if he suddenly wore a hideous mask. It was startlingly familiar, like how Octavia looked during her late night visit to her sister.

Sera jumped back, the arm of the couch stopping her from going any further. "What the hell was that?"

The sound of fabric ripping filled the air as his nails dug into the couch. He growled, low and menacing.

"I'm-I'm not playing games," she managed to stutter as she cowered before him. "I assumed you had stolen it."

Did his eyes really just do that? Are the dreams driving me crazy?

Lorenzo stared at her, his eyes red-rimmed and burning. He flew to his feet before she could blink and confronted Solomon. "*Why* did you bring her to me? Did you not *think* to check before you wasted my time?" he yelled up at Solomon's face.

"FIND IT!" He upended the conference table, chairs flying in all directions as he stormed his way out of the room, not waiting for a response. His howls of frustration echoed down the hall.

Sera stared with wide eyes at the table, a solid oak table that must have weighed several hundred pounds.

"Well, that didn't go well," Alexander said with a low whistle.

Solomon stood there looking at her with furrowed eyebrows, his lips pulled tight and his eyes lost in thought. Unable to think properly after what she just witnessed, she stared back at him.

"Let's go," he said after a few moments that felt like an eternity, turning on his heel and heading for the door they had come in.

Sera scrambled to grab her bag, which she had dropped onto the floor at some point, and hurried out the door behind him.

"What just happened?" she asked, her voice shaking as they all piled back into the car.

Alexander glanced at her in the rearview mirror as he directed the car down the hill, a smirk on his face. "You get to live another day. You're lucky he already ate today." He rolled his eyes in the mirror after Solomon growled a warning she couldn't hear.

"The dude has a wicked hangry side," Alexander said.

"Hangry?" She had a sneaking suspicion Nora would know what that meant.

"He gets very angry when he's hungry," he explained.

Sera giggled, then the giggle turned into a laugh, a laugh she couldn't stop. Tears ran down her cheeks as she laughed deliriously. The emotional toll of what had just occurred had caught up to her.

Solomon reached over and turned the volume of the stereo up, concealing the sound of her laughter, which quickly turned to sobs. She lay down on the backseat, tears falling onto the leather as she shook.

"Can we knock her out or something?" she heard Alexander mutter over the music.

By the time they pulled up to her apartment building, she felt oddly refreshed, like she had needed to release her fear and anxiety through tears. Sera snatched her phone out of Solomon's outstretched hand. Rage rose within her as she got out of the car, and she slammed the door behind her, hoping to inflict some damage on the expensive vehicle. How dare they make her feel so vulnerable, so threatened.

And for what? she thought. *Their own idiocy.*

She stormed all the way up to her door, ignoring the indignant scowl thrown her way by the lady next door when Sera failed to acknowledge her greeting. Why should she care what her neighbor thinks of her impolite behavior when she had just had her life threatened by a maniac? Her blood chilled at the memory of the overturned table as she let herself into her apartment.

Leaning back against her closed door, she stared at her phone. Calling the police had felt like the logical thing to do until she remembered that maniac had displayed unnatural, superhuman strength. It seemed like the worst idea ever to draw even more attention to herself.

Calling Nora was the next logical choice, but her thumb hovered above her contact image on the phone as she hesitated. Grumbling, she locked her phone. Nora would only worry, for Sera as well as herself, and it would probably be for nothing. It was pretty clear they knew Sera didn't have the amulet, and Nora had said she wouldn't give Solomon the time of day after his lies.

After triple-checking the locks on the door and all the windows, Sera curled up on the couch and pulled the throw blanket over her head, hoping to escape her thoughts and the world as she fell asleep.

* * *

The steady beat of the drums reverberated through Liviana's entire body as she and her friend reached the entrance to the massive temple. She gazed in awe at the scene unfolding before her inside—a dozen women and men she didn't recognize knelt on the temple's stone floor, forming a half circle facing the altar. The women had removed their cloaks and shoes, their simple white gowns spread out behind them like veils. The men had stripped down to their linen pants, their bare chests and feet exposed to the night's cool breeze.

A young woman came up to Liviana and Horatia with a warm smile on her face. She took their cloaks and pointed to where they could leave their shoes. An older woman led them to the left side of the altar where she motioned for them to kneel. Low murmurs filled the temple as those gathered spoke to one another before the ceremony began.

"Psst," came from behind Liviana.

She turned around and gasped. "Tavia!"

Octavia giggled as she held a finger up to her mouth.

Liviana had to hold back from flinging herself into Octavia's arms. It wouldn't be appropriate. "How are you here?"

Her sister looked how she remembered from before Octavia left home—her hair was artfully braided, her gown and skin were clean, and her eyes sparkled with mischievous intent.

"This is my home now, Livy. And maybe it will be yours, too, after tonight," she said with a wink.

A hush fell over the group as the drums ceased beating. The ceremony was about to begin. Octavia motioned for her to turn back around and watch.

Liviana could barely contain her excitement. Her sister was alive! Alive and well, from the looks of it. She wasn't the monster Liviana remembered at her window.

It must have been a dream after all, *she thought.*

As the procession started, two people at a time entered the temple, separating as they reached the first half circle. They formed a new half circle behind the first. There were far more attendees than Liviana had expected. The stream of men and women continued until the High Priestess of Bacchus stepped inside. The woman's golden hair flowed like a river down her back, a stark contrast to her dark eyes.

The High Priestess walked through the center of the two half circles of celebrants, her pinecone-topped thyrsus tapping the floor, and stopped in the middle of the temple.

Taking the offered chalice from a young woman and handing over the thyrsus, she held the gilded cup up to the altar before her.

"B—"

Beep! Beep! Beep!

It was stifling under the throw blanket. Sera sucked in a breath of cool, fresh air as she pulled it off of her, slamming her hand down on her watch to cease the alarm. She had fallen asleep on the couch, and if her stiff limbs were any indication, she hadn't moved all night.

Sera groaned in pain as she stretched, grumbling to herself as she remembered the reason she fell asleep on the couch in the first place. All she wanted was for the damn amulet to be found and for everyone to leave her the hell alone.

Her phone buzzing drew her attention—Hiro had left a video message. Despite her initial grumpy wake-up, she smiled as she saw his face.

"Hey, gorgeous." He grinned as he walked down the hospital hallway, wearing green scrubs and a stethoscope. "I'm sorry I snuck out the other morning. You just looked so beautiful sleeping, I couldn't bring myself to wake you. Anyway, I hope everything went okay with the police, and I'm glad Nora finally came around. You knew she would."

He looked down as the device attached to his front pocket beeped. "I've got to run, but I couldn't resist letting you know how much I love you." He winked before the message ended.

While her heart somersaulted inside her chest, Scra peeled herself off the couch to get ready for classes.

He really knows how to turn my day around. God, I love him.

CHAPTER 11

Solomon

Serafina flung herself out of the car when they pulled up outside her apartment, anger emitting from her body so thick he could almost taste it.

Your fury is nothing compared to the rage Lorenzo is about to face when he tells Danae, Solomon thought.

Racking his brain as they drove away from the apartment, Solomon tried to pick up the piece to the puzzle he had evidently dropped. He would have sworn on his Immortal life that the girl had the amulet. Like his maker, he could smell the god's pungent scent all over her. But watching her face during the encounter with Lorenzo, he knew it wasn't in her possession.

Danae hadn't given them much to work with, just that she had been tracking the god's amulet for centuries, and it had some kind of powers only a Council member of her station could wield. Or so she said. He knew from his own investigation that she almost had her hands on the amulet two decades ago, just after Alexander joined their ranks, but it had somehow disappeared. History seemed to be repeating itself.

"It really sucks we can't just make her give us the amulet. Or torture and then kill her. Where to?" Alexander asked, interrupting his thoughts.

Yes, killing her would be far easier and the kid would get to fulfill one of his sadistic fantasies. But if the god suspected they knew about the girl, he'd up and disappear. Again.

Solomon glanced at the clock. It was close to the time he was supposed to meet up with Nora. She had agreed to meet with him, presumably to give him an earful, but she was keeping it a secret from Serafina. He'd have to lie his way back into her bed if he wanted to get any more information from her about the girl and the amulet. A little bit of *influence* couldn't hurt, either.

"Drop me off at the museum. I'm going to try to pick up the guard's trail again," he said. "You head back to the house and make sure Lorenzo hasn't destroyed any antiquities."

Alexander snorted as he turned the car down the next street, heading for the museum. They both seemed to know that it was highly likely something invaluable had already been broken. Possibly several invaluables.

When the car was out of sight a minute later, Solomon walked straight toward the restaurant where he'd be meeting Nora. He knew the security guard's scent would be long gone by then, but Alexander wouldn't think about a detail like that.

A few blocks away from the museum, Solomon secured a table inside the restaurant and waited for Nora to arrive. He pulled out his phone to check the GPS tracker he had finally been able to place in Serafina's phone. She hadn't left her apartment. The dark-haired girl had turned out to be a creature of habit, which had made it easy for him to keep track of her whereabouts. Now, it would be even easier.

Solomon lifted his head as a familiar coconut oil scent caught his attention. Nora sauntered toward him in a skintight white dress that left very little to his imagination. Not that he needed his imagination after seeing her as the gods made her, but the eyes that followed her didn't have that privilege. And yes, it was a privilege.

She narrowed her eyes at him as she approached, even more so when he stood and pulled out the chair across from him.

"You can try to woo me all you want, but I do not appreciate being lied to." One of her perfectly shaped eyebrows arched upward as she sat in the offered chair.

Trying his best to show remorse as he returned to his seat, Solomon sighed. "I know, but I didn't want you to come to the wrong conclusion about our dates. I didn't even know you were friends with Serafina when we first connected." The lies came smoothly.

Nora pursed her lips. "Why didn't Vicari, your *employer*, just buy a ticket? Why use me for a date?"

"Mr. Vicari donated several tickets' worth to the event, but I hate going to those things alone. I found you by coincidence. Your picture was too beautiful to pass up." He took her hand and kissed the back of it.

Her mouth twitched slightly as she tried to hold back a smile. He knew he had won.

"Well, why didn't you tell me you invited her to that dinner when we met for coffee?"

"I got the sense Serafina didn't want you to know, and I didn't want to cause trouble between you two." It seemed like a reasonable excuse. "I had hoped she would've told you before the dinner." He ran his thumb along the back of her hand, tracing the blue veins. Her skin was always softer than it looked.

She turned away from his gaze. "Why do you always call her Serafina?"

"Isn't that her name?"

"Yes, but everyone just calls her Sera."

"I don't feel like I know her that well. If you haven't noticed, she kind of avoids me."

Nora rested a hand on his arm. "I don't think she's actively dodging you. She just has a lot going on."

He smiled as he won her over again, a smile he was sure she would misinterpret. But he was pleased he played the human part so well. It had been almost fun to flex those long-dead muscles.

"I heard the police are investigating faculty and students about the amulet. Have they questioned either of you?" he asked, placing his hand on top of hers.

"Just Sera." She snatched her hand from under his and looked him in the eyes again. "Did you have anything to do with the theft?"

He shook his head. "My boss is buying the amulet from the Italians. Why would we steal it?"

"To save money?"

The laugh came out unexpectedly. "I don't mean to laugh," he said quickly when he saw her eyebrow arch again. "But money is not something that concerns my boss. Someone as wealthy as Lorenzo doesn't need to save money."

Narrowed green eyes scrutinized him. "I suppose you're right."

"So, do you or Sera have any ideas of who did steal it?" he asked, playfully emphasizing the girl's name.

"None at all. Sera is super bummed because she's weirdly attracted to it."

The server arrived to take their order. After she left, Solomon pushed back his chair and slid into the one next to Nora. Wrapping his hand around the back of her neck, he pulled her to him, pressing his lips against hers. Her mouth parted beneath his as she returned the kiss, running her fingers through his hair and holding him to her. For a brief moment, he lost himself in that kiss, oblivious to their public surroundings and forgetting his true intentions.

Solomon pulled back, shocked that he'd had that reaction. It had been over 200 years since he lost control like that, when he and the plantation owner's daughter shared forbidden kisses beneath the moonlight. Her ivory skin had glowed next to his own dark skin as he made love to her on the blanket.

Nora stared at him, breathless.

"So, am I forgiven?" He ran his thumb down the side of her face to her lips. He would have to watch himself better with this one.

"Yes." Looking up at him through thick lashes, she bit him lightly on the thumb before drawing it into her mouth.

"Okay, we're getting out of here." Solomon took out his wallet and dropped a few crisp bills on the table. Pushing his chair back, he stood and pulled Nora behind him, a mischievous smile on her face.

CHAPTER 12

Serafina

Sera's jaw clicked from the force of her yawn as she stepped off the Metro escalator. Glancing over her shoulder every few minutes, she headed in the direction of her apartment. The last few days of classes since she had been so rudely kidnapped had been hell.

First, she had stepped in a muddy puddle just after reaching the university grounds one morning, far too late to go home and change or even buy another pair of slacks. Then, Chad had visited her classroom not once, not twice, but three times with no real purpose except to harass her and drive her crazy. Whatever his reason for avoiding her previously, he had gotten over it. As if that wasn't enough, her laptop crashed in the middle of a lecture, and she had no backup materials prepared for the day. Her Friday night plan was to take a hot bath and climb into bed.

Reaching the top step of her apartment stairwell, Sera stopped with one foot raised. Her door stood wide open. It couldn't be Hiro. She was almost certain he was on a two-day rotation at the hospital and wouldn't be available until the next day.

Goosebumps rose on her arms. Lorenzo couldn't possibly still think she had the amulet...could he?

Looking around for something she could use as a weapon, Sera spotted an old wooden broom leaning on the wall outside her neighbor's door. She grabbed it with clammy hands and moved closer to her apartment, straining her ears to hear if the intruder was still inside.

After waiting several moments and hearing nothing, she peeked inside her apartment, her heart threatening to leap out of her chest. Her furniture and belongings were scattered everywhere, and glass from picture frames littered the floor. She stood there for a moment taking it all in, devastation finding its way out through her tears.

"Sera, are you okay?"

She nearly jumped out of her skin hearing Hiro's voice behind her. Dropping the broom, she ran to him in the hall, burying her face in his shirt as he wrapped his arms around her. She started to sob as his familiar scent enveloped her.

"Did you call the police?" he asked.

She shook her head against his chest. Logic wasn't on her side after the exhausting week she'd had.

"Wait, why are you here? You're supposed to be working." She pulled back to look up at him, his face blurred through her soggy eyelashes.

"I knew how tough the week was for you, so I switched shifts with someone. Did you go inside?" His voice dropped to a whisper.

Shaking her head, she wiped her wet cheeks with the palm of her hand. Hiro released her and motioned for her to stay put. Setting down a plastic grocery bag, he picked up the broom and disappeared inside the apartment.

A tangy scent in the air caught her attention. She looked down at the bag he brought—dinner from one of their favorite Chinese restaurants. Tears sprang to her eyes again. Switching his shift and bringing food when she had planned on having a packaged ramen noodle night was such a Hiro thing to do.

Sera chewed on her bottom lip as the seconds ticked by. It was taking way too long for him to check an apartment that size. Just when her imagination was getting the best of her, thinking he had been killed inside, Hiro reappeared.

"No one's inside. Let's call the police." Replacing the broom next to her neighbor's door, he picked up the food and her bag and led her inside.

"We can't call the police," she protested.

"Why not?"

Sera hesitated. Lorenzo had to be responsible for the break-in after the "visit" she was forced to have earlier in the week, but she hadn't told Hiro about it yet. It was one thing to tell him about Chad, the normal kind of asshole, but Lorenzo was something else. He flipped that table like it was a quarter in a coin toss. Putting Hiro in danger wasn't an option.

Shaking his head, Hiro took out his phone and dialed. "We're definitely calling the police."

Less than a half hour later, he opened the door to let the police in. Sera's heart sank when Theo Pratt and Julia Dixon walked into her apartment, followed by two technicians. She was going to have to tell them about Lorenzo, and she dreaded being caught in a lie.

"Yikes, I'm so sorry to hear this happened to you, Sera." Julia slowly unbuttoned her black peacoat, taking in the scene around her. Her curly red hair had been pulled back into a ponytail over a chunky blue scarf.

Her partner carefully stepped through the glass to check out the rest of the apartment. The technicians started to dust various objects and surfaces in her apartment to collect fingerprints. The click of their cameras could be heard every few minutes.

"It's pretty clear this isn't a typical burglary—your TV and other valuable items are still here." Julia nodded in the direction of the TV hanging on the wall before taking a seat in a chair next to the couch where Sera sat. "So, the most basic question we always ask is if you have any idea who would be looking through your stuff and what they would be looking for."

Theo returned to the living room, removing a pair of latex gloves. Despite the warmth of the apartment, he kept his black coat buttoned and leaned against a wall.

Sitting next to her, Hiro squeezed Sera's hand. She had filled him in on the abduction while they waited for the police to arrive. Now, he wanted to murder two people because of her, and he wasn't exactly her biggest fan at the moment. But their schedules made it difficult to connect some weeks, and she didn't want to tell him via phone. Besides, she knew he'd be worried sick, which could affect his focus on his patients. Nothing else had happened, and she thought she was done with them for good. Until this happened.

"Lorenzo Vicari," Sera said. The two detectives exchanged a surprised glance. "Well, maybe not Vicari himself. But the men who work for him. They think I have the amulet."

Julia's eyebrows came together. "Why would they think that?"

"Vicari had invited me to a dinner for collectors of antiquities the night before the amulet was stolen. He was interested in learning more about it," she explained.

"Huh," Julia said as she jotted down some notes.

"And then after it was stolen, these men—Solomon and Alexander—basically kidnapped me and took me to Vicari's house. He was convinced I had the amulet at that point and was *very* angry when he realized I didn't." Hairs on the back of her neck stood on end as she recalled the man's transformed face. Her hand trembled as she pushed loose strands of hair behind her ears.

"Wait, they kidnapped you?" Julia frowned. "Why didn't you call us?"

"They didn't actually *do* anything to me, and I thought it was over," Sera said with a sheepish shrug. The image of him flipping over the wooden table flashed through her mind. She gripped Hiro's hand a little tighter. "Vicari's a powerful man. I didn't want to risk making him angrier."

Julia stared at her a moment longer before nodding. "I see. So, Vicari thought you would have it, which means he probably doesn't have it either." She tapped her pencil against her chin. "But you think they still believe you have it? Or will at some point, and that's why they broke in?"

"Right."

"Interesting," Julia said. "Do you have last names for Solomon or Alexander?"

"No, they never mentioned any, and I haven't thought to ask." Once again, she wished the incident with Chad at the gala had never occurred so she could have gotten to know Solomon better before all of this happened.

A low sound, almost like a growl, rolled through her mind. Or was she hearing something? Distracted, she tilted her head to the side.

"We have a few more questions about the amulet," Theo chimed in, startling Sera. She had nearly forgotten he was there.

Turning a stern stare toward her partner, Julia shook her head.

"Now is not—" she started to say, but Theo cut her off.

"We've been reviewing the security footage from the museum, and it appears you've visited the amulet on several occasions, sometimes for hours," he said, his dark eyes focused on Sera's. "Care to shed some light on the purpose of those visits?"

Sera stared at him with her mouth agape, unsure of how to respond. How could she explain to this cop that she felt drawn to the amulet? Or that she heard whispers when she was in its presence? They would both think she was crazy.

"Uh. It's hard to explain…" she said, stumbling through an explanation she didn't really understand herself. "Because I was the one who found it and studied it, I feel connected to it. In a sense. I guess I'm just excited because it's my first big find? I wasn't there studying the security or anything…" She trailed off when Hiro squeezed her hand. She was rambling.

"Uh-huh." Theo regarded her with an unreadable expression.

"Anything else you want to share, Sera?" Julia interjected, casting a glare at her partner.

Sera shook her head, feeling lightheaded and dizzy as she did so. They must think she had something to do with the amulet's disappearance. She put a hand to her perspiring forehead. Was she a suspect now? Her stomach rumbled, interrupting her thoughts.

Julia smiled sympathetically. "We'll let you guys eat your dinner in peace. You're welcome to clean up now that the crew has collected what they could. We'll be here for a bit talking to neighbors, but call us if anything comes up."

The two detectives stood and followed the technicians out the door, Hiro closing it behind them.

He grabbed the bag of Chinese food and set the containers on the coffee table. "Do you want me to heat it up?"

Sera shook her head and shoveled noodles into her mouth.

"Well, I'm glad you didn't lose your appetite," Hiro said with a chuckle as he watched her devour her meal. At least he wasn't holding a grudge.

She gave an apologetic look over her chopsticks. "Do you think they consider me a suspect? Because I visited the amulet?" she asked in between mouthfuls.

Hiro shook his head. "No way. If you could steal something like that, you wouldn't be living in this hellhole you call an apartment."

He smiled as she glared at him over her food. She had turned down his offer to move in with him before the dig, mostly because his reasoning had been for her to save money and move to a safer neighborhood. Call her a romantic, but she wanted to live with him when he couldn't imagine being apart any longer. Besides, she loved having a tiny sanctuary to call her own.

It had been the only point of contention between them for months. Well, that and his mother. Mrs. Saito had planned out Hiro's entire life for him, including his career. It had put quite a kink in her plans when he met Sera and didn't give in to his mother's demands to end the relationship and marry a more suitable Japanese girl.

"I'm going to schedule a cab to pick us up. We'll stay at my place tonight and clean this place up later," he said, pulling out his phone.

"I can't thank you enough for being here and for changing your shift and for being my protector and for bringing food and for keeping me sane." Sera heard herself rambling again. She set her now-empty container back down on the coffee table. "I'll go pack up some things."

Less than ten minutes later they were on the road, driving the few miles to Hiro's apartment. He lived close to the hospital where he had his residency for practical reasons—he was almost always on call if not working. When they finally crawled into bed, Sera's head barely hit the pillow before she fell asleep.

* * *

"Bacchus, we come to you with this offering," the High Priestess called out, bowing her head toward the chalice she held toward the statue of the god looming above her. She brought the cup to her lips and took a sip. Stepping forward, a young woman took the chalice and offered it to each person in the half circle.

Liviana accepted the cup when it was offered to her and took a sip—wine. She licked her lips as the woman moved on to Horatia.

"We also bring before you two additional offerings," the High Priestess gestured toward the girls.

What did it mean to be an offering to a god? Octavia wouldn't let them sacrifice her... Would she? Liviana gulped, fear constricting her throat.

"Hear our prayers and grace us with your presence."

The temple fell silent but for the chirping of the crickets outside. Liviana bowed her head as she saw the others do and waited. For what, she didn't know. For many moments they knelt, quiet, until a breeze began to blow through the temple. It turned into a windstorm, and she was forced to close her eyes and raise her arm against the sheer force of it. Her gown whipped out behind her, heart racing at the phenomenon.

Just as suddenly, the wind stopped.

"Ah, my loves, is it that time again?" a deep voice boomed from the center of the temple, startling her. Footsteps turned in her direction. Her body trembled, eyes still tightly closed. Cool hands touched her arms from behind.

"Open your eyes, Livy," Octavia's reassuring voice whispered in her ear.

Taking a deep breath and trusting her sister, she opened her eyes. She followed the pattern of the floor to the barefooted man who stood before her. A gasp escaped her lips as she raised her eyes and saw his face. Her fear tingled as it melted, like frozen hands held before a fire.

It was Bacchus. There was no mistaking the likeness of the god's bearded face to the murals and statues she had grown up with. He was both there and not there, his body shimmering like a mirage. She could see the other celebrants through the hazy figure.

Bacchus smiled benevolently upon Liviana. "You always bring me the most delectable treats."

Standing at his side, the High Priestess nodded in deference.

He held out his hand to Liviana. She reached out tentatively, not knowing what it would feel like to touch a god. A solid, warm hand gripped hers. He pulled her to her feet as her friend stirred next to her.

"No, just this one," Bacchus said as he turned her around in a circle, inspecting her like a prize.

Liviana could hear Horatia protesting as she was escorted from the temple, but her eyes were only on Bacchus. At that moment, she wanted nothing more than to please him.

"Do you accept your role as an offering?" he asked, stroking her cheek. His touch scorched her skin, but the pain she expected didn't come. Instead, new sensations coursed through her body as she leaned into his hand. She craved more.

"Yes."

The drums began to beat again as Bacchus led Liviana to the center of the temple. Two men came forward and lifted her under arms and legs, placing her supine on the altar. Her gaze never left Bacchus, staring at him in awe and wonder as he smiled down at her. His hand stroked her hair as the High Priestess reached forward and turned Liviana's head to the side, exposing her neck.

Bacchus's eyes flashed a brilliant gold, and a wicked smile came to his lips. "This is going to hurt quite a bit."

* * *

Sera shot up in bed, clasping her neck where she could still feel the pain from her dream. Shudders wracked her body as terror gripped her insides. Lying back down, she pulled the blankets up around her shoulders and snuggled closer to Hiro. She replayed the dream over and over in her mind, unable to sleep as she imagined what was to become of that girl.

CHAPTER 13

Solomon

"The girl's in for the evening," Solomon said when he and Alexander joined Lorenzo in the library. "We'll head back out in the morning."

It had been nearly five days since the amulet disappeared without leaving any trail to follow. The god's scent continued to lead them to the girl, but Serafina had done nothing except go to the university and return home every day that week. Predictable and boring. They had been watching her closer than ever, knowing that the god would make his presence known soon. Killing her before that happened was out of the question.

Solomon and Alexander had returned to the mansion for a meal after the dark-haired girl had disappeared into her apartment building that evening. GPS confirmed she had stayed put.

The antique rotary telephone rang. Lorenzo reached over the arm of the brown leather chaise on which he lounged to pick up the handset and held it to his ear.

Solomon still didn't understand the ancient Immortal's obsession with "the good old days," as his maker put it. Collecting antiquities of all different eras, Lorenzo actually enjoyed making use of them. Solomon much preferred the quick pace of modern-day life with a library, the latest news, and a theater in the palm of his hand. Cellular phones were easily one of his favorite inventions.

"Yes?" Lorenzo asked into the receiver. Only one person called that line these days—his contact at the police station.

It drove Solomon mad that he still didn't know who the contact was. He watched his maker's face as he listened, trying to anticipate what news he could be getting and from whom. But even with heightened senses, Solomon couldn't hear the other person speak. That was another thing he loved about the modern world and cell phones—he could hear full conversations from across a room. Something about a landline interfered with and muted the sounds.

"I see," Lorenzo said, his eyes narrowing. A moment later their maker hung up the phone. He steepled his fingers together in front of his face, eyes deep in thought.

"It seems we have a problem, boys," he said after a few tense moments. "The young woman has decided to involve us in a police investigation after an unknown party rifled through her belongings." Lorenzo's piercing blue eyes flicked between them with steady intent. "Do either of you know anything about that?"

Solomon glanced at Alexander. Surely, he wouldn't have been *that* stupid, would he? But the look on his face said he was just as innocent. For once, he seemed to know his place.

"We would not stoop to such undignified measures, and without her consent, it would be next to impossible," Solomon said. "We've already confirmed she's not in possession of the amulet."

Lorenzo moved his hands to the arms of his chaise and gripped the fabric, his long, yellowing fingernails digging gouges into the leather.

"You two had better hope this was a coincidence. If someone else is after the amulet, I will rip them apart," he spat out, his eyes burning red.

"If someone else is after the amulet, he's doing a piss-poor job of staying undiscovered," Alexander chimed in. "We'll track him down. Do you want us to bring him back here to question before killing him? I've been wanting to try out some new tools."

Solomon sighed inwardly. The kid never seemed to remember the need for their kind to remain invisible to humans. Too many deaths in one area drew unwanted attention, and there had been more than a few over the last month—Lorenzo had been in a foul mood.

Lorenzo flashed his white teeth in a grin, though his eyes remained bright with anger.

"I always enjoy your spirit, Alexander. But no, caution must prevail," he said, flicking his wrist in dismissal. "Go.

Find the intruder. Let him know who controls this town. Do not return without answers."

Solomon checked the GPS tracker on Serafina's phone as they drove to her apartment.

It better not have been an Immortal, or else they'll face my wrath. Whoever it was, dishing out a good mauling would feel good after years of inactivity.

The girl had relocated to her boyfriend's house. He clenched his jaw, thinking about all of the opportunities for something to occur they'd missed by returning to the mansion. Who was stupid enough to interfere with the Council's plan? Was this a random act of coincidence?

"The police are still here." Alexander pulled the Maserati into an open parking space across the street, nodding toward the building.

Like most neighborhoods in the District, Shaw saw its fair share of crime, which meant no one walking or driving by stopped to gawk. It was just another day on the block.

The two detectives who'd been interviewing students and staff at the university stood outside talking to two others carrying camera bags and toolboxes. A few moments later, the detectives turned and got into an unmarked sedan, and the technicians loaded their gear into a van.

"Stay here," Solomon said, pushing open his door after both vehicles drove away. He strode across the street, knowing Alexander would listen. Laziness had its benefits.

As he climbed the stairs toward Serafina's apartment, a putrid scent like rotting garbage wafted past his nose. His nostrils flared against the smell, and he groaned as he recognized it. He knew who had been in the girl's apartment.

"We need to head to the Wharf," Solomon said as he slid back into the passenger seat of the Maserati. As predicted, the kid had remained in his seat, scrolling through images on his phone.

"Care to share what you discovered?" Alexander pulled the car back onto the street and made an illegal U-turn.

"It's Leif Karlsson."

Alexander snorted. "No way. That guy still hasn't learned to stay out of Lorenzo's way?"

"Apparently not."

"You think he's stupid enough to be at his house?" The sedan turned south.

"Yes."

The house was dark and empty when they arrived. A thin layer of dust covered every surface of the historic home, and large spider webs obscured more than one dark corner. Leif's scent, a combination of sour milk and mildew, filled the air. He had been there recently.

"Ugh, does the dude ever shower?" Alexander gagged into his hand as he walked into the living room next to the front entryway. He leaned against the window frame and looked outside.

Entering Leif's home hadn't been a problem since their last encounter—Lorenzo had required him to invite all Immortals in as part of their settlement agreement.

"That's not human filth you smell. That's a decaying mind," Solomon said.

Leif had been a thorn in the Council's side for over twenty years. *Twenty years?* he thought. *He's been a nuisance almost since the day Alexander received his immortality and our powers started waning.*

He didn't have time to consider it further. The front door opened, and a figure encased in shadows shuffled into the darkened hallway, plastic bags hanging from each arm. Wrapping his hand around the man's throat, Solomon pinned him to the wall before the door had time to shut. The bags clattered to the floor, glass breaking.

"You were warned to stay away." A flash of red lit up Leif's gasping face as Solomon's power flared from his eyes. He couldn't let Leif know how much of his Immortal *influence* he had lost since their last encounter.

A maniacal chuckle gurgled out from the man in front of him. Solomon dropped Leif to his feet, where he bent over wheezing and rubbing his throat. Being that close to the unkempt man meant Solomon got a strong whiff of his internal decomposition. He resisted the urge to take a step back.

"I knew you'd show up," Leif said with a grin, his nasal voice strained even further from the throttle. He adjusted his thick-lensed glasses before bending down to collect the bags, grimacing as he looked inside one. "You didn't have to break my jam."

The man looked the same as he always did, wearing dirt-stained khakis and an untucked button-down shirt. The only visible change was his hair, which had turned completely white since the last visit.

"We're not here to catch up," Solomon said.

"We?" His head swiveled to the window, catching sight of Alexander standing in the moon's glow.

"Oh, you brought the newbie." Leif rolled his eyes at the young Immortal's growl. He started to head down the hallway. "Come, join me in the kitchen."

Solomon caught the man's arm, his grip causing Leif to wince.

"As I said, we're not here to catch up. You're playing a dangerous game by involving yourself with the girl," he said.

"Relax, old friend," Leif said as he tried to remove the hand from his arm. "I'm only trying to help."

"Help? How could you possibly help?"

"I'm going to get the amulet back from the girl and give it to the Council. Get back in their good graces," Leif explained. Jam dripped onto the floor at his feet.

Solomon raised his eyebrows. "The girl doesn't have the amulet. And you were never in their good graces. You never will be. Cease your attempts to *help*, or there will be consequences."

"Ooo, so scary." Leif narrowed his eyes. "You know I don't scare easily."

"No?" Alexander asked.

Leif jumped slightly as the kid appeared at his side, extended fangs glinting in the light of the moon through the window.

"Nice trick, newbie," he said with a giggle. "She does have the amulet. She's just hiding it—"

Less than a second later, Alexander had him pinned against the wall again, gasping for breath. A bright flash of light and clap of thunder filled the entry hall, blinding Solomon for a moment, followed by a billowing plume of smoke and two loud thuds.

Waving his hand in front of his face, Solomon tried to clear the smoke enough to see what had happened. Alexander was on the floor of the living room, his face full of surprise. Leif was nowhere to be seen. Leave it to

Alexander to act without thinking. The witch may have actually known where the amulet was.

"Leave the girl to us. The consequences will be fatal this time," Solomon said, knowing the deranged man would hear him.

A chuckle echoed from every corner of the house, its source's location unknown.

CHAPTER 14

Serafina

Dull throbs pulsed through Sera's head.

Cracking an eye open proved it was daylight. Sleep must have overtaken her sometime in the early morning.

She closed her eye again and pulled a pillow over her head, hoping the darkness would ease the pain in her temples. She should have known she'd wake up with a headache after the stress of last night, not to mention the dream.

When Sera opened her eyes again, the pain was gone. And so was most of the day. After a quick shower to wake up, she sat down on the edge of the bed, still wrapped in a towel, and dug through her bag for clean clothes. Her hand closed on a metal chain, cold to the touch.

Every fiber of her being froze as she pulled the amulet out of her bag.

Goosebumps rose on the skin of her arms and up the back of her neck. Her bag had been empty when she packed it the night before. She was sure of it. Did someone break into Hiro's apartment while they slept? Was she being framed? Questions rolled through her mind faster than an avalanche.

Sera dropped the amulet onto the comforter like it bit her, and she scooted off of the bed. Grabbing her phone, she stared at the artifact, almost expecting it to move.

"Nor, I need you to come to Hiro's," she said when her friend picked up, doing her best to hide the panic rising in her throat. The amulet didn't leave her sight.

"I was just about to meet up with some of the girls. Want to come?" Nora asked. Keys jangled on the other end.

"No, I *need* you to come to Hiro's *now*. It's SOS-level urgent. Emergency. Life or death," Sera stressed, her hand almost crushing her phone as she continued to stare at the amulet. It hadn't moved.

"What's going on, girl?"

"I can't tell you over the phone."

Silence stretched between them.

"I'm on my way. But you owe me big-time." The line went dead.

Sera pulled on her clothes, her eyes never leaving the amulet except for the brief moment she pulled a shirt over her head. She froze again as a new fear arose. If someone had broken in to frame her, there was a chance that person was still in Hiro's apartment. She couldn't imagine her heart being able to beat any faster than when she found the amulet, but it threatened to break a few ribs when she envisioned someone still inside the apartment with her.

Grabbing the small canister of mace she kept on her keychain since the abduction, she crept to the bedroom door. She peered out. The hallway turned left to get into the living room, which hindered her sight into the rest of the apartment. Cursing the layout, she tiptoed down the hall, gripping the mace in her hand and ready to spray if she needed to.

After a thorough search turned up nothing, Sera returned to the side of the bed. She wiped her sweaty palms on her leggings as she glared at the amulet. This damned necklace had made her life a living hell. She sat down next to it again, her mind replaying the weird events that had occurred since the amulet had been brought home from Italy.

The gemstone began to glow, a reddish hue so faint it could have been a trick of the light from the setting sun's rays falling across the bed. But Sera was sure it was coming from the amulet itself. Brushing her mind like a feather's caress, the whispering voice she had heard in its presence before came back. It called to her by name. Unable to resist, she reached forward to pick the necklace up.

Knocking at the door startled her out of the trance. She blinked and shook her head. The amulet looked the same as it always had. Only now it gave her the creeps.

"All right, what's going on?" Nora asked, removing her gloves as Sera let her inside the apartment.

She took Nora by the hand and led her to Hiro's room, unable to get the words out. She pointed at the bed.

Nora's eyes widened, her expression stunned. "*You* stole the amulet? How?" Disbelief and possibly even respect crossed over her face.

"No, of course not." She looked around as if someone else was listening. "I just found it in my bag this afternoon."

Nora blinked at her. "You just...found it."

"I know it sounds crazy, and I feel like I am literally losing my mind because of this thing." She waved her hand at the amulet.

"How did it get in your bag?" Nora arched an eyebrow.

Sera stared at her friend in exasperation. It was like she wasn't even listening. "That's what I'd like to know. I *know* my bag was empty when I packed it at my place. So, whoever raided my apartment didn't do it."

Nora's hand shot up to stop her from talking. "Hold up. Did you just say 'raided'?"

After filling her friend in on the trip to Lorenzo's, the break-in, and the police visit, tears pricked the corners of Sera's eyes.

"For Christ's sake, I just agreed to give Sol another shot, and here he goes screwing it up again." Nora shook her fist at the air. "Good lord, Serafina, what is going on with you this year?" She pulled Sera in for a tight hug. "We need to go see Renee."

Sera stepped back from the hug, confused. "Renee? No, I need to take this damned thing to the police."

"You're a suspect, Sera. If you take the amulet to the police after questioning you like they did last night, they'll assume you're turning yourself in. Like your guilt got the best of you," Nora explained.

"But…" Sera stopped as she glanced at the amulet. Her friend was right. She looked back at Nora, eyebrows furrowed. "Why Renee?"

"She told me to come to her if I ran into any trouble, and she knew a lot about the amulet when you talked to her. Maybe she can tell us more about it, and why Vicari is trying so hard to get his hands on it." Nora shrugged.

"Well, we definitely hit trouble. Can you drive us?"

* * *

Saturday night meant they had to park several blocks away. Partygoers and tourists from all over, including from the neighboring states Virginia and Maryland, flooded into the heart of the city for the weekends, and Renee's historic row house on Capitol Hill stood near a popular bar-hopping street. It was full dark when they walked up Renee's front steps. Her smiling face greeted them a moment after Nora rang the doorbell.

"Something told me you'd be coming," the grey-haired woman said, wrapping a black shawl tighter around her shoulders.

Sera and Nora exchanged a look, both foreheads crinkled in confusion.

"A little psychic humor. Come in." Renee chuckled and waved them inside. After they hung up their jackets and scarves, she led them down the hall.

Sera continued to clutch her bag tightly to her chest all the way from Hiro's apartment, terrified she would lose the amulet but also wishing it would just disappear. They followed Renee into her library, the old wooden floors creaking underfoot. The crackling fire provided a natural warmth to the room, which lacked any modern heating, and a smoldering oak scent filled the room.

"Tea?" Renee asked as they sat in the purple wingback chairs. She must have seen something on both their faces. "Or does this conversation call for something stronger? I've got brandy in the cabinet." Without waiting for a response, she opened up an oak cabinet and pulled out three snifters and a bottle of brandy. She poured them each a glass before sitting down herself.

Sera closed her eyes and breathed in the delicate, floral notes of the drink before taking a sip. Warmth ran down her throat like honey, soothing her nerves. She would have preferred a nice full glass of red wine, but she wasn't going to complain.

When she opened her eyes, both women were staring at her in expectation. She set her glass down on the table beside the chair and opened up her bag. Too terrified to touch it with her bare hands, she'd wrapped the amulet in a hand towel.

Renee gasped as Sera opened the towel to reveal the amulet. "Well, I certainly didn't see *that* coming." The crystal strands holding the glasses around her neck made a gentle tinkling sound as she placed the frames on her face. Leaning forward, she inched to the edge of her chair. She stopped as she reached out a hand, looking up at Sera over her glasses.

"May I?"

"At your own risk," Sera said with a quirk of her lips, trying to interject some humor into the tense situation. Although, she may have been the only one in the room afraid to touch it.

The corners of Renee's lips lifted into a smile as she gently picked up the amulet. Holding her breath, Sera half expected the amulet to glow.

"It's even more beautiful than I remember," Renee murmured, turning the amulet this way and that.

Sera released a breath in relief when nothing happened.

"Than you remember?" Nora asked with a look of bewilderment.

After returning the amulet to the towel, Renee removed her lavender-framed glasses. She rubbed the bridge of her nose then smiled at them.

"I hate wearing these darn things." She tapped her glasses.

"You can't seriously be thinking of avoiding the subject." Nora raised one of her eyebrows dramatically.

Renee chuckled. "No, no. I'm just collecting my thoughts. I haven't had to have this conversation in many years." She leaned back in her chair.

"Where to start? Let's see. I first discovered I had the Sight when I was a young woman, closer to your age but younger still. I was very naive back then, living in rural Georgia. When the visions came to me, I thought I was going crazy or even demon-possessed. It wasn't until I attended courses at the local university that I learned others had the Sight and how to control it. I wasn't alone anymore."

She paused as she gazed at a picture frame on the wall. A group of college-aged friends in the photo laughed as they threw their arms around each other.

Sera pressed her lips together to stay quiet. She didn't know how any of this related to the amulet, and her anxiety was already through the roof.

"Through the friends I made, I discovered a new religion and way of life—witchcraft. Having the Sight made it far easier to come to terms with the fact that magic really does exist in our world, which may be harder for you two to hear and accept. But bear with me. We banded together to form a coven. Some had the Sight like me, others could move objects with just their minds, and our leader, the High Priestess, could commune with the dead—a very dangerous undertaking. Speaking with the dead can invite unwanted attention from the underworld," Renee said, her eyes narrowing, "as well as the living dead.

"Now, I don't mean zombies are walking around." She shook her head. "But there's a monster out there that does exist, and the amulet—" She eyed the delicate chain lying on Sera's towel. "The amulet is a part of that monster's creation."

Sera and Nora looked at each other, eyes wide. Chills ran up her spine at the mention of a monster, and the hair on her arms prickled as goosebumps spread like wildfire.

"What do you mean by 'monster'?" Sera asked as she turned her attention back to Renee.

"Roughly twenty years ago now, many years after I joined the coven, my High Priestess did a favor for a very close friend of hers and tried to locate where someone had died. This individual was rumored to be the last known handler of the amulet. As a fairly new coven, we didn't know much about it, only that it was a powerful relic. When she located the body, my coven went to find it and we hoped the amulet as well.

"But we weren't the only ones who sought it. One of these monsters, an 'Eternal' as they're called, had been tracking the amulet for millennia. Yes, millennia. She followed us. The person who had last worn the amulet had died deep within a cave, and we found both the body and the amulet, untouched for almost a century.

"But, when we tried to leave, it was a…" Renee paused, her eyes unfocused. "Massacre. We weren't at all prepared for a confrontation like that. Only a few of us escaped. We collapsed the entrance to the cave with magic hoping to seal the Eternal in forever."

"Wait, my mom died when a cave collapsed twenty years ago. And you said you'd met her," Sera interjected as the similarities clicked into place.

Renee nodded, gazing at her with sorrowful eyes.

"Are you trying to say my *mom* was the close friend of your High Priestess?" Shock registered through her system, cooling her blood to ice. She barely heard Nora's sharp intake of breath.

"I'm sorry you have to find out this way, Sera. But yes, your mother was also a witch, and she died at the hand of a supernatural creature. A vampire."

Her blood defrosted as quickly as it had frozen as she processed those words. The woman was making some sort of sick joke. She stared at Renee, then at Nora, who looked shocked and scared, then back at Renee before bursting into laughter.

"Vampires? Are you for real?" she asked incredulously when she finally stopped laughing. "Listen, I really appreciate all the help you've been with my dreams. Witches, I can believe. I know all about rituals like Drawing Down the Moon—I experimented as a kid, too. But vampires?" Sera snorted, wrapping up the amulet and thrusting the towel back into her bag. Her hand shook in anger as her shock shattered like a dropped glass.

Standing, she slung her bag over her shoulder. "I'm out of here."

"Sera, wait—" Nora reached out a hand to stop her.

"No, Nor, I'll take the Metro," she snapped at her friend before leaving.

This crazy woman seriously tried to bring Sera's mother into her supernatural fantasy, and Nora even seemed to be in on it. She grabbed her scarf and jacket and continued out the front door without putting them on.

"Sera!" she heard behind her but didn't stop.

CHAPTER 15

Serafina

The chilly, fall night air whipped against Sera's unprotected face, adding to the rage that fueled her brisk stride. She wound her scarf around her neck too tight in response. The pocket of her jacket buzzed as the garment fought with her attempts to put it on, the Metro still several blocks away. She punched the red button on her phone with her thumb to decline the call and shoved her phone in her bag. Nora.

She had trusted that old woman. Trying to make light of her mom's death using vampires went way too far, and Nora opened her big mouth far too often. Why did she think it was okay to tell that woman about her mom? Nora knew how hard losing her had been on her and her father. And why wasn't Nora just as angry as she was? Was she really more gullible than Sera thought she was? Wasn't *Sera* usually the gullible one?

Vampires. She snorted. *What is she going to come up with next? Werewolves? If this woman seriously believes in vampires, she needs to get some professional help.*

She muttered into the frosty air, her breath puffing out in steamy clouds before her. Shadows filled the residential street she walked down as the city hadn't installed any streetlamps yet, and the overcast sky hid the moon's shine. The glow from porch lights didn't quite make it to the sidewalk beyond the gated front yards, and the illuminated sign of the Metro entrance stood another block away.

Two figures stepped out of a darkened doorway and blocked her path, close but not close enough for Sera to see their faces. She stopped short, breath catching as she realized how reckless it was to be walking alone at night in an unfamiliar neighborhood, especially after her abduction. Sliding her hand into her bag, she readied the mace.

One of the figures raised his arms toward his face. She heard a click as a lighter flared to life, the end of his cigarette burning. She recognized the light hair—Alexander.

"Solomon?" she asked the other man warily. His chuckle echoed in reply.

"Hello, Serafina." He lifted his face toward the dark sky and took in a deep breath. "I believe you have something that belongs to us. I can smell it."

"You want the amulet? No problem." She released the mace and dug through her bag, doing her best to ignore his weird comment. Who could smell a piece of jewelry? "I'm tired of this thing wreaking havoc on my life." Pulling out the bundled towel, she grasped the amulet in her other hand as the two men stepped toward her in anticipation.

The amulet burst into a brilliant crimson light, flooding the area in a bloody hue. Sera glanced up at Solomon in fear, expecting him to take the amulet. Only it wasn't the Solomon she knew—his canines now protruded from his upper lip, twice the length they were before, and his catlike, vertically-constricted pupils glowed a fiery red, smoldering from the inside. They both stumbled back as she raised the amulet in reflex.

"He's chosen you." Solomon lifted an arm, covering his face from the amulet's glow as if it stung him somehow. He and Alexander backed away.

Headlights from a car coming down the street fell across Sera's body, drowning out the crimson haze of the amulet and making it difficult for her to see the two men as they withdrew.

"Who? What are you talking about?" She pleaded after him, forgetting for an instant the monster she had seen in his face. They disappeared into the shadows of an alley as the car passed by.

Sera looked down at her hands. The amulet had returned to normal.

Holy shit.

* * *

Renee's sigh of relief when she opened the door hit Sera like a punch in the gut. She had been so rude after this woman revealed a dark secret, and she had been right. And here she was welcoming Sera back into her home again like nothing had happened.

"Nora isn't with you?" Renee asked as she looked over Sera's shoulder.

She shook her head, numb from the revelation of the encounter.

The grey-haired woman helped her remove her coat. "She left after you did, also needing some time to decompress. You look like you've seen a ghost," she said gently, leading Sera to a table outside of the galley kitchen. "What brought you back?"

Sera slumped down into a chair, resting her head in her hands. Thoughts flew by like blurred scenery out a train window.

Putting a kettle of water on to boil, Renee sat across from her at the tiny two-person table just outside the kitchen. Not much else fit in a row house of that age.

"You were right. How is this even possible?" Sera lifted her head. "Solomon and Alexander. They're…they're not human."

Renee nodded.

"That means Vicari is one of these creatures, too?" she asked.

"He is, and very old. He's not an Eternal, but he works for one. She's his maker," Renee explained.

Sera rubbed her face with her hands. "I think you're going to have to back up a bit."

The kettle's piercing whistle announced it was ready, and Renee's chair creaked as she stood. She poured them each a fresh teacup.

"Let's go sit somewhere more comfortable. This could

take a while." Renee nodded her head down the hall.

A few steps later, Sera sat in one of the worn wingback chairs in the library and kicked off her boots, tucking her legs under her. Sipping the tea, she let the warmth run through her, soothing her muscles and nerves. The steam slowly defrosted her nose.

"Let me start with what I know about these creatures. Let's continue to call them vampires for simplicity's sake, but I'm not entirely sure the term is correct," Renee began. "I've done as much research as I can, but without directly interviewing one of them, I've only gathered so much."

Sera gave a half smile at the thought of interviewing a vampire, still adjusting to the fact that they existed. Or at least something like a vampire.

As Renee shared what she knew about the supernatural creatures, a wave of nausea washed over Sera. How could she have been this blind? She had been so close to Lorenzo, and he had overturned a heavy table like it weighed nothing. She'd probably come close to being his next meal.

"Today's vampire, however, is much weaker than twenty years ago. They still have extraordinary strength when compared to a human, and some can do light mind control if the human is vulnerable enough. But that ability weakens year by year. They won't burn up during the day, but having heightened senses makes them strongest at night—"

"Why can't they do any of that stuff anymore?" Sera interrupted, drawn into the story.

"When we escaped from the cave with the amulet, we agreed it should be hidden and protected at all costs. The amulet houses some kind of magic, and an Eternal is trying to get her hands on it. We knew it must be powerful, but we needed to learn more about it. And with only three of us left, we wouldn't be strong enough to protect the amulet from the vampires. We decided one of us should go to your mother's coven for help."

Sera's brows pulled together. "Why didn't they help find the amulet to begin with?" Shivers ran down her back at the thought of her mother being a part of a coven. It made her memory seem different somehow, ethereal.

"Rachel had been the only member of her coven who believed in the amulet's existence. She tracked its proximity close to where we lived in Georgia, which is why she reached out to us. Her High Priest thought it was a fool's errand. Sadly, he was mistaken." Renee sighed.

"Why did only one of you take the amulet? Wouldn't it have been safer with all three of you?"

Renee shook her head. "You would think so, but in the magic world, the opposite holds true. Witches emit a magical signal that other witches can pick up. The more of us that are together, the stronger the signal. The Eternal who destroyed my coven seemed to be able to track it as well."

"Wow. Sorry to keep interrupting. Please continue," Sera said, her thoughts trying to run in a million different directions as she took in all of this new information.

"Well, from what I've been told by their High Priest, which wasn't much, the pompous old fool," Renee's face darkened as she continued, "the coven performed a spell with the amulet's help that stripped vampires of most of their supernatural abilities. My coven member disappeared after the spell, taking the amulet with him. Ever since then, vampires have become less like the vampires you read about.

But they know the amulet is the key to restoring their power."

Chills ran up her spine, causing the tea to ripple in her cup. "I take it the Eternal got out of the cave?"

Renee sighed. "Yes. Had we been a full coven sealing the cave, no way. But the three of us just didn't have enough power."

"How did you three escape?" Sera asked.

A pained expression crossed Renee's face.

"I'm sorry. I don't mean to bring up old wounds, but...I have to know. Please."

"You deserve to know." Renee leaned her head back against the chair, as if to steady herself. "The Eternal ambushed us in the cave as we were leaving, not far from the entrance. She was incredible." Her face took on a look of awe, her eyes unfocused.

Sera arched an eyebrow. That incredible vampire had killed her mom.

"Not necessarily in a good way," Renee explained when she caught Sera's reaction. "But you haven't seen a vampire in action yet. And one that old moves with inhuman grace and speed that is simply remarkable, even with how small she seemed to be. She killed several coven members before we could even register what was happening. The three of us made it to the cave entrance before she could follow. We made the split-second decision to collapse the entrance, seal it with magic to imprison her, and hopefully kill her of starvation." Her eyes stared at nothing, unfocused.

"The screams of rage that came from within after the cave was sealed chilled me to the bone. I've never heard anything like that in my life, nor since. We ran into the woods, heading in opposite directions in case our magic couldn't contain her and reconvened at our safe house."

Sera's heart pounded. "Why hasn't she come after you?"

A grim smile pulled at her lips, her eyes gleaming. "Oh, she has. But without her original powers, she's not the force that we faced in the cave. After several stalemate confrontations, we have a tentative agreement to leave each other alone. However, I'm sure neither of us trusts the other to keep that agreement should the right time present itself."

Sera sipped her forgotten tea. It had cooled significantly during the story but still warmed her chilled bones.

"How well did you know my mom?" she asked suddenly as her whirling thoughts took her back to the cave.

Renee shook her head, her eyes full of sorrow as she looked at Sera. "Not well. I only knew a little bit about her research on the amulet from my High Priestess before we left. We met for the first time at the cave. I could *see* Rachel was a powerful witch, and she was one of the few who seemed to be giving the vampire any trouble. My coven never really needed to be strong. We knew vampires existed, but up until then, they didn't trouble us, and we didn't trouble them."

Holding back tears, Sera stared at her bag, imagining her mom fighting for her life against a monster that shouldn't exist. Despite the pain, pride flared through her as well.

"It lit up when I encountered Solomon and Alexander," Sera said to change the subject.

Renee leaned forward. "Lit up?"

She nodded. "It was like the blood in the stone came to life—a red light burst out of it like a flashlight. It scared them off. And the car that passed by had great timing. But that's when I saw his teeth. His…fangs."

"I see."

"Solomon said 'He's chosen you' before he ran off. He didn't mean Vicari, his tone made that clear, but I don't know who else he could have meant."

Renee furrowed her eyebrows as she relaxed back in her chair. "Interesting. My knowledge of the amulet is still fairly limited. Your mother had been the one with all of the information, and I still don't know where she got it. She wanted to obtain the amulet as proof of whatever it was that she researched, then present it to her coven. But all of that knowledge died with her. The magic within may be a spirit of some sort." Renee paused for a moment. "Perhaps even related to a god."

"Related to a god? Like Bacchus?" Sera recalled her research and dreams.

The woman nodded. "That would make the most sense."

"Are you saying Bacchus was a real god?" Her teacup rattled as her hands shook. She wasn't sure she could handle that thought just yet. Vampires and witches were enough for one night.

Renee smiled and spread her hands. "Who's to say? I worship Diana, the Roman goddess of the hunt and moon. I believe she's real, and the source of my Sight. There are still many of us who worship the gods and goddesses of ancient times. Even Christianity can be considered ancient."

Sera stared at her tea, the leaves settling on the bottom of her cup, the water stilling. Her eyes lost focus as she considered the possibility of a spirit, or a god, somehow working through the amulet. She found some peace in the knowledge that her mother hadn't died in a freak caving accident and disappeared off the face of the earth.

If only her father knew. Maybe she should tell him that her mother had been trying to locate a magical amulet, which had then been used to disarm the very vampire who killed her. She was a damn hero. But she didn't know what her mother was trying to prove. Besides, he probably wouldn't take it well.

What was so important about the amulet that this vampire killed her mother and the other witches when they normally left each other alone? She needed to find out what happened after the cave was sealed.

Thinking about the vampire who killed her mother, the Eternal, Sera's cheeks burned with rage. It seemed like such a senseless act of violence. She understood vampires weren't the good guys, but a being that powerful didn't need to destroy an entire coven. It sounded like the creature could have just waltzed in and practically taken the cursed thing out of their hands. Was the Eternal afraid of exactly what happened coming to pass? Did she cause a self-fulfilling prophecy by involving herself?

Catching sight of Renee watching her, she realized she had been lost in her thoughts for some time. She gave a half-hearted smile, exhaustion not allowing her to smile further, and set down her empty teacup.

"Sorry, I'm just amazed that this whole other side to life, and death, exists, and I never knew. I never even had an inkling. I wish my mom had told me," Sera said, dazed as she realized how much she still didn't know.

What else is out there?

"Most people don't," Renee said with a sympathetic smile as she stood. "I want you to stay here tonight, where it's safe. Let your boyfriend know. If he's working, he should be safe at the hospital."

"But—"

"I'm not taking no for an answer," she said. "This house is protected by magic, his is not. At least not yet. I'm going to put some magic into a few crystals that you can give to anyone you think the vampires may go after to get to you."

Sera blinked at Renee, slowly registering what she said. "They'll come after me. Of course—what am I supposed to do?" Drawing her knees to her chest, she wrapped her arms around them and dropped her head, desperation filling her mind.

Renee walked over and squeezed Sera's arms. "Don't panic, first and foremost. We'll come up with a plan tomorrow, but for now, you need sleep." After some gentle encouragement to help Sera stand, Renee walked her back into the hallway and pointed up a flight of stairs.

"First door on your left. The bathroom is the second door on the left. You can't really get lost in this place," Renee said. She hesitated before asking, "May I study the amulet tonight?"

"Be my guest." Sera dug in her bag, retrieving the amulet wrapped back up in its towel. Handing it to Renee, the slightest of tugs pulled at her heart as she let go.

Renee opened the towel and gazed at the amulet, shaking her head.

"I truly never thought I'd see this again." She smiled, then motioned for Sera to head upstairs.

She followed Renee's directions and found the guest room exactly where she described. The small space was furnished with a simple, full-sized bed covered with a floral comforter, a nightstand holding a tall vase filled with a few dainty snowdrops, and nothing else. Situated in the middle of the house, the room was warm despite the frost outside due to the lack of a window. She dropped her bag next to the bed and climbed in, not even bothering to remove her clothes.

* * *

The god's teeth sank into the flesh of her neck, burning like fire and ice all at once. Liviana gasped in pain and surprise. Cold hands held down her arms and legs as the instinct to fight kicked in. Within a matter of moments, the sharp throb melted into a simmering warmth that radiated through her whole being.

Her life drained away through the openings in her neck, but she didn't fear it. The sensation was not as painful as Bacchus made it seem. In fact, it was downright pleasant. Liviana relaxed into the moment, feeling loved as she and her sister locked eyes. She hardly noticed when he moved away, her body limp and lifeless.

The High Priestess stepped in front of the altar, obscuring Octavia from her view. Holding the chalice to Liviana's lips, the woman lifted her heavy head to the brim. The strong metallic scent of blood within made her stomach turn and nostrils flare. She didn't have the energy to refuse.

The liquid, which she thought would be as foul-tasting as it smelled, danced its way across her tongue and down her throat, engulfing her senses in pure pleasure. Nectar-like in texture and wine-like in flavor, it drew her in, and she drank eagerly. When the chalice was drained, the High Priestess stepped away.

Liviana lay there, still weary down to the bone, but a new life force flowed through her body. Her veins, muscles, organs—every inch of her—started to thrum as the god's blood coursed through.

Then her body began to smolder, from within.

CHAPTER 16

Solomon

"Um, what just happened? Why didn't you just take the amulet from her?" Alexander asked as they walked back toward the Maserati. They had parked far enough away from the witch's house that they wouldn't be seen. Even though it was dark out, a car like that was hard to miss.

The walk gave Solomon a chance to regain control of his emotions, reining in the anger stimulating his fangs to prepare for hunting. Frustration continued to roll through him like thunder as he clenched his fists.

"Our lives just became exponentially more difficult," he replied, opening the car door. "And possibly forfeit."

Alexander raised his eyebrows as he climbed in and

started the engine. "For what?"

"Did you smell the difference in her scent tonight?" he asked, trying to be patient despite their failure to obtain the amulet before now. The kid didn't know the whole truth about their waning powers yet.

Alexander made a face. "Yeah, she definitely had a vinegary smell. Like outside the museum. Bacchus?"

Solomon nodded. "The god has claimed her. He's going to do everything he can to protect her."

"You lost me." Alexander pulled the car away from the curb.

"You know the origin of our kind, but you don't know the origin and history of the amulet. Lorenzo will tell you when he thinks you're ready," Solomon said. They drove the rest of the way in silence as they each mulled over the night's confrontation. Or at least, he assumed Alexander thought about it the way he did.

"But, we're basically screwed is what you're saying," Alexander said as he parked the car in the mansion's back driveway.

"Right." Solomon opened the car door.

Music hit their ears as they entered the mansion. Lorenzo had apparently decided to throw a party while they were out. Solomon's shoulders relaxed, knowing the distraction of young blood would help keep their maker calm. As calm as he could be with more bad news, anyway.

They followed the music to the expansive living room, which doubled as a party room on nights like that. But living room was an understatement—it was the size of the average American's entire house. The middle of the room sank several feet into the ground and provided a generously sized dance floor, surrounded on all four sides by three steps leading down. The people dancing there could easily be seen and chosen by the Immortals in attendance.

The room opened up onto an equally large back patio, the swimming pool complete with a hidden grotto and slide. Lorenzo's pool may have been the inspiration for Hugh Hefner's, but Solomon couldn't be sure and never cared enough to ask.

Feeling a nudge on his arm, Solomon looked at Alexander, who motioned to Lorenzo's favorite corner. The Immortal sat with several young men and women, all of whom were vying for his attention. He had that effect on money-hungry humans, even without his additional *influence*.

When Lorenzo saw them approach, he smiled broadly and opened his arms in greeting. "Ah! My boys! You have good news." His eyes flashed in threat despite his smile.

"We've hit a complication," Solomon said.

Lorenzo nodded but didn't disentangle himself from his adorers, a sign he wasn't interested in the details. "I trust you will resolve the issue in a timely manner." A flick of his hand dismissed them before he turned his attention back to the adorers.

Knowing better than to say more while humans were present, Solomon dipped his head in assent and led Alexander back out of the room.

"You're not going to tell him what the 'complication' is?" Alexander asked in the hallway, running a hand through his blond curls. "Did we really just drive all the way here for you not to say anything?"

Solomon dug his nails into his palms. "We'll wait out the night here and track her if she leaves the witch's house.

As long as she doesn't wear the amulet, we still have a good chance of getting it without additional resources," he explained, trying to keep his voice level as Alexander rolled his eyes. "It would not be wise to anger Lorenzo to that degree with humans present. You know it'd turn into a slaughter, and I don't feel like cleaning up that sort of mess."

"Well, I'm going back to the party. I'm not going to mope around like I'm sure you will. Some of us actually enjoy our immortality," Alexander said as he opened the door to the living room again. "Come and get me when it's time to leave."

Narrowing his eyes, Solomon took a deep breath as his protégé disappeared into the crowd. The Immortal guard standing on the inside of the door raised a questioning eyebrow at Solomon, who shook his head in return. The guard pulled the door shut, leaving him alone in the hall.

Turning on his heel, Solomon followed the hall to the servants' quarters, needing to be as strong as possible in the morning. Most of the human servants in Lorenzo's employ wanted to become Immortals themselves. As part of their advancement to immortality, they signed a contract to allow the Immortals to feed off them whenever the need arose. The Immortals, in turn, agreed to only take as much as their bodies required and not enough to kill any human. Unless the human broke the life-binding confidentiality agreement outside the mansion, of course.

Solomon hoped the kid would feed on a stranger at the party as discreetly as possible. The Immortals had to ensure they weren't feeding off the same human all the time even though some tasted better than others. Human blood needed time to replenish, and too much blood loss meant a lower quality of work the next day. It was business, after all.

After he had his fill, he headed to the library. As much as he hated Lorenzo's passion for the old, there were some things he couldn't find on the internet because they had been "lost" to human history. Some truths were better kept out of mortals' hands.

Solomon browsed the shelves until he found what he was looking for. He pulled out an ancient manuscript, a relic from the Great Library of Alexandria, and his only source of information on Bacchus and their Immortal origins other than talking to Danae. But asking Danae was a fool's errand. She held her secrets close.

The wooden chair creaked as Solomon sat at one of the antique rolltop desks. He unrolled the manuscript and started to read.

CHAPTER 17

Serafina

*L*iviana writhed, curling up into a ball then stretching out, trying to escape the fiery pain as her blood boiled. Screaming for help as she was sure she would ignite, she fell from the altar to the stone floor. She shook and rolled in agony, blood-curdling screams echoing throughout the temple.

Just as Liviana reached out, trying to find something— anything—with which to take her own life, to end the torture, it stopped. She lay still, panting against the coolness of the stone, pressing her cheek against it to chill her inner flame. The pain had dispersed, but the dying embers within remained. She opened her eyes when she sensed feet approaching, a vinegary scent drifting toward her nose.

Bacchus held out his shimmering hand toward Liviana and helped her to her feet, her legs still shaking.

"Welcome, my child, to the Thiasus." His voice boomed in the temple.

Liviana's legs steadied beneath her as she stood, stronger than she remembered them being before. She looked up to his face and into his eyes. They were green, she saw. But veined with gold and glittering with an internal light. A god's eyes.

The squeal of a dying mouse drew her attention. She whipped her head toward the sound, curious to know what animal had gotten inside the temple to catch its prey. But the building was devoid of any animal predators.

Bacchus chuckled, a rumbling heard deep within his chest. *"Your senses have become godlike, little one. What you hear is outside the walls of this shrine."*

A lavender scent swirled in the air as her sister approached. Octavia took her by the hands.

"I'm so happy you've joined us, little sister," she said, her blue eyes a brighter hue than Liviana remembered, like the blue of an early morning sky. *"Things will be very different for you from now on. You will acclimate to the sensory overload soon."* She led Liviana to a corner of the temple where Horatia lay asleep on a blanket.

Confused, Liviana's forehead crinkled as her eyebrows drew together.

"We gave her herbs to sleep through the ceremony. But now, you need to feed on a living, mortal source to complete your transformation. Bacchus's blood only begins the change." Octavia knelt down next to the girl and brushed her hair away from her neck. Her friend sighed in her sleep at the touch.

Staring at the neck, pulsing with so much blood, Liviana knelt down. She could hear the girl's slow heartbeat. Steady, but strong. The need to feed was irresistible and excited her, but still she hesitated, balling her hands into fists. This was her friend. No, she couldn't do that to her. What would that even make Liviana?

"You're only going to drink enough to satisfy the hunger, not enough to kill her. She'll recover. But failing to feed will mean your own death at sunrise," Octavia explained as she rested her hand on Liviana's shoulder.

Not ready to die, she bent forward toward the lily-white spot Octavia tapped. Her nostrils flared as she got closer, picking up the scent of the beating blood beneath the delicate skin. Canines extending and protruding from her mouth in response, the hunger rose like a wave within her. She struck, surprised at how easy it was to release the sweet flow of liquid life. Liviana drank eagerly, feeling the change within her deepen and solidify with each gulp.

A hand on her shoulder gently pulled her away what felt like only a few moments later. "Remember, not too much. We want your friend to return to town unharmed." Octavia briefly put her thumb in her mouth to wet it, then wiped her saliva over the two puncture wounds.

The holes sealed and disappeared.

"We never want humankind to discover we exist as we do," Octavia explained. "Though we are fierce predators and not unlike the gods, humans vastly outnumber us and will destroy us if it ever came to war."

"Why did you come home after your change? Were you going to feed on us?"

She gave a rueful smile. "No. I was foolish, thinking I knew better than the others. I was wrong."

"What are we if no longer human?" Liviana asked, her insides fluttering.

"Invisible. Powerful. Immortal. We are Bacchae."

* * *

The welcome scent of cooked eggs and freshly brewed coffee met Sera's nose as she came down the stairs the next morning.

"I didn't think you drank anything but tea," Sera said with a smile, feeling refreshed for the first time in a long time. Something about her latest dream left her satisfied. Probably because the girl didn't die after all. Not fully, anyway.

Renee chuckled over the skillet, where she was busy scrambling up the last of the eggs. "There's toast and butter already on the table. Coffee and mugs are by the sink."

Sera helped herself to the coffee before sitting at the table. She liked her coffee black as night and hotter than a midsummer day. Wrapping her fingers around the mug, she inhaled the earthy aroma before slurping it slowly to avoid burning her tongue. Before meeting Hiro, she dated a guy who thought slurping was rude, even though it helped aerate the coffee to get the full flavor, much like wine. Sera ended things with him shortly after his pretentious comments.

"I had another dream," she said over the steam rising from her mug.

"Oh?" Renee brought over the eggs and sat down, scooping a hefty amount onto Sera's plate before taking some for herself.

"If my dreams are truly coming from the amulet, then I know how these creatures were created," Sera said.

"I would bet my life on that being true. Eat, then tell me what you saw." Renee tapped her fork on the plate.

Sera shoveled a few bites into her mouth before continuing.

"Bacchus created the Eternals, at his mystery rites. He chose new humans to become vampires—Bacchae is what Octavia called them. The god would drain them of blood, then they would drink *his* blood in return. I actually got to feel what Liviana went through in the transformation, which was, in the most understated comment of the century, unpleasant. And I saw the world through her Bacchae eyes." Sera shook her head slowly. "It's unreal. They really are supernatural."

"Ah. I heard you cry out in the middle of the night. Ouch." Renee tilted her head to the side as she took another bite. "Infused with a god's blood would make them more like demigods than the undead. Or they were before most of their power was removed," she said with a slight smirk.

As Sera chuckled through another mouthful of eggs, she nearly choked. She swallowed hard and coughed, her eyes watering.

So graceful.

"What do I do? I can't just give up the amulet—my mom died trying to protect it. I don't know how or why, but it found its way to me." Sera set her fork on the table, her stomach stuffed to the brim. "Did you learn anything about it last night?"

"Unfortunately, no." Renee stood and retrieved the amulet, still wrapped in the towel, from the counter. She laid it on the table between them, flicking the edge of the towel over to uncover the amulet. "Whatever is in there is keeping itself hidden. I'll be right back."

Sera glanced over her mug at the amulet. A prickling sensation washed over her, and she shivered.

Renee returned holding a small cloth bag decorated with a smiley face pattern all over it.

"Don't mind the print. I was on an emoji kick a while back." Renee chuckled. She poured out the contents onto the table next to the amulet—clear marbles and thin leather threads about a foot long. At least, they looked like marbles, only flatter.

Sera picked one up to see it closer but dropped it with a gasp.

"I forgot you haven't seen one of these before," Renee said with an apologetic grimace. "These are crystal wards, imbued with defensive magic to protect the bearer from offensive magic, as well as supernatural creatures like vampires. Ba—what'd you call them?"

"Bacchae. Like bock-eye."

"Right. Anyway, they've got a bit of a zing to them. I just gave them all a tune-up last night—my entire coven created the wards years ago, which means they're especially effective."

"Wait, you said creatures. As in plural? There are other things out there?" Sera blinked at Renee.

The woman smiled. "Let's handle one thing at a time, shall we?"

Returning her gaze to the table, Sera agreed internally that any more world-altering information would have to wait.

"What do I do with it?" She picked up a crystal again, more cautiously this time. Her fingers tingled where she held it.

"Ideally, wear it," Renee said as she grabbed a leather thread. She put the crystal within the small pouch sewn onto the middle of the thread then tied it around Sera's neck. No tingling sensation this time.

"Another amulet," Sera murmured as she touched the crystal through the pouch.

"The others are for Eleanor, your father, and your boyfriend. Is there anyone else you can think of?" Renee asked.

Sera shook her head, relieved for the first time to be so focused on her studies that she didn't have many close friends who could be used for negotiation with immortal terrorists.

"Nora will be easy because she's already aware, but my dad and Hiro... What do I tell them? How do I get them to wear one of these?" Sera cringed at the idea of telling either one of them the truth. She'd have to tell Hiro soon, though.

"Did you forget you had these authentic Italian leather necklaces to give them as gifts? They're all the rage in Italy." Renee winked at her. "You can always tuck it into a wallet if the fake gift idea doesn't fly. They have a pretty decent radius of coverage from wherever they sit."

Sera's phone buzzed.

Nora: "Can we talk tonight?"

Sera: "Yes! Our usual spot? 7?"

Nora: "Make it 8 & we've got a date. Smooches."

"I'm meeting up with Nora tonight, so I'll be able to give her a crystal then," Sera said. "I'll have to take the train out to see my dad as soon as I can." Being able to afford the luxury of having a car in a city like the District didn't come with her teaching arrangement, nor did she usually need one with the convenience of the Metro and her own two feet.

"I've got a car that never gets used. I prefer to walk around town. I don't go far. You'll be doing me a favor by taking it out, so I don't have to do my monthly trip around the block to keep the engine alive," Renee said.

"How would I get through this without you, Renee?" Sera reached across the table and squeezed one of her hands.

"You wouldn't, kiddo." They both chuckled at the witch's attempt at humor, but Sera knew it was true.

Sera stood from her chair then promptly sat back down again, her eyes wide. "How am I supposed to just pretend like everything is normal? I have classes to teach all this week before Thanksgiving break, and an Eternal vampire-like creature is trying to hunt down the amulet, which has chosen to be with *me* of all people." Gripping the table, her voice rose in pitch as she spoke.

"Breathe, Sera. It's going to be okay. Things will never be 'normal' again, at least not your current one. But you'll adjust to a new normal, and each day will get easier and easier," Renee said in a calm voice.

Nodding, Sera willed her heart to slow its pace and took a few deep breaths.

"All right, I can do this." She bundled up the amulet before placing it into her bag once again, the smiling bag of crystals and threads along with it.

* * *

Once she turned off the interstate on the way to her father's house, Sera passed beneath tunnels created by long tree branches. The drive became a rain of fire as foliage of all colors floated to the ground around the passing cars.

Fall always reminded Sera of her mother's hair—browns, golds, and reds intermixing in the most mesmerizing way. When it had been cool enough to roll the windows down on their old hatchback, long since gone, her mother's hair would flutter like leaves on the wind, her laugh music to Sera's ears as they both relished the crisp, fresh air.

Life had changed as drastically as those leaves and in a similar amount of time. Soon the branches would be bare as all the leaves finished their descent to the ground. A shiver ran up her spine as she hoped her life wouldn't follow suit.

Fall Sundays in the Finch household were football days. The sounds of the referee whistles, crowds cheering, and sportscasters debating the plays filled their home. That was the church Sera knew growing up. So, she didn't doubt she would find her father in his usual worn-out easy chair parked in front of the TV.

Before she even reached the front door, Sera heard him yelling at what she could only assume was a fumble that should have been caught. She smiled at the familiar sound as she let herself in, closing the door behind her.

"Hey, Dad," she called out over the volume of the TV.

His hand lifted up in "hello," but his focus remained on the play. He groaned when it ended and leaned back in his chair, looking up with a smile as she walked into the living room. It had been almost six months since she last saw him thanks to her summer and school schedule. But besides being more grey in the beard and slightly rounder in the belly, he looked the same as he always did.

"Long time, no see, honey. What brings you out to the boonies?" Teasing her about loving the city life as much as she did was a favorite pastime of his, but it was also a jab at how little she visited. She always told him it went both ways—he had never seen the inside of her apartment and she had been there for over two and a half years, since she started graduate school.

"I forgot I had a gift for you from Italy. I found it when I was packing up to stay at Hiro's." The smooth lie surprised her as she pulled the leather thread out of her pocket.

He took the offered necklace from her and stared at it. "I'm sorry, honey. What do I do with it?"

"It's a necklace. Made from authentic Italian leather. I've got a matching one." She pulled her scarf down slightly to show him her own.

He nodded as he looked between the two threads. "I'll be the talk of the town wearing 'authentic Italian leather,'" he said with a mock accent. He winked, then held his back out to her. "Would you put this on my nightstand for me? I don't want to forget it in the morning."

She held in her sigh. It had been a long shot. "Sure, Dad. I'll be right back."

Taking the necklace, Sera headed upstairs to his bedroom. Knowing he wouldn't actually wear it, she slipped the crystal out of the tiny bag before setting the thread on the table next to his bed. The crystal's energy thrummed against the palm of her hand. She located his wallet in a drawer and found a spot to hide the crystal. Thankfully, he hadn't changed wallets in years, probably decades, so the leather was supple to the point of being a wonder it still held together. She couldn't even tell the crystal was inside. Now just to hope it wouldn't fall out.

Catching sight of her favorite picture as she came back downstairs, Sera stopped. A trail ran through the dust as she traced the lines of her mom's face with a fingertip, warmth spreading through her to her core. Her mother had been a witch. A powerful one. Was she planning on telling Sera when she got older? That damn amulet was the reason she'd never know.

She glanced toward her bag lying near the front door, her blood running cold just knowing the amulet was in there and some mythical monster turned real was coming for it. She shivered and blew a kiss toward her mother's face before returning to the living room.

Watching her father from the doorframe, she reminisced about her childhood in this room, enjoying football together as she cuddled on his lap. Sera missed those days when they were closer, when her mom was alive and baking some tasty treat in the kitchen, the scent of cocoa and vanilla wafting through the house. Now, it smelled old and slightly musty. It needed a good airing out and a deep clean. She added that idea to her mental list of Christmas gifts.

"I can stay for a while, if you like. Maybe we can do dinner together before I head back to the city?" she offered on a whim.

He seemed surprised at the suggestion, making her wince on the inside. It shouldn't surprise him that his little girl wanted to spend time with him.

"Sure, honey, that sounds great." The skin around his eyes crinkled as he smiled. "You know you're always welcome to stay here. Your room is just how you left it."

Kicking off her boots, she sat on the couch next to his chair and tucked her legs beneath her. She wished she could take him up on his offer, spend some time getting closer to him, but there was no way she was going to bring any supernatural attention his way if she could avoid it. She would do better going forward, once she figured out this mess with the Bacchae, anyway.

She glanced at him out of the corner of her eye. Could he have known her mom was a witch? Did he know about the world of the supernatural? Nah, there was no way.

"That commute for school would kill me," she said, then nearly choked as she realized a vampire was actually trying to kill her. He reached over and patted her on the back to ease the coughing fit.

"Just choking on my spit, graceful as usual," Sera said when she could breathe.

Although his eyes drifted back to the TV, he smiled at her old joke. She'd been klutzy since birth, she was sure. Probably fell out and landed on her head. Some things never die.

"Sorry to hear that thing you found went missing." He turned to look at her, his brown eyes soft. It wasn't an invitation to talk about her work, but she appreciated his attempt to show he paid attention to her life.

After her mother disappeared, her father refused to leave the house for almost six months after. When he did, he worked long hours and avoided contact with Sera. She could count on one hand how many school activities he made time for and how many birthday parties he planned. Going to college had caused a deeper rift between them because she continued to pursue her dream to be an archaeologist like her mother.

She and her father loved each other of course, but she found it difficult to talk to him about her life because the unbearable grief would return to his eyes as he looked into hers. She may have gotten her darker hair from him, but Sera's steel grey eyes were all her mother's.

"Yeah, it's been a real bummer for the entire department." Not to mention the havoc it wreaked on her life.

"Did Hiro tell you he stopped by earlier this week?" Her father had turned his eyes back to the game, but he wore a hint of a smile.

Sera blinked at him. "No…" That was *very* odd for Hiro to do. He had only interacted with her father four times over the past two years. Why in the world would he have trekked all the way out here?

"Said he was in the neighborhood. Nice kid. I always liked him."

As Sera's mind reeled with the possibilities for her boyfriend's visit, their team scored a touchdown. Her father shouted loud enough to make her jump in her seat.

"Beer time. You want one?" he asked as he stood from the recliner.

She shook her head, too stunned to speak, and watched him disappear into the kitchen next door. It would be completely like Hiro to visit her father to ask for his daughter's hand in marriage. He was super traditional that way. Thrills of excitement coursed up her spine at the thought. Maybe it was finally time for her happy ending. Mrs. Saito would *not* be happy. The thought took some of the wind out of her sails. But only a bit.

The rest of the afternoon was spent yelling at the game and catching up on all the neighborhood happenings. For brief periods of time, she was able to forget the amulet altogether.

It was one of the best afternoons she'd had in a long time.

CHAPTER 18

Solomon

The sharp scent of aged wine clung to the insides of his nose as Solomon slid into the passenger seat of the Maserati. He'd been watching Serafina and her father inside the house for the better part of the day while Alexander waited in the car. This was too big of a deal to let the kid mess it up.

"She didn't remove her scarf inside. If she's wearing the amulet, we're going to need a lot more power than just the two of us." He'd learned a thing or two from the manuscript he studied.

Alexander sighed as he tapped out a beat on the steering wheel. Much to Solomon's annoyance, the kid had been a wannabe drummer in his past life and carried his so-called passion into his Immortal one. If Lorenzo hadn't done so already, Solomon would have killed the younger Immortal's past handler for letting him maintain such traits.

They continued to wait. The sun set early these days, and it was nearly dark out when the front door opened again. Alexander groaned when they saw Serafina bundled up, hugging her father before heading to her car.

"We'll keep following her until we have confirmation the amulet's not yet worn. Let's go," Solomon said.

The two men followed the girl back to the city, not overly concerned if she noticed someone behind her. Chances were she wouldn't, even a car as distinct as the Maserati. Parking normally wasn't an issue on a Sunday night, but an event at the convention center meant the streets nearby were lined with cars.

They parked in a restricted alley close to where Serafina finally found parking. The custom plates on the Maserati would ward off any ticket or towing-happy cops. Lorenzo's exalted status within the District's political and social elite ensured that. He supplied the police department with generous donations, and they looked the other way. Business as usual.

Strolling behind the girl as she walked at a brisk pace down the street, Solomon noted with pleasure that the sidewalks were virtually free of other humans. Whatever event was going on at the convention center must have already started. They'd have to take the risk of exposure with the passing cars.

"She's headed for The Morning Grind a block away, probably to meet Nora. It's their usual meeting spot," Solomon said.

Just then, the girl unwound her scarf. The smell of salt in her sweat drifted toward them. Walking in the city caused a lot of heat for humans, even in the middle of winter. No amulet, just a leather necklace. He couldn't help the grin that came to his face, his fangs extending with delight.

The chase would end tonight.

She stopped without warning and whirled around, facing them as they approached. The look of fear in her grey eyes turned to one of steely determination when she recognized them.

"Come to suck my blood, have you?" she asked.

The slight shake in her voice betrayed her firm stance, but Solomon slowed his pace anyway. She knew what they were now and how dangerous confronting them would be, and confidence wasn't her typical demeanor. Something was off.

Alexander grinned at her, his fangs glistening in the streetlights. As usual, he probably hadn't picked up on the change in Serafina's behavior.

"Just give us the amulet, and no one gets hurt," the kid said.

Solomon rolled his eyes upward, unable to hide his distaste at the awful cliché. He could be such an embarrassment to their kind.

"This will all be over as soon as you give me the amulet. You can go back to your boring human life with your boring human boyfriend," Solomon said as he stepped forward.

She scoffed. "He's not boring. He's perfect."

Fangs brushed his lower lip as he smiled. "Let your life return to normal. Hand it over." He held out his hand.

Her arm covered her bag protectively. "Over my dead body. My mom died at the hands of a vampire-Bacchae-thing because of this damn necklace. Or claws. Whatever you have. I'm not about to give it up to another one of your kind," she spat back at him.

Solomon raised his eyebrow at her use of the word *vampire*, but it certainly wasn't the first time a human mistook him for a mythical creature. He could smell her fear dissolving as she grew angry.

"As you wish." Solomon spread his hands in mock sympathy. He gave an almost imperceptible nod to his protégé.

Alexander rubbed his hands together before lunging at the girl, who threw her hands up in defensive instinct. But instead of ripping her to shreds, he hit an invisible wall a few feet away from her and fell backward, his body hitting the ground with a loud thud. A blue sedan screeched to a halt.

Jumping back up to his feet as gracefully as a cat despite his weight, Alexander circled her, unable to break the force field surrounding her each time he tried.

Solomon narrowed his eyes, ignoring the bald man yelling at them from his car. How was she able to block Alexander's attempts?

"You're not wearing the amulet," he accused her.

Serafina peeked her eyes open and lowered her arms. Her breath released with a rush. "No, I'm not."

"The witch," Solomon snarled. The girl's smirk confirmed it. He should have anticipated the witch's help, but he was losing his edge after years of little to no action.

"Hey, what's going on here?" a gruff voice asked. The older man from the car had gotten out and walked toward them with hesitating steps.

Solomon's lips pulled back as he bared his fangs at the interloper.

The man stopped a few feet short, his eyes opening wide. "What the—" Before he could complete the sentence, Alexander descended upon him, tearing into the soft flesh of the man's neck. Within a matter of moments, the gurgling sounds and twitches ceased.

"Damn it, Alex."

Lifting his head from the neck, the kid's mouth and chin were covered in the crimson life force. "What? He saw us." His fangs retracted as he let the limp body fall unceremoniously to the ground.

"Have a nice night, fellas!"

Both Immortal heads whipped toward the girl's voice as she disappeared around the corner. Solomon put a hand on Alexander's arm to stop him from following her.

"It's no use. She's protected with a ward," he growled as Serafina disappeared around the corner. His nails bit deep into the palms of his hands as their key to remaining alive vanished. "We need a new plan."

Alexander gaped at him, blood still dripping from his chin to the ground. "You don't even want to try? What if we both attack her at once? Our combined strength, especially at night, has to be good for something, right?"

"A defensive ward isn't like wearing a suit of armor where there are gaps between the plates. Its protection is absolute. We need to figure out how to bring the entire shield down," he said.

Alexander crossed his arms over his chest. "And how do we figure that out?"

"Research." He pointed to the body. "Bring that. You're cleaning up any mess it makes." Turning around, he headed toward the alley where they parked.

A groan came from behind, but the kid did as he was told. The sound of boots scraping along the ground followed them.

* * *

Solomon glanced up over his book as Alexander walked into the library.

"It's been over twenty-four hours," the kid said, leaning against a bookshelf. "Lorenzo's starting to get restless. Getting the amulet from the girl should have been easy. Have you figured anything out yet?"

Solomon glared back at him. He had been going through all of the manuscripts he could find on witchcraft, but so far he was striking out. A reminder of his failure wasn't helpful.

"This would go a lot faster if you would sit down and crack open a book yourself," he said.

Alexander shrugged. It was obvious research wasn't his thing.

"As far as I can tell, the wards are impenetrable. We would need a more powerful witch to perform a deactivation spell, and witches are few in number these days. Even fewer will assist Immortals in bringing down a god."

A sigh escaped him. He had really been enjoying all that modern technology brought his way until this despicable relic showed up. He didn't want his Immortal life to end just yet, but failing to retrieve the amulet may result in just that. The past century was made for him, made for his human brothers and sisters as well.

Lorenzo had purchased Solomon from his previous owner in the early 1800s, having been a prize amongst slave owners because of his strength, quiet determination, and lighter-colored skin compared to his kinsmen. Born a bastard, Solomon knew his father had been one of his mother's owners, but he hadn't found out who before he himself had been sold at the ripe old age of ten.

It hadn't taken much, if any, convincing for Solomon to readily accepted the contract of immortality in return for lifetime employment to his maker. Even back then, life in Lorenzo's employ was luxurious in a way most folk only dreamed of. And, unlike Alexander, Solomon had put in years of blood, sweat, and tears before Lorenzo had finally considered him worthy of the change.

He had fought for freedom during the American Civil War and bathed in the blood of his final owner. In 1963, he had traveled hundreds of miles with his brothers and sisters several generations removed, marched up to the doorstep of the new nation, and demanded equal rights. Decades later, his human race still struggled to achieve equality, but he could see a new wave of activists rising to finish the dream. He wanted to live to see them succeed.

"Maybe Danae can do it." Alexander picked dirt out from under his fingernail and flicked it away.

"Danae?" He must have heard the kid wrong.

"She's a witch. Maybe she's more powerful than the human." Alexander shrugged with indifference.

Solomon stared. "What makes you think she's a witch?"

"I don't think it, I know it. Lorenzo told me one night after an especially juicy dinner."

If he had kept such human traits, Solomon's mouth would have hung open in shock, but most were long since gone. It infuriated him that Lorenzo would confide such an important detail to an Immortal as green as Alexander.

"Well, that both simplifies and complicates the matter," he said once his initial shock wore off. "We'll need Lorenzo to contact Danae, which means admitting we have run into an obstacle that wouldn't exist if we had gotten the amulet by now."

Solomon closed the book. At least they had a solution.

They found Lorenzo swimming laps in his private indoor pool. Even though the cold winter water of the outdoor one wouldn't bother him, Lorenzo preferred to swim in a balmy 98 degrees. It came complete with a retractable glass roof, a sauna big enough to hold an entire football team, and a fully equipped gym for stress relief. Luxury.

They waited for him to finish his laps.

"I can tell by your faces that you have something interesting to tell me," he said, pulling himself out of the water, which ran like rivulets down his body to collect at his feet. A servant stepped forward to hand him a towel.

It's possible the ancient Immortal had been considered attractive as a human in his own time. His chest and back were covered in a thick, coarse, black rug, his classic Roman nose was far too large for his narrow eyes and thin lips, and he would be lucky if he stood five feet tall. Solomon didn't often think about his maker's looks, but when the Immortal was standing there almost naked in his European-style swimsuit, it was hard not to wonder what attracted women and men to him when he didn't use his *influence*. It had to be his money.

"We need Danae's assistance in breaking through a defensive ward," he explained.

Lorenzo paused in the middle of drying off his face and arms. "That *is* interesting. Danae will not be pleased to involve herself."

Solomon spread his hands. "We need a powerful witch to counteract the human witch's magic. Alexander tells me Danae is such a witch."

"He is not wrong. Very well, I will let her know what you need. Is there anything else?" Dropping his towel at Solomon's feet, he didn't wait for them to respond before walking past him to the sauna.

Solomon's jaw clenched. He was losing Lorenzo's favor, and it was all due to this damned amulet. This whole situation needed to end, and soon.

CHAPTER 19

Serafina

S era turned the corner after the confrontation with the two Bacchae, Solomon's intense glare disappearing from view. Collapsing onto the steps leading up to a darkened front porch, her heart beat at least twice its normal rate and wanted to leap out of her throat.

She could have died at any moment confronting them like that. But as she saw them standing there, demanding the amulet like it was their right, the amulet her mother had died defending, rage had replaced any fear.

Just like she didn't believe these creatures existed until she saw the truth in the flesh—and fangs—Sera hadn't fully trusted the crystal's ability until she saw Alexander go flying backward like a mime who hit an invisible wall. She hadn't thought to ask Renee what she meant by "defensive magic." Their identical looks of disbelief were glorious until Alexander killed that man coming to her rescue.

That poor man *died* because of her. And horribly. She had never seen anyone killed before, and the image seared itself like a brand behind her eyes. Trying to shut out the bloody scene and the guilt accompanying it, she squeezed her eyes closed, her insides clenching.

Not wanting to dwell on it any further while alone in the cold and dark, Sera rubbed her face with gloved hands and stood from the stoop. The Morning Grind, the diner where she always met up with Nora, stood just a street away. Nora would know how to handle it, she always did. She stayed in the light of the streetlamps as she walked, glancing behind her every few feet.

The tiny diner squeezed in between two office buildings. Most people passed it by without giving a second glance, probably assuming it was a window to one of the offices. But Sera and Nora knew the staff on a first-name basis.

The bell above the door rang as she entered, and she breathed in the familiar smells of frying bacon and hazelnut-flavored coffee. But instead of feeling relief, her stomach churned as she once again thought of the dead man, who would never get to enjoy such things again. Shuddering, she scanned the small space for Nora.

"Hey, Cheryl, have you seen Nora yet?" she called over to a middle-aged, African-American woman leaning against the bar top that overlooked the kitchen.

Cheryl shook her head. "No, ma'am. Take your usual table, and I'll get you a coffee while you wait."

Removing her scarf and jacket, Sera hung them on the coatrack by the door before taking her seat at their booth. She checked her watch, 8:10, and glanced out the window. Even after a run-in with supernatural monsters, she managed to beat Nora to the diner.

"Here you go, darlin'," Cheryl said as she turned over the mug on the table and filled it with plain black coffee. Her artfully braided hair swept up into a bun on the top of her head, and her apron was as white as a freshly fallen snow— she must have just started her shift.

"Thanks, Cher. You on night shift?" Sera hoped the conversation would distract her from seeing the dead man's face. She wrapped her icy fingers around the mug for warmth.

"Yup. And on a Sunday." Cheryl snorted. Sundays were notoriously slow. "You doin' okay? You look like today's been a rough one."

Sera had a sudden urge to tell her, to tell anyone, that vampires existed, and she had just had a skirmish with two of them, but her magical crystal ward kept her safe. And then a man died... Her nose tingled as she held back tears.

"Yeah, it has been," she replied instead, taking a sip of the coffee. The bell over the door rang again, and both women looked over. It wasn't Nora.

"Any food?" Cheryl asked as she turned to go greet the new customers.

Sera shook her head. She pulled out her phone and checked it for what must have been the millionth time since she had parked. 8:14. No new messages.

Sera: "Where are you??"

Sitting back in the booth, she sipped her coffee as she

stared out the window, focusing on anything but the confrontation.

The bell dinged again.

Oh, shit. Sera's heart skipped a beat as she looked up. *Do they already know about the man who died?*

"Ms. Finch," Theo addressed her formally as he and Julia walked over to her booth. They slid into the bench across from her without asking if she was expecting anyone.

"Hello, officers. Er, detectives? Right? How can I assist you today?" Sera asked.

Am I being awkward? I'm definitely being awkward.

"We received an anonymous tip that we would find you here." Julia glanced at Sera's bag on the table. "With the amulet."

Sera's mouth dropped open, shock freezing her in place. Did Nora call the police on her? Or was she being framed for the actual theft?

"He also said you'd be here alone. And here you are, alone," Julia continued.

Sera snapped her mouth shut. *He?* So, not Nora. Who was setting her up? Solomon?

Theo dropped a warrant in front of her and opened up her bag, pulling items out and inspecting each one before setting it on the table.

"Hey—" Sera started to protest, but his stern gaze met her own, and she stopped. For a younger-looking man, he sure had the scolding father look down.

"Let's not make a scene," he said and continued to pull items out. Sera didn't carry much with her, so it didn't take him long to finish. She steeled herself as he reached his hand in one last time and felt around, his eyebrows pulling together in a look of confusion. He looked at his partner and shook his head.

"Where is it, Sera?" Julia asked, her voice lowered and threatening.

"I don't know," she answered honestly, blinking at them both.

"Did you put it in your pockets?" Theo asked.

Sera blinked at him again. "These are leggings. They don't have pockets."

The detectives exchanged a glance before sliding out of the booth.

"It would be in your best interest to return the amulet as soon as possible," Julia said as they walked away. The bell dinged over the door as they left the diner.

Sera turned her head to look at her bag, her heart racing. Did she lose the amulet? She opened her bag and flipped open the towel.

There sat the amulet.

What the... she thought in confusion. It was right in front of her, and yet he had missed it. The magic within the amulet must have hidden it somehow. That was the only explanation. Right?

"Everything okay over here?" Cheryl's voice startled her back to the present.

She slammed her bag shut.

"Yeah, peachy keen." Sera tried to conjure a smile to reassure Cheryl, but frazzled nerves made her lips quiver.

She glanced at her phone, 8:35, no new messages. It wasn't out of the ordinary for Nora to run behind schedule, but being this late with no heads-up was cause for concern.

Sera shoved her things back into her bag and slid out of the booth. "I've got to run. Can you tell Nora I'll be at her aunt's house if she shows up?"

"Sure thing, love. You stay warm out there." Cheryl walked the coffee carafe to the kitchen.

Sera bundled back up and headed to Renee's car, walking as quickly as she could without drawing attention. She held her bag tightly to her chest as she looked behind and around her every few feet, still expecting an attack at any moment.

Damn Bacchae.

* * *

"Is Nora here?" Sera asked as soon as Renee opened the door.

"No…" Renee took a step back to let her in. "Wasn't she meeting with you?"

"She didn't show up at the coffee shop. But the police did. They said they got an anonymous tip that I would be there alone." She handed Renee her bag and shrugged off her jacket.

"I almost thought it was Nora who tipped them off, which wouldn't make sense, but then the cop said 'he,' so obviously not Nora. But then the other cop, or detective, whatever their title is, opened my bag and didn't find the amulet. He practically dumped everything out and dug around inside, and nothing. It was right there." Sera could tell by the look on the other woman's face that she was rambling. She took a deep breath.

"Let's go sit in the library before you hurt yourself," Renee said as Sera struggled to unwind her scarf.

Freeing herself with one last yank, she threw the scarf on the coatrack.

"Oh, and your ward worked," she continued as they walked down the hall. "The Bacchae showed up, and Alexander tried to attack me, but he hit some kind of barrier we couldn't see. You should have seen the look on their faces." A giggle escaped her lips, quickly cut off by her gasping breath as she remembered the man.

"Then they *killed* someone! Right in front of me!" Tears sprang to her eyes as the reality of what she saw hit her full on.

Helping her find her way to one of the wingback chairs, Renee knelt in front of her. "Who?"

"I don't even know," she said, sniffling through sobs. "He was coming to help me, and Alexander practically ripped his throat out. There was so much blood, and they killed him because of *me*."

Renee shook her head, taking Sera's hand in her own and squeezing it. "You can't think that way. These creatures are dangerous predators. I know it's terrible to see, but what they did is on them. Okay?"

Wiping away tears with the back of her other hand, Sera nodded. Though she wasn't sure she agreed. Not completely, anyway. Walking around the city alone with an ancient relic that supernatural creatures were trying to take from her probably wasn't the smartest idea.

"Has Eleanor messaged you at all?"

Sera took out her phone to check again before shaking her head. "Nothing. It's not like her. She always lets me know if she's behind schedule, which is always."

Renee tilted her head to the side. "Well, let's not jump to any assumptions just yet. You both have classes tomorrow?"

"Tomorrow? How am I supposed to wait until tomorrow? What if something bad happened to her?"

"I don't get the sense that the Bacchae have her. It seems strange to me that they'd attack you on the street if they had leverage," Renee said, shaking her head.

Relief passed through her as the older woman brought order to the chaos of her mind. She sniffled. "Okay, then I should see her tomorrow."

"Why don't you stay here again tonight, and you can grab your things before class?"

"As safe as I feel here, I need to get this ward to Hiro before anything bad happens." Her skin prickled. She hoped it wasn't too late already.

Renee nodded. "Do you want to borrow my car?"

Her heart warmed at the woman's generous offer. "No, parking around Hiro's place and the university is such a pain in the ass. I think I'm pretty well protected now thanks to you." Sera touched the leather thong around her neck.

"Get going then, before it gets too late." Renee stood and shooed her toward the front door.

Hugging the woman on a whim, Sera sought the comfort she wished she could have gotten from her mother. Renee squeezed her tightly in return.

"You be safe, kiddo," Renee said after she helped with her jacket and scarf.

Sera headed for the Metro.

* * *

Hiro's apartment was dark and silent when she let herself in. Knowing how long and difficult his shifts could be, and that he'd be getting up early the next day for his flight home to Seattle for Thanksgiving, she wouldn't dare wake him. Instead, she watched him sleep for a moment, trying to guess how he would react to the news that vampires and witches existed when she finally had a chance to tell him.

Despite her initial reaction, Sera didn't find it that hard to believe—she had been a fantasy junkie since birth. Her parents had always encouraged her active and sometimes wild imagination. But Hiro grew up in a strict household where imagination was shunned and logic prevailed. Becoming a doctor had been his mother's dream for him, and he'd fulfilled it.

She headed to the bathroom to brush her teeth before calling it a night herself. Clothes lay in a heap on the bathroom floor, which was unlike him. Order ruled his world. Her heart ached as she thought about the day he must have had to just leave his clothes like that.

A few minutes and a clean mouth later, Sera climbed into bed beside Hiro. He stirred and turned toward her, opening one eye to peek at her.

"Hey, you," he said, still half asleep. His eye closed again.

She smiled at the man she loved. "I have a gift for you. Don't take it off, okay?" she whispered, slipping the leather thread around his neck and tying it.

His eyes still shut, Hiro nodded and nuzzled her before falling back asleep.

Sera sighed—missing him, loving him, and not knowing when or how she'd tell him about everything she'd learned. Not to mention Nora going incommunicado. Those creatures better not have done anything to her best friend. She would have to trust Renee for now.

She stared at the ceiling, counting shadows to quiet her anxious thoughts. Time was slipping away from her.

CHAPTER 20

Serafina

Thanksgiving week meant half the students were already gone and the other half were too restless to pay attention. Even Sera found it difficult to pay attention with Nora missing. Hiro had headed home to Seattle for the week and the long holiday weekend, even though he'd offered to stay until Nora turned up. As much as she wanted him to, there was no way his mother would understand. Mrs. Saito already had a difficult time with her perfect son falling for a girl who wasn't Japanese.

As usual, Sera had made holiday plans with her father. Neither of them cooked, however, so they planned their annual reservation at the restaurant down the street from his house. It'd been their tradition since her mom died. Maybe someday she'd learn how to cook a big, fat bird, so they could enjoy a home-cooked meal. But someday was not today.

By the afternoon, Nora hadn't turned up, and Sera started to panic as she imagined the worst. Nora's mom had even sent a text, asking if she knew why her daughter was giving her the cold shoulder. If something terrible had happened, she'd never be able to forgive herself.

"Renee, I have a really bad feeling about this," she whispered into her phone between classes.

"Come over. I'll do a locating spell, but it'll be more effective with your help," Renee answered on the other end just as Chad walked into her classroom.

"Okay. Gotta go." Sera quickly ended the call.

"Where is Nora? She hasn't shown up to teach any of her classes today, and she's not returning calls. She's acting completely unprofessionally." He folded his arms across his chest.

"First of all, I'm not Nora's keeper," she snapped at him, her blood boiling. "Second, you are a visiting scholar, or had you forgotten? You do not run this department."

Chad unfolded his arms, her response clearly not expected. "Serafina, you would be wise to—"

"To what? Be careful what I say around you? Are you going to force yourself on me again? Try to end my career?" Sera advanced toward him, her eyes narrowing. Her skin tingled as a surge of energy rushed through her. How dare he come into her classroom demanding *anything*.

"I don't know wh—"

"Oh, yes, you do, *Dr. Lambert*. You know exactly what I'm talking about." She closed in on him as he bumped into a desk, trying to back away.

She poked him hard in the chest. "You stay away from me. I'm not putting up with your shit any longer. Do you understand me?" She poked him again, harder. "Stop threatening me. Stop harassing me in my classroom. Stop *looking* at me."

She was close enough to him that she could see her reflection in his eyes. Her own looked wild and menacing, and she could've sworn they glowed gold for a moment.

His mouth hung open. Sera was pretty sure no one had ever talked to him like that in his life.

"I—" he stammered.

She used her poking finger to point toward the door. "Out. *Now.*"

Chad scurried out of the classroom.

Still fuming, Sera took a deep breath. That felt good. Really good. Where in the world had that come from? It was what she'd wanted to say to him from the very start, when he began making inappropriate comments to her. But she'd been afraid of making him angry, afraid he would hurt her or her reputation if she offended him.

Bastard, she thought with a roll of her eyes. Students started filing in for her next class.

"Class is canceled," Sera said to the closest student before grabbing her bag and leaving.

* * *

Locating spells in the twenty-first century apparently involved using a map app on Sera's phone. Renee wasn't a fan of modern technology, which meant she only had an ancient flip phone that wasn't built with accessible GPS. So, Sera's smartphone and the amulet lay in the middle of the small kitchen table, surrounded by a ring of candles. The two women sat on either end of the table.

"Can't you just snap your fingers or something?" Sera asked as Renee lit each of the candles with a match. Having no idea what to expect from a real magic spell, she attempted to smile, but her quivering cheeks interfered.

Renee chuckled, dancing flames reflecting in her eyes. "That would make my life far easier, wouldn't it?" After lighting the last candle, she blew out the match, a tendril of smoke drifting up from the end. She reached across the table and around the candles to take Sera's hands in her own.

"I'm hoping the amulet chooses to assist us in finding Eleanor." Renee gave a suggestive glance at the amulet. It didn't respond. "Okay, now this may feel silly, but close your eyes and concentrate on Eleanor. Think about anything you want to, as long as it's about her." She closed her own eyes and began to hum.

Sera did, in fact, feel silly closing her eyes, but she would do anything to find Nora. Her hair came to mind first—those blonde ringlet curls that framed her face in a short bob. Sera had always been envious of Nora's hair, so unlike her own dark strands that didn't respond to the toughest of heat. Straight hair wasn't as great as everyone tried to say it was.

Renee continued to hum.

Memories of their childhood crept in next. They would dress up together in their mothers' clothes, stumbling around each other's bedrooms in heels that would take years to fit. Giggling sessions ended in laughing so hard they had tears streaming down their faces. She was beyond blessed to have found her soulmate in her best friend. Before recent events, Sera hadn't been a strong believer in any higher power or supernatural beings like ghosts. Or vampires. But if vampires turned out to be real, then Nora was definitely her soulmate. Who said soulmates had to be lovers?

Hiro amazed Sera in every possible way, but she wouldn't call him her soulmate. A thrill of excitement coursed through her as she imagined sharing this new side to the world with him. He'd believe it when he saw it.

Renee's humming intensified.

Oh, right, Sera thought as she refocused on Nora.

Realizing the humming had stopped, she cracked an eye open. Renee stared intently at the phone.

"I don't like the look of this," she muttered as she rolled the crystal strands of her glasses' straps between her fingers.

"The look of what? What do you see?" Sera leaned forward toward the phone.

Renee pointed to two dots of light pulsing on the phone's map—one white and one red—near the Wharf in the southwest quadrant of the District.

"The white one is Eleanor. The white symbolizes a traditional, non-magical human being. The red is a witch," Renee explained.

"Why would she meet up with another witch?" Sera tried to recall if Nora knew anyone living in the Wharf, but no one came to mind.

Renee looked thoughtfully at the map, chewing on the end of her glasses. "I'm not sure. Witches aren't as common as we once were. We typically introduce ourselves to other witches or at the very least announce ourselves with a magic pulse whenever we enter a new territory."

Sera arched an eyebrow. "A magic pulse?"

"We can send a small blast of power through an area to announce our presence and intentions to other witches. It's a common courtesy, especially in a city the size of the District. The problem with this witch is he or she didn't make any kind of announcement, which makes me think ill intent or reckless. I'm hoping the latter."

"What about a new witch? Someone who just figured out they had power?" She didn't want to consider Nora with a witch in either of the scenarios Renee laid out.

Renee shook her head. "A red dot indicates someone who has a coven and considerable power. A newer, untrained witch would have more of a pinkish dot."

"Okay, so she's not answering her phone, she's been MIA since Sunday, and she's with an established witch who isn't you—what do we do?" Sera blinked at the other woman, her heart fluttering with fear.

"*We* don't do anything. I'm going to go get Eleanor, and you're going to stay here." Renee gave her a stern look before blowing out the candles. Wisps of smoke curled upward.

"There's zero percent chance of that happening." Sera leaned back in the chair and crossed her arms.

"If this is in the worst-case-scenario category, you're going to end up getting hurt. Or worse."

"Won't this ward protect me?" Sera tapped the leather thread.

"It depends how strong this witch's magic is. If they're as strong or stronger than I am, then it might not hold."

Renee paused and tilted her head to one side. "But the amulet…"

"You want to use the amulet?"

"I want you to wear it."

Sera blinked. "Come again? Wear it? After what happened when I touched it last time? How do we even know that's safe?" Her heart raced at the thought of wearing the amulet, for fear of the unknown, but also excitement. Wearing the amulet had been all she could think about whenever she was around it.

"The amulet has protected you from harm already by announcing its intentions to the Bacchae. My instinct as a witch is telling me whatever's inside has chosen you," Renee said.

"That's what Solomon said," Sera remembered out loud. "All right look, I'll wear the amulet *if* I need to. But this may end up being something totally harmless, and I'm not showing up wearing a stolen invaluable artifact to what could potentially be an elaborate trap by the police."

"Fair enough," Renee conceded. "Let's get ready."

After leading her upstairs, Renee pulled the attic ladder down. A slight buzz coursed over Sera's body as she climbed up, leaving her skin tingling.

"That was the secondary protection spell on the house," Renee explained the sensation. "If someone came up here without my consent, they would just see a dusty old attic." She pulled the string attached to the light when they reached the top.

Sera gasped, her eyes opening wide. The entire attic had been converted into a combined storage room and lab.

Stepping past the shelves, she stared at jars filled with murky liquid and unidentifiable inhabitants, vases of plants and flowers, boxes of dried herbs, and books. Lots and lots of books. She ended up standing at the table next to Renee, who was busy putting items into the pockets of a black trench coat hanging on a wall hook. The table was exactly as Sera remembered from high school science classes—home to Petri dishes, flasks, and even a burner.

"This is straight up out of a movie." Sera shook her head slowly in disbelief.

"Where do you think their inspiration comes from?" Renee winked then walked over to a tall filing cabinet. She rifled through the drawers and took out specific objects.

"Magic isn't as simple as waving a wand and saying some word or phrase, although that would be incredibly useful at times," she explained as she looked for items. "You've heard the phrase, 'Do as you will but harm none'?"

Sera nodded.

"The 'will' part is much deeper than it first sounds. It's the power to focus your intent and visualize what you want in order to make it come about. Witchcraft is the process of bending, weaving, and changing the reality we currently live in into what we want it to be."

A tremor shook Sera's body. The thought of changing the world with a mere thought, albeit a strong-willed thought, filled her with fear laced with excitement.

Renee continued to rummage through the drawers. "In most cases, magic needs to be prepared in advance of using it—potions, wards, and runes, for example. Potions are pretty elementary when it comes to magic, but they sure come in handy in a bind."

It made perfect sense, although it would have been nice to not need the preparation. Sera tried to figure out each item's use as Renee held them up for a quick inspection.

"To steady the nerves?" she asked as Renee put a drinking flask into an inside pocket of the coat.

Renee smirked. "It's filled with Dragon's Fire, a potion that will turn to flames when spat at or thrown on an enemy."

"Of course it does," Sera said with a wide-eyed nod, amazed that such a thing really existed. The normalcy of her previous life continued to melt away the more she learned about this hidden one.

Renee opened up the biggest drawer at the bottom of the cabinet and took out a pair of hand axes, grinning when she saw Sera's questioning look. "Tomahawks for throwing. Or chopping. If your magic fails, you always need a backup plan."

"You actually know how to use those things?" Sera was starting to feel wholly inadequate as a human specimen.

"I did once upon a time. Let's hope my old bones don't need to use them. Anything you need to grab?" Renee asked, sliding the axes into holsters attached to her waist. She grunted as she pulled the coat around her shoulders. A grim look crossed her face as if ready to go to war.

"Uh, nope." Sera had already grabbed her bag with the amulet packed safely inside and tucked her phone with the map into the back pocket of her jeans.

Renee nodded. "Let's hit the road."

CHAPTER 21

Serafina

The two locator dots brought them to an old house in the neighborhood surrounding the Wharf. Because the District had become such a transient hub for college students and young professionals, it meant much of the city became a ghost town for family holidays like Thanksgiving. Not having to search for parking after the sun went down was one more thing to be thankful for that year.

"Which house number is it?" Renee threw her gloves back into the car before shutting the door.

"2242," Sera said after consulting the map one more time. Shaky nerves made her doubt herself even though she had the number memorized. A cold breeze stirred up some leaves on the ground, creating an eerie rustling sound. She scrunched up her nose as the wind also delivered the scent of freshly caught fish from the actual wharf a few streets away.

Renee handed her a belt, which held a knife with a short blade encased in a leather sheath. "Just in case."

Sera blinked as she accepted the belt. "I literally have no idea what to do with this."

"For starters, wear it." Renee grinned. "Worst-case scenario, remove the blade from the sheath and wave it around wildly. Your sporadic moves might scare someone off."

"Ha ha." Sera rolled her eyes as she secured the belt through her belt loops, the sheath hanging down her hip. She took a deep breath. Hopefully, her inner klutz wouldn't try to get her killed.

"Ready?" Renee asked.

Sera looked up at the house. The siding was in desperate need of a power wash and had fallen off in multiple places. Wooden front steps looked more like death traps with jagged shards threatening to puncture shoes and feet if one dared to approach the door. Whoever lived there obviously didn't care about the disrepair. Or maybe it was abandoned.

Despite the fear clinging to her like a leech, she turned her head to Renee and nodded. The two women walked up the steps, avoiding the crumbling holes, and knocked on the door. The light next to the front door was either off or out, so they waited in the dark and silence for what felt like an eternity. Not even crickets kept them company.

No one came to answer the door. Sera didn't know if she was relieved or terrified. Leaning over the railing of the front porch, she peeked through the dingy front window.

Nothing could be seen in the darkness inside, but her skin bristled like she was being watched. She shook her head at Renee.

Pulling a small vial out of her inner coat pocket, Renee sprinkled some of the powdered contents into her palm. She rubbed her hands together, then placed one hand on the door handle and the other just above it where the deadbolt would be. She took a deep breath and exhaled onto the lock. Sera could feel the witch *push*—not with her body but with her mind. A small pulse of energy burst out like sonar from the witch's hands, causing the door to ripple in Sera's vision. A moment later she heard the familiar click of a deadbolt turning, and Renee opened the door.

Sera's pulse raced, her adrenaline rising as she added breaking and entering to her mental list of things she never thought she'd do in life. Right next to hiding a stolen amulet from the cops and witnessing magic firsthand. She almost giggled from her growing panic when Renee pointed two fingers toward her eyes, then motioned toward the house and put a finger to her lips, speaking to her in a universal language of make-believe spies. She didn't even know what she found the most funny—the breaking and entering, or the fact she could sense the magic used to break in, or the idea that they were about to face a witch of unknown power.

We're really doing this. Holy shit.

She followed Renee into the house. Standing outside was one thing, but going in set her skin crawling, like hundreds of tiny spiders had dropped from above.

As was common in the District, the house they entered was old, and the floors creaked beneath their feet regardless of how lightly they tried to tread. Cold sweat formed on her body as they crept toward the back of the small house in the dark, checking each room and door as they went—Sera with her phone's flashlight app and Renee with an actual flashlight. It didn't seem like anyone was home, nor had been for some time.

Almost bumping into Renee when she stopped, Sera's breath caught in her throat. The woman pointed toward the back of the kitchen, where a faint light shone under a closed door.

They listened for a moment. Nothing but the sound of their own rapid breathing and pounding hearts. Renee slowly turned the handle on the door. It opened up to stairs leading down to the basement, a single lit bulb hanging over the steps.

It had to be the basement, of course.

Renee pulled the flask of Dragon Fire out of her pocket and unhooked the lid. As Sera's pulse raced faster at the thought of the witch actually needing to use the liquid, the steady cadence beating in her ears threatened to drown out any other sounds. She followed Renee down the stairs in a slight crouch, trying to see past the overhanging wall as soon as possible.

The room appeared to be empty. Sera blew out the breath she held and sagged against the wall in relief.

Then she saw Nora.

Her friend lay curled up on her side on top of a dirty mattress—which might have been white once—in the corner of the basement, her mouth gagged. A faded blanket riddled with holes covered her body but left her bound hands and feet exposed, all of which were red, cracked, and raw.

"Nora," Sera whispered urgently, rushing past Renee toward her friend.

Her eyes shot open as Sera knelt next to the mattress. Nora looked and smelled like she hadn't bathed in days. Her hair stuck to her face, both covered in a few layers of dirt and oil. Sera's eyes watered, stinging, as she caught a whiff of what could only be described as a teenage boys' dirty locker room. Anger flared inside her like a lit match as she imagined what had befallen her best friend and cursed herself for her stupidity. If only she hadn't run from Renee's, then none of this would have happened.

Nora shook her head, her eyes wild with fear.

A nasally chuckle sounded from a darkened corner of the room. Renee moved next to them, the flask held behind her back. Taking a slow breath to calm her shaking limbs, Sera got to her feet.

"Well, well, well. My trap worked," a man said as he stepped forward out of the shadows into the pale light.

"Leif?" Renee asked, shock written across her face, her mouth popping open.

The man who stood before them looked like a mad man—he had wiry white hair that stood out from his head in random places; khaki pants and a half-tucked-in, button-down shirt, both of which looked like they hadn't been washed in a week; and his eyebrows, the same white color as his hair, overhung and threatened to obscure his eyes below. But his eyes were the worst part of his appearance— menacing dark pupils looked even larger behind thick, wire-framed glasses. They moved erratically between Renee and Sera, then landed on Sera's bag at her waist.

"I want what is rightfully mine." Licking his lips, Leif held out a hand toward the bag.

Renee stepped in front of her, keeping the flask hidden. Speaking in a low tone, she said, "Leif, it's me, Renee."

His eyes shot back up to Renee's face. "Oh, I know who you are. You needn't have come. The girl did her job bringing me my amulet."

"You don't seem like yourself. Where have you been for the last twenty years? You disappeared after the ritual." Renee's voice remained calm despite the obvious threat in his.

He scratched at his neck with his nails, black from the dirt that caked beneath them. "He called to me after we collapsed the cave. Tempted me with dreams of grandeur. Then as soon as he got what he wanted from the coven, poof! He vanished. For twenty years, I have been searching for him. For twenty years, he's eluded me, hidden where I couldn't find him. But now, he's surfaced once again, and he's toyed with me for the last time. I've won." A maniacal cackle wormed its way up his throat.

"Who is the 'he' you're referring to? Bacchus?" Renee asked.

"Give me the god, and you can all leave without harm." He took a step toward Sera, his lip curling up with a snarl.

"There's no reason to get violent. Let's talk this through. The amulet has chosen Sera—"

His roar of fury cut her off. Lunging toward Sera, he immediately hit the invisible barrier protecting her.

Sera staggered back from the force of his attack, like an earthquake had rolled underfoot.

Well, that isn't good.

Renee took a quick swig from her flask. A scorching flame flew like a stream of water from her mouth toward Leif as she unleashed the Dragon Fire. Feeling it from where she stood, Sera shielded Nora from the blazing heat.

The wild man's own protection spell deflected the rain of fire, and embers fell to the floor, scorched spots on the concrete marking where they fell. Sera thrust her hand inside her bag, grabbed the extra leather thread holding a crystal ward, and pulled it over Nora's head.

"Leif, stop, you don't want to harm me or these girls," Renee said, wiping her mouth with her sleeve.

He raised his arms, two black stones in each hand, and chanted in a language Sera didn't understand. Before she could blink, he hurled the stones toward her. She raised her arm instinctively, but the stones hit the barrier. Instead of bouncing off as he had, they embedded themselves into it. The barrier became visible, a crackling sphere surrounding her like a sizzling bubble. Holes formed where the black stones hit, the openings stretching outward.

Renee gasped. "Sera, the amulet! Now!"

Without a second thought, Sera snatched the amulet from her bag and wrapped it around her neck, feeling for the clasps at the ends. As her fingers fumbled, the ends of the amulet connected and sealed on their own, just as the last of her barrier dissipated like evaporating water.

When he saw the amulet, Leif charged at her again, his rage-filled howls paralyzing her with fear. Before he made it across the room, Renee threw a powder at him that exploded in his face. His magic protected him from any real harm, but he stopped short, his arms covering his face.

Somehow focusing amidst the turmoil, Sera used that moment to pull the knife out of the sheath at her waist. Her hands shook as she cut through the rope holding Nora as fast as she could. At least she knew how to use a knife for that purpose. She thanked her lucky stars he hadn't used magic to bind Nora.

Duck, a voice whispered in her head.

"What?" Sera squinted at Nora, who blinked back, the gag still in her mouth.

Invisible hands yanked Sera to the side just as Renee yelled her name. Something that looked like a bolt of lightning flashed over her head where she had been only a moment before and continued right through the basement wall, burrowing itself into the concrete where it continued to smolder.

Staring at the hole in the wall, her jaw trembled.

That could have been me.

The amulet lit up like a lighthouse—if a lighthouse used scarlet to call the ships to shore—bathing Leif in its bloody hue. A look of shock crossed his face.

"No. No, it can't be! It's mine. He's *mine!*" Spittle flew from his mouth as Leif roared again, his face transforming into a mask of rage.

A burst of energy rippled through Sera and down her arms. She could *see* the energy like a stream of wavering air crossing the distance toward Leif. The witch's defensive barrier illuminated as the force she emitted hit it. The forcefield crackled once, then dissolved into thin air like a popped bubble.

Leif's mouth dropped open for a moment before he turned and ran for the stairs. Sera was on her feet and after him before she could even consider her next course of action.

"Sera, stop!" a voice called out behind her, but her feet chased him up the basement stairs, down the hall, and out the front door. She wasn't in control of her body, but she didn't try to stop or even think about whatever was happening to her. The raw fury she felt toward this man threatening her life and the lives of her friends fueled her to give in. Clenching her jaw and her fists, she ran.

They both jumped over the broken front steps, Sera landing more smoothly than Leif, who tripped over his own foot and nearly fell. He recovered quickly, gaining traction on the pavement of the street. Still holding the knife, her arm readied it for throwing as she chased him.

Their feet beat a steady rhythm against the asphalt, but Sera was gaining on him, her breath coming out in short bursts. The veins throbbed in her neck as she kept up an unnatural speed. She couldn't remember running a day in her life, but it was glorious.

As they neared the Wharf, she could see crowds of people heading for the water's edge through the gap between two tall apartment buildings. There must have been a concert at the Anthem that night. Leif ran straight across the busy street without stopping, horns honking as cars screeched to a halt to avoid hitting him. Sera's arm raised to release the knife.

"*Stop!*" Willing her arm and body to obey, her arm fell back down to her side as she slowed to a stop. She tucked the knife back into the sheath before anyone could see it. The street was too crowded, too many people would see her act or get caught in the fight. She jogged across the street to follow Leif, her eyes narrowing as she surveyed the unfamiliar faces. She had lost him in the sea of people.

You better stay gone, she thought with a huff.

When she returned to the house, Nora and Renee were waiting beside the car. Nora rubbed her wrists where the ropes had cut into her skin.

"Oh my god, what were you thinking?" She grabbed Sera by the shoulders and shook her. Sera simply wrapped her arms around the tiny blonde and hugged her tight in return.

"Nor, you stink," she said as she squeezed Nora one more time. They both smiled then started laughing, from exhaustion and relief. The thought of losing her best friend was unimaginable.

"Okay, back to the house before anyone or anything else shows up with a claim on that amulet." Renee opened up the back door of the car and motioned them to get inside.

The adrenaline and whatever other energy residing in Sera started to fade, and her legs turned to jelly after the intense chase, barely keeping her standing. It took everything in her power not to slump over and pass out when she climbed in. Instead, she rested her head on top of Nora's, who had already fallen asleep with her cheek against Sera's shoulder.

* * *

An hour later, Renee and Nora sat across from her in the row house library, staring with equally wide eyes as she conducted a one-sided conversation. That or Sera was going crazy. At least that's what she was sure it looked like to them.

I can speak through you, if you would like, Bacchus said after she blundered through an attempt at explaining an ancient god was talking in her head.

"Now you tell me." Sera threw her arms up in the air, exasperated. "Yes, please talk so they can hear you, too, and we all know I'm not going insane."

Are you so sure about the latter? A rumbling chuckle rolled through her mind as the light within the amulet amplified and a tingling sensation coursed through her body.

Relax, he whispered. *It's easier when you're not so tense.* She stopped herself from rolling her eyes in response. As if relaxing after that fight and finding out she could talk to a god in her head was an option.

"Greetings, Witch." Sera's mouth moved, but a man's booming voice sounded in her ears. Bacchus's voice from her dreams.

This is going to be weird, she thought.

This is going to be fun, he replied.

Renee bowed her head respectfully, though her eyes remained wide. Nora stopped scrunching her curls, still wet after her much-needed shower, and gulped.

"Bacchus, it's an honor to have you in my home." Renee stared into Sera's eyes.

"I was about to give Serafina the missing puzzle pieces to the story of how I came to be within this amulet," Bacchus said. "Would you care to listen?"

"We would be delighted."

"Excellent. As I told Serafina, you may think of these creatures as vampires, as I am sure much of vampire lore is based on their likeness and behavior. But to me, they will always be Bacchae, in honor of yours truly, of course. I have heard they like to call themselves Immortals these days. Vampires, Immortals, Bacchae—they're all the same. The name may change, but their appetites never do." Sera's shoulders moved as Bacchus shrugged.

"I required the utmost discretion of my creations, as I went against Jupiter's wishes creating them in the first place. For the most part, they obeyed—much to the annoyance of your modern archaeologists."

He was right about that. Very little could be confirmed about the mystery cults, which drove Sera and her colleagues crazy.

"One of the High Priestesses of my Thiasus near Salerno, the temple where you found my amulet, was also a witch of exceptional power. In time, she convinced me to give her and the others the greatest gift of them all—the ability to create new Bacchae by infusing their own blood instead of mine. She was—and still is—a master manipulator."

Sera's arm reached over to the glass of wine she had poured for herself, and she took a sip.

I feel like a puppet. Her nostrils flared at the thought. Letting someone else control her body wasn't something she generally agreed with—even if that someone was a god.

"Ah, delicious." He smacked Sera's lips together before continuing. "I gave my children rules to follow. Simple ones. But they disobeyed all the same, as all children do." He chuckled, an intense vibration in Sera's chest she had never felt before.

This is definitely more weird than fun, she thought.
Hush. It's rude to interrupt a god.

Sera held back her snort, thankful she was too exhausted to truly process what was happening to her. To all of them.

"They were to limit the amount of immortal life they passed on, but in time, their number began to grow to a point where the very ecosystem threatened to become unstable. The earth cannot have too many predators, you see, or other predators may rise. Kill too many sharks, and the octopus will become king of the ocean."

Even though the words came from her lips, Sera shuddered at the thought of octopuses taking over the ocean. Some people were afraid of sharks, she was petrified of tentacles.

Really, octopuses? But they're so scrumptious, Bacchus questioned inside her head.

"Yes, the thought of their slimy, suctiony arms rising from the deep to pull a ship down under gives me the heebie-jeebies," Sera said out loud. "He's making fun of my fear of octopuses," she explained as she caught the questioning look from Nora.

"I think it's a reasonable fear," Nora chimed in. "They can grow up to, like, thirty feet, you know."

"That's not really helping." Bile rose in her throat.

Nora shrugged in a half apology, a smile on her lips.

Bringing the wineglass to her mouth, she drained it, almost gagging. Modern wine was meant to be sipped, not chugged. Her arm raised the glass for more.

Renee scrambled to her feet to fill the glass.

I'm a lightweight, Bacchus. You're going to get me drunk, Sera warned him.

Good, you need it.

"What was I saying?" he asked out loud, taking back over in his deep baritone voice. "Ah, yes. As the rise of Christianity flooded the world, my power, and the power of all the ancient gods, began to wane. And so, I sought the help of a powerful coven of witches. Together, we encased my entire essence, all of my power, into the amulet, to keep it sealed and protected from fading altogether. The blood inside is mine.

"But doing this also meant I could no longer act alone. Over the centuries, I selected individuals with qualities that appealed to me and used them to whittle down the Bacchae whenever they became too confident and too numerous, disobeying my rules in their hubris. I needed to remind them who was in charge."

Sera's lips pulled up into a smirk.

"I grew weary of this game after many years and decided to put an end to their ability to multiply. I called out to another coven's strongest witch—your mother—from my resting place deep within a cave."

Her heart fluttered at the mention of her mother. Had her mother spoken to Bacchus as she had?

"I am truly sorry you lost your mother to one of my creations. Together, we can get vengeance for her death."

Sera blinked as he finished, shivering as he released control of her limbs. "How did you, the amulet, whatever, get into my bag?"

Of all the things you could ask me right now, and you choose that? he asked with condescension so strong she could taste it.

"I'm sure we all have questions for you, but I really am curious to know how you ended up in my bag, which I know was empty when I packed for Hiro's."

The security guard, he replied.

"The security guard works for you?"

All three women looked confused.

The tingling sensation coursed through her body as Bacchus took over her speech once again. "I am able to control humans with weak constitutions for a limited time without their having to wear the amulet. I used the security guard from the museum to transport myself from the case to your bag. Despite his portly figure, he can be quite stealthy when he puts his mind to it. Or when *I* put his mind to it." Bacchus chuckled at his own joke. "He has no memory of any of it."

Ouch. "Are you saying I have a weak constitution?"

He sighed in response, her chest rising and falling with the breath. "No, Serafina. Apparently, you have not noticed I can only control your actions when you wear the amulet and allow me to take over. It's far easier to do so when you're in a weakened mental or emotional state, however. Drunk helps."

Had he just complimented or insulted her? Perhaps a mix of both.

"If I may?" Renee asked.

Sera's head tilted forward in assent. Raising the wineglass to her lips again, another tingling sensation made itself known, this time from the quantity of wine she had consumed. She would need to stop drinking soon, or there was a good chance she'd black out.

"How exactly do you intend to exact this 'vengeance' against the High Priestess?" Renee asked.

Yeah, that was probably the better question to ask right away.

"A witch and an Immortal she might be, but she's still no god. With Serafina's assistance, we will bring her empire down," he replied.

"What am I, just a host?" Sera snorted at the thought. If she had to share her body with a god, she'd rather be partners.

"In a sense, yes. You are the vessel through which I will channel my power. But you're much stronger than you give yourself credit for," Bacchus said.

Her cheeks grew warm as she blushed, in delight at the praise and embarrassed she so often doubted herself.

"I'd like to offer my help in any way I can," Renee offered. "It worries me you have chosen Serafina, who has her whole life ahead of her. She's young, accomplished, and in love," she said with a smile at Sera. "Let me take her place."

Despite the enticing offer, her heart clenched at the thought of giving up the amulet. She knew now that the desire came from Bacchus calling to her, but knowing didn't make the thought of parting any easier. And what about her mother? Bacchus might have more information.

"With all due respect to you and your power," he replied before Sera could, "your age is one reason I cannot use you. As Serafina has already found out, it takes a physical toll on her human body whenever I exert my powers as a god. I'm afraid you and I would not make it to our grand finale."

Fear and excitement rippled through her.

"What does that mean exactly? Are you slowly killing her?" Nora spoke up, a frown on her face.

"No, no, nothing like that. She will recover each time because she's young and in her prime. Although, she may feel like she's dying from time to time." Bacchus said the last in an offhand manner.

Oh great, Sera thought sarcastically. *This is going to be fun.*

I told you. She could almost see his devilish grin.

"Yeah, I'm not sure how I feel about you torturing my best friend," Nora said. "But can we back up for a sec? Who the hell was that guy?" She pulled the blanket she had wrapped around her even tighter. The red marks around her wrists looked better after her shower, but they would be bruising by morning.

Another question that probably should have been asked before how the amulet got into her bag. At least they were asking them now.

Renee reached out and rubbed Nora's back. "That was Leif Karlsson, the witch from my coven who took the amulet and disappeared after the spell to remove the vampires'—er, Bacchae's—ability to create new Bacchae. Although, that's not the Leif I remember. What happened to him?" She looked at Sera.

"Leif did what many have tried to do over the centuries. He tried to control me through my amulet, finding out the hard way what happens when you meet a god's wrath." Bacchus's anger simmered beneath the surface of her mind as he spoke of the other witch. "I would not have expected him to go so far as to destroy your apartment and kidnap your lovely friend."

Flashing a dazzling smile at the compliment, even though it was coming from Sera's mouth, Nora seemed to have gotten used to a god's voice speaking through her.

It didn't seem likely that *she* would ever get used to it.

"It wasn't the Bacchae who broke in?" Sera hadn't even stopped to think it might be someone else.

"No. Leif knew sooner or later I would find my way to you. I fear he will continue to be a pest until his broken mind completely shatters or his body gives out from overuse of magic. Bacchae are many things, but careless is not one of them. You would have had to invite them into your home for them to return unnoticed—one of my safety measures."

That explains why they abducted me on the street, she thought.

"So, what now?" Nora asked.

"Now, I would like to ask Renee's assistance in contacting a few friends of mine. A god I may be, but we will need as much help as we can get. Danae will have an entire army at her disposal," Bacchus replied.

Renee nodded. "Anything I can do to help."

"First and foremost, we need more wine." He raised the empty wineglass and shook it.

Her head spinning from the alcohol as well as all the new information, Sera let out a groan. She wasn't sure she could take much more of either.

After a refill of all the glasses, Bacchus and Renee discussed what he needed for the communication ritual, although he wouldn't go into detail about who he wanted to contact. It would take Renee a few days to gather all of the necessary items. The four of them continued to talk into the night until Sera felt like she was going to drop dead, or at least pass out mid-sentence. Renee must have caught her wobbling.

"All right, everyone. We know our immediate plans. Let's get some much-needed rest before we have to pretend life is normal tomorrow." Renee rose from her chair.

Nora followed Sera up to the guest room, not willing to stay by herself on the pull-out couch in the basement.

Sera didn't blame her. She wasn't sure any of them would look at basements the same way ever again. As she laid her head on the pillow, warmth infused Sera's bones.

Sleep now, my darling, Bacchus whispered.

She did.

CHAPTER 22

Solomon

Lorenzo's eyes narrowed to slits. A deep red simmered beneath the surface of his blue irises as they told him about the fight the humans had with Leif.

"Did you take care of that *witch*?"

"He was warned, but his warped mind doesn't seem capable of heeding it. He used magic to escape before we could kill him," Solomon said.

Leif always interfered sooner or later, but Solomon hadn't expected him to take on a witch as powerful as Renee Colette. Now that he knew how powerful the woman was, he understood why she and Danae were at a stalemate.

Things might change once Danae retrieved the amulet, however.

Solomon had spent more time in the library in the last few weeks than he had in the last few decades since Lorenzo had made the mansion his new home in the District. It would be time to move on soon—being Immortals who didn't age beyond their mortal years meant changing the scenery to avoid discovery. He would miss this particular library, especially because he wasn't sure he'd live to see the next one with all the failures obtaining the amulet.

Witches were always meddling where they weren't welcome.

"Did he get the amulet?"

Solomon shook his head. "No, they chased him off. But…" He hesitated, knowing his next statement may cost him his life right then and there.

"But?" Lorenzo's eyes flashed red in warning.

"The girl has to be wearing the amulet. Her scarf obscured the view to confirm."

Lorenzo's eyes returned to their original blue, all signs of anger dissolving. He smiled at Solomon, crossing one leg over the other casually. "I see. Well, it is a good thing Danae arrives in two days to fix your mess, sì?"

Confusion kept Solomon silent. He had grown used to Lorenzo's volatile nature and moods changing faster than a blink of his eye. But his maker usually went from calm to raging storm, not the other way around.

"You and Alexander continue to watch from afar. Do not confront her until Danae provides you with a solution. The last thing I need is two dead Immortal bodies to clean up." Lorenzo laughed, slapping his knee at what he considered a good joke. Nothing would be left behind to clean up. He returned to his book, a sign that Solomon was dismissed.

Replaying the conversation in his head after closing the library door behind him, the exchange left him more confused than he'd ever been. His maker must have faith Danae will get the amulet, regardless of who was wearing it.

* * *

Lorenzo pulled out all the stops for the Eternal's arrival on the night of Thanksgiving. Every square inch of his home was scrubbed until it shone, and he invited the highest members of the Council—both humans and Immortals. He also sent out a private invite to certain regulars he knew would make the finest meals. If he didn't know better, Solomon would have thought the royal family was visiting.

"It would be in both your best interests to let me do the talking," Lorenzo warned Solomon and Alexander as Danae's retinue arrived.

Solomon didn't need the warning, but he knew the kid would have trouble obeying the command with his constant desire to be seen as more important than he actually was.

The three of them stood outside the mansion as dusk turned the world as grey and grainy as an old photograph. Four black SUVs rolled into the back driveway that only the Immortals and house staff used. Danae preferred to keep all her comings and goings as quiet as possible from the human world.

Immortals in black suits and dark sunglasses stepped out of the vehicles. Each one took a position around the perimeter of the driveway, forming a fence of bodies. After taking a glance around the area, another Immortal, wearing several sets of daggers on her person—and more hidden, he was sure—opened one of the back doors and held out her hand to the Eternal inside.

Danae's signature blood-red stiletto ending in a steel tip caught Solomon's attention as she stepped down from the vehicle. It was said she wore them whenever she traveled from her home territory to ensure those she met knew exactly with whom they dealt. Some claimed the steel tip was dipped in silver, which acted like acid to his kind. He didn't want to find out if there was any truth to the rumor. At least not personally.

He had only seen Danae once before when she was confirming Alexander's transition to immortality two decades ago. It was from a distance as she exited her private plane and slid into the back of a limo. She didn't often have reason to cross to the East Coast.

Solomon's eyebrows lifted, creasing his forehead, as she stepped forward. Alexander sucked in his breath beside him. Not only was she quite possibly the most beautiful woman Solomon had ever laid eyes on, though much younger-looking than he had realized, but the power emanating from her brought the three men she approached to a knee in genuflection. It was no wonder Lorenzo had been unfazed in the library.

"Buona sera, la mia bella signora." Lorenzo rose to his feet and took her hand, kissing the back of it.

Unlike the rest of her entourage, Danae did not wear sunglasses. Her eyes reminded Solomon of a winter sky—

light blue with streaks of silver, and cold as ice. They focused on his maker.

"Where is it at this moment?" Her girlish voice belied her true age.

Solomon had to remind himself that this girl—this woman—had more than two thousand years on him. Maybe even more.

"The girl continues to keep the amulet with her. She is in Virginia for the American holiday—" Lorenzo stopped when she raised her hand.

"I assume you have someone who can show my people the way while you and I catch up." Her frozen orbs narrowed, a storm threatening to unleash its fury.

Lorenzo nodded casually, unfazed. "Sì. Certo. Solomon and Alexander know exactly where to find her."

Danae glanced at four of her guard, who got back into one of the SUVs. She held out her hand, and another one stepped forward. He tipped a small bag over and dropped two black crystals into her waiting palm.

"The counter-defense crystals are not easy to make. I do not plan to make more than two." For a brief moment, her eyes met Solomon's, and his breath caught in his throat before she looked away. He couldn't be sure if he had felt excitement, or something else. She placed the crystals back into the bag, the Immortal cinching it closed before handing it to Solomon.

Solomon and Alexander climbed into the back of the SUV with the others while Lorenzo led Danae inside the house. As he reached out to close the car door behind him, Solomon's gaze lingered on the Eternal, identifying the strange sensation coursing through his body, a feeling he hadn't had since his mortal days.

Fear.

CHAPTER 23

Serafina

Because the tiny guest room lacked windows, it was dark save for the sliver of light showing under the door. Sera had no idea what time it was or when Nora had snuck out. She lay still in the empty bed, staring at the ceiling, thinking back over how her life had so drastically changed in such a short amount of time.

You'll get used to it, Bacchus's voice chimed in. She still wasn't sure she'd ever get used to *that*.

"I can't believe I'm not hungover," she said as she turned her head side to side, amazed it wasn't pounding like a jackhammer at the movement. Although her tongue tried to stick to the roof of her mouth. The last time she'd had that much to drink, she was down for a whole day recovering.

Just one of the many benefits of having me by your side. Or in your head. A thank you is always appreciated. Bacchus's chuckle rumbled through her mind.

"Are you always going to be present? Or is there a way to turn you off?"

Don't be a goop. I'm only trying to help, came his teasing reply.

"I just mean there are going to be situations where I'd like some privacy in my head," she explained.

Would a safe word work?

"Like for kinky sex?" Her cheeks grew warm. She enjoyed an adventurous romp as much as anyone, but gossiping about it was more Nora's realm.

That is one popular use for safe words, yes.

Random words started drifting through Sera's mind: marshmallow, donut, pineapple, app–

Why are you only thinking of foods?

"I'm hungry, okay?" That was a bit of an understatement—she was ravenous and parched.

Bacchus's deep laugh rolled through like distant thunder.

Let's just start with, "I need some privacy, please." Nice and polite. Now, go eat.

When Sera stumbled downstairs, her legs still weak from the sprint the night before, she found Renee had already made grilled cheese sandwiches, hot tomato soup, and fresh coffee. The smells were as welcome as the warm bed had been the night before.

"Can I just live here forever?" she asked as she inhaled a sandwich, burning her tongue in the process. As a graduate student focused too much on her research, she hardly ever ate an actual meal, and home-cooked even less so. Not even grilled cheese sandwiches.

Renee smiled over her cup of tea. "You are welcome to stay as long as you need to while you become more knowledgeable about this world. But then I'm going to need my space back." She winked.

Sera nodded, her mouth too stuffed with another sandwich to reply.

"And how is our ancient friend this morning?"

Peachy, Bacchus replied in her mind.

"He said he's doing wonderful, and to thank you for asking, as well as for your hospitality," Sera replied after she swallowed the last of the sandwich.

I didn't say any of that. Had I known you told tales I wouldn't have chosen you, he said, a hint of humor in his voice.

She ignored him. "Where's Nora?"

"She implied my shower hadn't been up to snuff to rid her of the smell of her captivity," Renee said between sips of tea. "She took a taxi home and said she'd call you later once she had a chance to process everything that happened."

"How was she this morning?" Sera asked before taking a bite out of a third sandwich.

"She seemed shaken, as expected. I'd be worried more about how well she's doing if I wasn't so close with her and her mother," Renee answered with a smile. "The Eisler women are strong women."

Her mouth too full to respond, Sera simply nodded. She'd also been a little worried about how accepting Nora had been with all this information. Not to mention being kidnapped by a crazed witch.

"I know you've got some additional help now, but I want you to wear another ward as a backup. At least until we know more about Bacchus's powers." Renee handed her another leather thread.

Sera slipped the necklace over her head with one hand, the other still holding a sandwich.

"Do you have plans for Thanksgiving? I'll be heading to a friend's, but you're welcome to join me," Renee offered.

Leaning back in the chair, Sera groaned at the thought of eating more after just stuffing herself full of sandwiches.

"How do I keep forgetting it's Thanksgiving this week?" she asked. "I'm not good at this whole pretending to be normal when my world has been turned upside down thing. I'm going to mess up in front of my dad."

I'll be here to guide you, Bacchus reminded her. *Like a spirit guide.*

"A spirit guide?"

Renee cocked an eyebrow at her. Sera pointed to the amulet and shrugged.

"I suppose I'll have to get used to this style of half conversation," Renee said with a chuckle.

"You and me both." Sera reached forward and grabbed another sandwich.

* * *

"Babe, I have so much to tell you when you get back," Sera said to Hiro's image on her phone as she climbed into bed.

It was Tuesday evening and they'd scheduled a video phone date while he was away. Amazingly, she made it through her day of classes without any supernatural issues. Respecting her request, Bacchus had even remained quiet to help her adjust. Mostly.

"Your 'boring' life suddenly filled with excitement?" He grinned as he threw her own words back at her. Far too often over the last two years, she had complained about missed social events as she immersed herself in her research. She almost regretted it now.

A flash of anger surged through her as she recalled Solomon's similar words to her outside the diner.

"You could say that. How's Seattle?"

"It'd be better with you here. My mom has been asking nonstop when I'm going to make an honest woman out of you." His wink sent Sera's heart into a state of flutter, although she was pretty sure his mother had said nothing of the sort.

He looked at something over his phone and sighed. "I've got to run already. The guys and I are getting together for a game of flag football. Tell your dad hi for me, okay?"

"Will do, same to your family." Her heart beat double time as she blew him a kiss, wishing she could feel his warm lips beneath her own. Tingles spread through her body at the thought of their last night together. It had been steamy.

I'll say, Bacchus interrupted. Her cheeks burned as they flushed, forgetting once again that the god could read her thoughts.

"I love you, Sera."

"Love you, too." Click.

Well, isn't he just a treat, Bacchus commented.

Rolling her eyes, she turned out the light.

* * *

Two days and zero supernatural occurrences later, Sera borrowed Renee's car for the drive out to her father's house. It was fall, her favorite time of year for that drive, but she couldn't enjoy it. Even though relieved she had grown accustomed to having an ancient god in her head and life, the reality of her situation hit her like Mount Vesuvius blowing its top.

Sera had asked Bacchus to give her some privacy on the drive over, to be alone in her thoughts. Knowing the truth about her mother's death brought buried feelings to the surface, but she wasn't sure she had it in her to enact vengeance of the magnitude Bacchus suggested. Watching a man die was hard enough. But purposefully taking another person's life felt wrong. Even if it was an evil Bacchae. Who'd killed her mom.

Groaning as her mind flip-flopped, her thoughts drifted to Hiro. She still hadn't explained any of this to him, and she wasn't even sure how to approach it. A god's baritone voice speaking through her would be a bit much for her logical boyfriend to handle. It would sure prove her story though.

At least she had Nora to talk to. As promised, her best friend had called later in the evening. Nora told her how Leif had approached her on the street near the diner, pretending to be lost. When she walked away, he attacked her from behind, holding a chloroform-soaked rag to her nose until she blacked out. It must have happened right as Sera confronted Solomon and Alexander, just two streets away.

Those goddamn Bacchae!

Nora had been staying at her mom's house, although she admitted she'd had nightmares and woke up in cold sweats more than once. During the day she felt fine. Sera shook her head as she turned off the interstate, relieved she and Renee had found Nora and the lunatic hadn't done any permanent harm to her best friend. Physically, anyway. Her eyes narrowed as she thought about Leif escaping into the crowd at the Wharf.

He better stay away if he knows what's good for him, she thought.

Okay, maybe she could take a life.

Feeling better after going through that cathartic mental exercise, Sera pulled the car into the driveway, rocks crunching beneath the tires. She took a deep breath to steady her nerves.

"I'm definitely going to need your help," she said to Bacchus.

I'll be here, came the soft reply.

The game was already on the TV when she walked in.

"Hey, Dad."

"Hey, honey, saved you a seat," he joked as he motioned to the couch next to his recliner. Their usual spots for their usual day.

"You're late," he said, not really complaining. Just stating a fact.

"Yeah, I was up late studying, and there was traffic." Studying, discussing evil witches, not too different.

Sera took a seat as he yelled at the TV, disagreeing with a flag called by the referee. It had been their Thanksgiving tradition to watch the game before dinner, even when her mom had been alive. Not much different than their Sunday tradition. Football pretty much ruled their lives during the fall.

A herd of men in battle gear running into each other? What a delight, Bacchus commented. *Where's the popcorn?*

Sera couldn't stop the snicker that slipped out, but her dad was too focused on the game to notice. Thankfully.

"Should we walk?" her dad asked when the game ended an hour later. He stretched out his legs as he stood.

She chuckled to herself. Of course they would walk. They always walked there and back to "get some exercise" before they stuffed themselves silly.

"Definitely. It's not too cold today."

Pretending everything in her life was normal was much harder with her father than with students and peers. But with Bacchus's help, she managed to fake it well enough while they walked to the restaurant.

When they arrived, the warmth inside welcomed them from the outside chill, even as mild of a day as that one. The staff greeted them by name when they arrived, happy to have had their business for the last twenty-plus years. Clinking silverware and the sizzle of frying food accompanied the multitude of conversations being held by the other patrons. Despite a nearly full house, their usual table was ready and waiting.

"How's that professor you told me about—Chad something?" her father asked after they were seated.

Sera's nostrils flared out in distaste as she thought about Chad.

Easy, killer, Bacchus commented through a chuckle.

Her father must have caught the look. "Not good, huh?"

"He's a pig. He knows the students fawn over him, and he uses it to take advantage of them. We exchanged some words. Well, I said some words to him anyway." She smirked as she remembered telling Chad off.

"Good for you, honey." He had always been an advocate for her standing up for herself. She wasn't sure why it had taken so long to actually do it.

The server, who didn't actually look old enough to be working yet, arrived to fill up their water glasses. He nervously asked if they needed anything, but the holiday menu was pre-set so they had no need to worry about perusing entrees that day. They shook their heads, and the server scampered away.

As a family-run business, the restaurant had been a staple of their neighborhood since the '70s. The couple who owned the place passed it down to their son when they got too old to run it themselves, and the servers, cooks, dishwashers—pretty much all of the staff—were related somehow.

"Something about you seems different. Did you get a haircut?" Her father squinted at her slightly.

"What? No. Nothing's different." She was hiding an ancient god within a stolen amulet under her scarf, a god who was being hunted by a really old Bacchae witch. But no, nothing much was different about Sera. Her fingers itched to move.

Relax, Bacchus whispered in a soothing tone.

Easy for you to say, she thought back.

Ask him about his life. Get his mind off you.

"How's retirement treating you?" she asked out loud, taking Bacchus's suggestion. Her father had been the neighborhood mechanic her entire life, but an injury to his back over a year ago forced him into early retirement. He still tinkered around as often as he could.

"I'm doing some work on Mrs. Ramsey's car. Her daughter just had a baby, so she needed it fixed as soon as possible to go visit." He continued to talk about his life until their food arrived. The delicious smells of toasted cornbread, mashed potatoes drenched in butter, and roasted turkey, perfectly golden, wafted over Sera, conjuring memories of her life growing up at that very table.

That smells divine, Bacchus said.

You would know, she thought back.

Savor it for me, will you? I'm going to pretend I eat human food.

They devoured their meal in what felt like record time, even though Sera really did give a valiant effort to slow down on Bacchus's behalf. It was just too good.

An hour later, the streetlamps cast their yellow glow onto the darkened sidewalk when they approached the door to leave, stopping to chat every few feet with other neighborhood regulars. As they bundled up to face the cold walk home, two women around her father's age walked in. His face lit up as he greeted them, but he turned most of his attention on the lovely redhead.

"I'm going to head back, but I'll walk slowly," she called back to her father as he caught up with his lady friend. He waved a hand to let her know he had heard. Catching the excitement in his voice as he talked with the woman, Sera smiled. Maybe there was some happiness to be found there. It'd be about time.

Sera began the short walk back to the house, breathing in the chilly evening air, which held the lingering scent of pumpkin pie from the restaurant behind her. It had been a really good pie. It always was. Walking would help wake up the rest of her body a bit before the drive back to the city. At the moment, her body focused on her belly, leaving her stroll sluggish.

Food has changed, Bacchus interrupted her thoughts to comment.

"Yeah, we have these wonderful things today called factory farming and mass production. We're all getting fat and dying of cancer because of it," she answered out loud since the street was empty. Shadows danced on the sidewalk as the wind moved bare branches above her.

Better than dying of dysentery and consumption, I suppose.

"Is it?" She shook her head at the idea of comparing diseases one could die from.

Most of the neighborhood was comprised of older, single-family homes with wrap-around porches and white picket fences out front. Despite the descending darkness, the sounds of laughter and children playing games rang from various backyards. More than one football flew by in Sera's periphery as she walked. The days may have been shorter and colder, but that didn't stop families from enjoying one of the best American traditions.

A black SUV pulled out from a driveway, blocking the sidewalk in front of her as it stopped. As the doors opened, goosebumps rose along her arms, making her skin crawl. Four men dressed in black suits stepped out. As they fanned out around her, Solomon and Alexander exited the vehicle.

"Seriously? Haven't you learned that I'm not giving you the amulet?" she asked, trying to sound more confident than she felt. She put her hands on her hips to make her point. A flush of warmth infused her bones as Bacchus silently backed her up.

Solomon held out his fist, opening it to reveal a black rock. It was a crystal, similar to the one Leif had used. He closed his hand and crushed the crystal into fine dust, letting it fall slowly from his palm and into the wind. The crystal in the pouch of the leather thread she wore around her neck started to shake. A crack resounded as the crystal shattered.

Not again. She groaned.

Solomon nodded at one of the black-suited men. He charged at her, his face contorting into a monstrous mask as his mouth revealed extended fangs. The amulet flared to life beneath her scarf, and a rush of energy flooded through her, every limb tingling for a brief moment as Bacchus took control of her body.

Countering the Bacchae's outstretched hands with the god's help, Sera swatted them aside with little effort. A look of surprise flashed across his face, probably matching her own. She pulled him toward her as she stepped to the side, using his momentum to send him flying to the ground behind her. Leaping back up to his feet, he growled at her.

Whoa. That was awesome! Exhilaration coursed through her veins.

"You would attack a human in the middle of a street? You have sunk too low, my children," Bacchus's voice boomed from within her body.

Within seconds, Solomon's face moved through shock, fear, and anger.

"I'm guessing that's not a good sign," Alexander said.

All four Bacchae in suits came at her at once. Instinctively, she ducked as the closest one swiped at her with an outstretched hand. The duck turned into a tumble as her body tried to go a different direction. She winced as she banged her elbow on the cement.

Stop interfering, Bacchus commanded her.

Cut me some slack. Being controlled by a god is new for me, Sera thought back as she scrambled to her feet. She took a deep breath and released her body to Bacchus's control.

"This ends now, my children. Return to your mistress, and tell her I'm coming for her. No one needs to die tonight," Bacchus spoke again as the Bacchae circled Sera.

Unnatural strength and power coursed through her limbs as one of them disregarded Bacchus's message and flung himself at her again. She grabbed him by the throat, lifted him into the air like a ragdoll, and launched him at the white picket fence of the house they stood in front of.

He landed back first onto the sharp wooden points, which continued through his body and out his chest with a sickening crunch. The Bacchae's body vibrated, shaking the entire fence before he died, his body dissolving into glittering dust that floated to the ground and disappeared into the grass.

The remaining three Bacchae stopped, eyes wide, mirroring the shock Sera felt at what she just witnessed. What she herself had *done.* The Bacchae exchanged glances. It probably wasn't often that they saw one of their own die. Instead of heeding the warning of impending death, they charged at her once again.

They really don't listen, do they? she thought to Bacchus.

Nope.

She reached over and grasped the stop sign from the street corner. Every inch of her body strained, her muscles screaming from the effort, as she pulled the metal pole from the ground and its cement base. Dirt and roots fell back toward the hole when it came free.

Sera brought the sign down on the closest Bacchae's head, stunning him, then spun in a circle and used the sharp edge of the octagon to slice through his neck, decapitating him. His eyes and mouth opened wide as his head slid from his body.

Unlike the first, this one didn't instantly dissolve. Within a few heartbeats, his skin had turned grey, muscles atrophying. Pulling away from his bones, his skin melted to the ground, evaporating as it touched the cement. The skeleton that remained crumbled into glittering dust, dissipating into the air.

Holy shit, she thought, realizing she had just taken not one but two lives. Technically, Bacchus did, but using *her* hands. What if someone had seen?

Bacchus turned Sera to face the last two suited Bacchae, her stomach twisted into knots.

Before they could act, a nearby house's floodlight clicked on, bathing the yard and the sidewalk in bright white light. The Bacchae all shied away from the light in reflex. A tiny dog announced its presence inside the house with its high-pitched yaps as the front door began to open.

The remaining Bacchae looked in her direction once more before making the decision to return to the SUV. Solomon lingered, his eyes calculating as he stared at her.

"She will come after you, again and again, until she has that amulet," he said. "Trust me when I say you do not want this fight in your life."

Sera snorted as the god relinquished control of her body. "Trust you? I don't think so, bud. Head on back to your master like a good dog." She shooed him away with her hand, trying to hide its trembling with movement.

Solomon's eyes narrowed even further at her taunt before he turned around and climbed inside the vehicle. The black SUV pulled away from the curb with screeching tires.

"Was that a friend of yours?" Her father's voice beside her made her jump.

"No, they were just lost," Sera managed to get out with only a slight stutter. "Who was that lovely lady you talked to?"

Despite having control of her own body again, Bacchus's anger bubbled inside her like a boiling pot about to overflow. One by one her limbs started to shake as the adrenaline and the god's power wore off. She had just *murdered* two men. Clenching her jaw to keep it from quivering too visibly, she pushed the thoughts away. Overanalyzing the encounter could come later, not in her father's presence.

"That was Susan. I've worked on her cars for years now. She's a nurse at the hospital." He continued to talk about Susan the rest of the walk home, a smile never leaving his face. Sera did her best to focus on his words, but her mind kept returning to the fight, nausea threatening to ruin her meal.

Movement at a window caught her eye, and a little girl, five or six years old at most, stared back at her, blue eyes wide. *Shit.* She must have seen the entire fight, including the glittery deaths. The little girl looked over her shoulder for a moment, before looking back. She gave Sera a thumbs-up and a grin before disappearing inside. The curtain fell shut.

Sera's mouth fell open.

She won't be an issue, Bacchus said, his anger dissipating into mirth. *Maybe I should recruit her instead.*

Be my guest. She snapped her jaw shut.

"I've got to head back. Studying never stops," she told her father when they reached the driveway. He reached over and drew her into a big hug. Hopefully, he wouldn't notice her shaking.

"I'm so proud of you, Sera. I know I don't say it enough," he told her before letting go.

Sera blinked back tears at the unexpected praise. "Thanks, Dad."

He frowned as he pointed to a tear in her jacket. "That wasn't there earlier."

"Uh, yeah, I caught it on a tree branch that came out of nowhere." Her lips quirked up in a smile. It must have happened in the fight, but she knew he'd believe her lie thanks to her clumsy childhood. Well, clumsy life. She hadn't really grown out of it yet.

"Sneaky trees." He chuckled as he walked toward the house, waving to her from the porch when she got into the car and started it up.

The cold clung to her like icicles from a gutter, and she turned the heat to full blast. By the time she had backed the car out of the driveway, an intense lethargy filled her bones.

Are we going to make it home? she asked in her head, too exhausted to speak out loud.

I will make sure of it, Bacchus replied.

The weariness tugged at her body, begging her to lie down and sleep, but Bacchus kept his promise.

CHAPTER 24

Solomon

Danae gazed past Solomon as he finished explaining the encounter with Serafina, her expression unreadable. The Immortals who had survived the fight returned to find Danae in the throne room, where she had all but claimed the throne. Lorenzo stood at her side, his knuckles white as he clenched his fists.

They all knew it had only been a matter of time before the girl put on the amulet. Solomon wondered if Danae would kill them all outright, draw the deaths out, or actually allow them to live.

Danae's eyes shifted to her two Immortal guards who had returned. She spoke to them in a language Solomon didn't know.

"So, she got away," Danae stated after their conversation.

Solomon nodded. "Yes, with Bacchus's help. She's wearing the amulet."

She looked thoughtfully at Solomon and Alexander, her eyes moving between them. Other than her shifting gaze, the Eternal was all but a statue with how still she sat.

"I am displeased you confronted the human girl in broad daylight, so to speak. We cannot risk alerting the human population to our true existence until we regain our powers." With a slight tilt of her head, she addressed Lorenzo next. "Do they know?"

"No. I have honored your command."

Her eyes, more grey than blue in the throne room light, met Solomon's directly before settling on Alexander. In that brief moment their eyes connected, the hair on the back of Solomon's neck stood on end as he felt her power move through his consciousness, like water turning to ice.

"Alexander was the last Immortal we were able to create. Bacchus and his coven of witches," her upper lip curled up at the reference, "stole our ability to pass on immortal life. He is the reason our powers are dwindling. We cannot risk angering the humans and being wiped from history while we are so vulnerable."

He'd wondered why it had been so long since they created any new Immortals. The usual time frame was only a few years, if that. There were certainly plenty of candidates. He glanced at Alexander briefly with disgust. They had wasted their last transformation on such an unworthy choice. His father, William, should have been the last.

William had been a high-ranking member of the human side of the Council and had forfeited his own transformation after his son became gravely ill. Shortly after the change, William died from a heart attack.

Alexander had been, and still was, the typical narcissist. He had a sense of entitlement because of who he was, not because of what he had accomplished. Solomon was of the mind that Alexander had not earned his place to be an Immortal, but Lorenzo's vote tipped the scale.

Danae stood and walked as lightly as a cat to the edge of the dais, making no noise even in her red stilettos. Moonlight filtering in through the high window washed over her olive-toned skin. Lorenzo thought she hailed from Macedonia or Crete, but he wasn't positive. Her origin was another secret she kept to herself.

"Controlling the amulet means we will reclaim what is rightfully ours. Gifts should be given out of love, not to control and manipulate as he has done." Danae gazed at each of the gathered Immortals in turn, diving deep into their souls. "We will show the god he created us well in his image. We will create an army of Immortals, and we will let ourselves be known to the world."

A stirring rose within Solomon as her *influence* washed over him. He longed to follow her to the ends of the earth and back, slaughtering any who stood in her way. If she had been at the height of her power, he wouldn't have been able to fight it the way he did now. But something about her plan didn't sit right with him. Unease settled around him like an ill-fitting jacket.

"Humans will become our livestock—some will be eaten, some will be bred, and some will be honored with the gift of immortality. We will rule this earth, and I will be your queen."

As she said the last, her Immortal guard knelt before her, bowing their heads in assent and submission. Lorenzo flicked his hand at Solomon and Alexander, indicating they do the same as he also knelt.

Solomon took a knee, not entirely liking the prospect of their kind ruling the world. It was right up Alexander's alley, but Solomon enjoyed the world the humans had created, particularly over the last century. He wasn't convinced his kind had the motivation and drive to create what mankind did in their lives of finite mortality. There was something about knowing one only has so much time in life that pushed a mind to the outer reaches of imagination.

An earthy, salty aroma like saffron greeted his nose, and Solomon found himself staring down at a pair of red stilettos.

"You'll join me this evening," Danae said above him.

Solomon looked up. A storm brewed in those blue-grey eyes, mixed with an animalistic desire. She turned on her heel and headed for the guest quarters. He may not be convinced her world domination plan was for him, but he had no hesitation following her to the bedroom. He wondered if she would taste as bitter as saffron.

* * *

Dismissed after sating the Eternal's primal desires, several times, Solomon found himself drawn to the servant's quarters to feed and replenish his energy. Danae wasn't one for small talk or sharing her bed for sleep.

Turning in a constant state of confusion, his thoughts had drifted to Nora more than once that night while with Danae. It was nearly impossible to compare the two, but he felt oddly guilty spending time with the Eternal, a feeling he had almost forgotten. He found himself wanting to crawl back into Nora's arms and breathe in her sweet, coconut scent as he buried his face in her hair. He wanted to see if her blood tasted as sweet as she smelled.

Solomon returned to the library after he fed, determined to distract his mind from his churning thoughts. He found Lorenzo there, speaking quietly into the antique telephone. Why was he talking to his police contact now that Danae had arrived? Lorenzo's eyes darted up to meet his, and he waved Solomon closer.

"Whatever you need to do, just see it done," Lorenzo said sharply before replacing the handset on the base. He steepled his fingers together in front of his face. "We will have visitors tomorrow night. Human visitors. Ensure the cellar has been set up for an extended, yet uncomfortable, stay."

Solomon raised an eyebrow. "Who?"

"Let us consider it a surprise. You know I love a good surprise." Lorenzo's mouth pulled up into a wolfish grin.

That was only true when the surprise wasn't directed at him. Solomon nodded to his maker, turning to leave the room he had hoped to find solace in.

"Make sure even you cannot pull the chains free," Lorenzo's voice called out as he reached the door.

CHAPTER 25

Serafina

Too sore to do much else, Sera peeked out from under a pillow. The sliver of light under the door told her daytime had arrived. An hour of the day when the sun was up and probably had been for a while.

"Why don't I have those dreams anymore?" She rolled onto her back, groaning as her muscles reminded her of just how out of shape she was.

Good morning to you, too, came Bacchus's reply. An internal warmth enveloped her muscles like a hot bath, soothing the aches away.

Sera smirked at the ceiling, clasping her fingers behind her head now that her arms didn't resist the movement. It was weird having someone else speak in her head, but she'd discovered she enjoyed the constant sense of not being alone. Not to mention the perk of quick healing from a god. It comforted her in a way she hadn't expected, much like her boyfriend did.

Hiro… She sighed. He'd be getting back from Seattle later in the day, then back to work the next. She had a limited window of time to talk to him that night about everything that'd been going on in her life. Explaining the supernatural world and magic existing weren't topics of conversation she ever thought she'd be having. Let alone that a god lived inside the amulet and spoke through her. Speaking of which…

"Hey, you didn't answer my question. Why did the dreams stop?"

Do you want to know what really happens at my festivals?

Images of the mostly nude sculptures and dancing satyrs from the gala lobby flashed through her mind, causing warmth to rise inside her. "Well, no. But what happened to Liviana? And Octavia?"

Liviana still lives. Octavia… she was one whose ambitions got the best of her. She did not enjoy obeying the rules.

It didn't surprise her based on the little she knew of Octavia from the dreams. "Where is Liviana now?"

As an Eternal, Liviana sits on the High Council. She has a much cooler head than Octavia ever did.

"High Council?"

With my encouragement, the Bacchae set up a system of government to keep their kind in check. The High Council is made up of only Eternals.

"Interesting. Was Danae the High Priestess I saw in my dreams?" She racked her brain trying to remember what the

High Priestess had looked like.

No. You would not forget Danae, Bacchus's voice had a loving tone to it, despite the underlying anger Sera could feel behind his words. *Danae had been the original High Priestess there, but she is older still. The woman you saw came after Danae moved on.*

"Why does Danae want the amulet so bad? She knows it's you, right?"

Are we playing a questions game?

Sera rolled her eyes. "Come on, I need to know this stuff if I'm going to help you bring them down."

Fair enough. He chuckled. *Danae knows my essence is encased within the amulet. She believes she can force me to restore their ability to create new Bacchae.*

"Can she? Force you?" She raised an eyebrow at the idea of controlling a god.

Yes.

Goosebumps crawled up her arms. "Why not just give the ability back and remind them what happens when they break the rules?"

Danae dreams of unmatched power. She wishes to rule the world with her immortal army. She will destroy the human race this time, and eventually the world if she gets her way.

Shivers ran up her spine at the thought of Bacchae ruling the world.

"Yikes. So, we're not just bringing Danae down, we're also saving the world. Awesome." Sera's stomach growled.

Let's start with breakfast, shall we?

Throwing on the last of her clean clothes, she headed downstairs to the empty kitchen. A note next to the already brewed coffee pot caught her eye: *Had to run errands for our friend. Food is in the fridge.*

Sera reached a hand up to the empty leather thread around her neck as she remembered the attack from the night before. "Crap. I needed to talk to Renee about the black crystal Solomon used."

She and I spoke last night. She's picking up supplies for a new ward we will do together. Stronger, this time, Bacchus said.

She blinked, her memory blank. "You did? I'm not sure how I feel about you talking to people when I'm not exactly present."

You'll get stronger over time and won't always pass out after we work together. But if you do not wish to reveal my existence, you'll have to get used to my help. She could almost see his shrug in her mind.

Even though his comments were logical, she didn't like the idea of him waltzing around town with her body while she was comatose. They would need to set some ground rules about what he could and couldn't do until she grew strong enough to resist the exhaustion.

Sera pulled the plate covered in plastic wrap out of the fridge. She wondered if this was what it would've been like having her mom in her life longer. Memories of her mom were usually special moments that stood out in her life, not the mundane, everyday stuff like food in the fridge while she ran errands. Although the thoughts made her heart heavy, Sera smiled. If this was as close to a mother as she would get, she would happily take it.

After inhaling the egg sandwich and draining the pot of coffee, she burped in satisfaction.

"Excuse me," she said out of habit.

You know, in many cultures it's a sign of respect to belch after a good meal, Bacchus commented.

"I'm going to make it my mission to bring that custom to America. After saving the world, that is," she joked with him. Despite the quest for vengeance looming ahead of her, things were looking up.

Sera cleaned up her dishes then headed for the door. Her plan was to head home for fresh clothes, then over to Hiro's to wait for him.

"I'm open to any ideas you have on how to talk to Hiro about all of this," she said to Bacchus as she skipped down the front steps.

* * *

A few hours later, Sera plopped onto Hiro's couch and turned on the TV. She couldn't remember the last time she had simply relaxed, but it felt good. Her phone buzzed with a text message a few minutes of channel surfing later.

Hiro: "Plane just landed. Be home to you soon. Be naked. Love you." She grinned as her stomach performed somersaults.

Isn't that darling. The god's voice in her head made her jump.

"Ugh. I forgot you were here for a minute. This is going to be one of those times I need privacy." She pursed her lips. "Real privacy. It's not going to be sexy at all having you talk in my head while I'm trying to have some naked time with Hiro."

Are you sure about that? Devious laughter lurked behind his words.

She rolled her eyes, heat rising in her cheeks. "Just make yourself scarce when he gets here."

Returning to channel surfing, she stopped when she found reruns of the reality show *Midnight Mediums*. It seemed appropriate with everything going on. Her eyelids grew heavy as she watched, snuggling under the blankets. Warm, comfortable, and content, her eyes finally closed.

* * *

Serafina. Bacchus's voice interrupted her dreams.

She rubbed her eyes and blinked. The TV was still playing episodes of the show, but it had turned dark outside.

"Where's Hiro?" She reached for her phone. No new messages.

He has not returned. Bacchus's voice held a strained note.

"What are you not telling me?" Sera sat straight up on the couch, adrenaline waking her up faster than a bucket of water to the face.

We should return to the witch's house. I do not like this feeling, he said.

Her skin crawled as goosebumps spread like wildfire. "Do you think something happened to him?" Sera could hear the panic in her voice and took a deep breath. It wouldn't help the situation to completely lose it.

I cannot say. Send him a message to call you, but we need to get to a safer place, he urged her.

The fact that Bacchus was unsettled scared her beyond words and set her heart pounding in her chest. She called Hiro, but it went straight to voicemail, which meant his phone had been turned off. He only turned his phone off when he was at work.

She sent him a quick text message to call her immediately and then dialed Nora. Voicemail. Dread dropped into her stomach like an anchor. Where the hell were they? After sending Nora the same message, she clambered off the couch and left Hiro's apartment, her bag slung over her shoulder.

Sera had only taken a few steps in the direction of the Metro station when a police car pulled up beside her. The window unrolled, and Julia smiled up at her.

"You leaving town?" the detective asked, brushing a strand of red hair off her face.

"What?" Sera looked at her in confusion.

Julia nodded at the bag of clothes.

"Oh. No, I'm staying at a friend's. I still feel weird at my apartment." That was mostly true. Mentioning the weird part being the vampire-like creatures stalking her for the ancient god she wore around her neck probably wouldn't go well.

"Let me give you a ride," Julia offered.

I've never liked her, Bacchus commented.

"Uh, that's a very nice offer, but I'm actually meeting my friend at the Metro." She didn't mean to outright lie, but she really didn't want to talk to the police right now while her boyfriend had possibly been abducted—or worse—by angry Bacchae or a psychotic witch.

"Get in the car, Sera. We need to talk." Julia got out and opened the door to the backseat.

She blinked at Julia. "Am I under arrest?"

"Should you be?" The detective's eyes moved down to her scarf covering the amulet.

Sera gulped, acutely aware the woman was staring at her moving throat. "Uh…no?"

Julia let out a resigned sigh. "We know you have the amulet. You can get in the car of your own volition, which will look good for you in court, or I can formally arrest you now. Which would you prefer?" Her eyes locked onto Sera's.

Well, this puts a kink in things. I can help you run if you wish.

Sera shook her head, in response to both Bacchus and the detective. As she climbed into the backseat of the police car, Julia closed the door behind her. She scrunched up her nose as she took in her surroundings, shying away from the middle of the leather bench seat, which had a large unidentifiable stain on it. The entire back of the car smelled like rancid body odor.

Fear set in as she realized what it meant to be heading to the police station while wearing a stolen artifact.

"Where's your partner?" Sera asked from the backseat when the detective had gotten back inside, trying to focus her racing thoughts. She wiped her sweating palms on her pants.

Julia pulled the car away from the curb and started to drive. "Back at the station."

Her reply was more curt than Sera expected. When Julia's phone rang, she held it to her ear, illegal in the District, rather than use the speaker or Bluetooth. Weren't cops supposed to obey the law, too? Not needing to add to her current predicament, Sera held in a snort.

"Yes, I have her." The detective's eyes flicked up to glance at her in the rearview mirror. "She still has it."

Something in her tone and behavior chilled Sera's blood.

"I understand. We'll be there soon." Julia tossed her phone on the seat beside her.

Sera checked her phone to see if Hiro or Nora had called or messaged, but she had no new alerts. Hoping to identify where they were headed, she looked out the window. She didn't recognize whatever route they were taking.

We should make a run for it, Bacchus said.

We can't open the door from inside, she thought back, pointing to the lack of a door handle.

I'm sure we could open the door if we tried. Bacchus sent a surge of strength through Sera's body, but she shook her head.

I'm already in enough trouble. If we escape now, I'm doomed to a life on the run. She's the police, maybe she has Hiro in protective custody?

It's your call, but I don't think that's the case, Bacchus replied.

Sera glanced out the window again as they turned off the main road. Her insides clenched, and she froze. They were heading up the driveway to Lorenzo's mansion.

CHAPTER 26

Serafina

"Why are you taking me to Vicari's?" Sera asked.

Julia nodded at the guard at the gate. The guard craned his neck to look at Sera in the backseat, then pressed the button to open the gate. It swung open in front of them, and Julia drove forward.

The detective reached over to open the glove box and set her holstered gun inside. As she settled back in her seat, Sera caught sight of two red puckering marks on the woman's neck. She blinked as the realization hit her over the head like a frying pan. "Do you *work* for Vicari?"

Julia's eyes narrowed in the rearview mirror as she adjusted her scarf to cover the bite marks.

"Why?" Sera asked. The Immortal was a monster. Who would willingly work for him? Maybe it was against her will...

"We have a deal. I deliver the amulet, and he delivers immortality," Julia explained as she put the car into park outside the house. Dark figures walked toward the vehicle.

Of course. Classic selfish human wanting to live forever.

She doesn't know he can't keep his half of the bargain. I won't let them regain that ability, Bacchus reminded her as her door opened.

"He can't—" Hands reached in and yanked Sera from the vehicle before she could finish.

Bacchae surrounded her. She yelped as one of them continued to drag her through the door.

"I can walk." She pulled her arm out of the Bacchae's grasp. The Bacchae hissed at her, his fangs extended.

"Yeah, yeah. You're a scary Bacchae." Sera glared back.

Serafina, be very careful here, Bacchus's voice warned her. *You may have me, but Danae brought backup. And it looks like a lot of it. We're severely outnumbered, and we're not invincible.*

Sera bit her lip as Bacchus's fear for her trembled through her. The Bacchae gave her one last push through a doorway, causing her to stumble slightly on the rough, stone floor before catching herself.

The room they entered was a long, rectangular hall with a slanted roof, and large enough to house an entire contingent of Bacchae, it seemed. They lined the hall from front to back, and the gentle hush of speech dwindled to a menacing silence as they noticed Sera's arrival.

Not a single piece of furniture was visible, aside from a chair—which looked like it belonged in a medieval throne room—sitting atop a dais. The woman on the throne gazed at Sera from across the hall.

As Julia led her toward the dais, Sera saw the woman turned out to be a young teenage girl, maybe fourteen or fifteen years old. A girl wearing dangerously high red stilettos. Black satin gloves disappeared up the sleeves of her dark sweater.

Looks can be deceiving. Tread very, very carefully, Bacchus whispered in her mind, his voice strained.

Unfamiliar faces flanked the girl on the left, but Lorenzo stood to the girl's right side, Solomon and Alexander to his right. Anger flared up inside Sera as she saw the two creatures who had turned her life into hell.

"Did you bring it?" The girl's voice sounded as young as she looked, but her blue eyes held a sharpness far beyond what her human years had been.

Someone kicked Sera's knees from behind, causing her legs to collapse forward. She winced as her knees hit the stone floor, jarring upward to rattle her teeth.

"Your Majesty, allow me to introduce Serafina Finch, the student who discovered the amulet." Julia knelt next to Sera.

Hands unwrapped the scarf at Sera's neck, revealing the amulet. Murmurs filled the hall. The girl on the throne held up a hand, and the room returned to silence.

"Serafina, I am Danae, one of the Eternals. But I believe you already knew that." Her eyes seemed to slice through Sera's skull to see Bacchus within.

Sera only nodded, afraid of what she might say to the Bacchae who had killed her mother and tried to have Sera killed.

"You look familiar. Who did you say her mother was again?" Danae tilted her head to one side.

Lorenzo grinned, his slicked-back hair glinting in the light. "Rachel Finch, one of the witches from the cave."

Warmth flooded Sera's neck and cheeks in anger. She clenched her fists to keep herself quiet.

"Ah, yes, now I remember," Danae said with a cruel smile. "The witch who thought she could outsmart me. To be fair, I did not anticipate that the survivors would seal the cave." She leaned forward in the chair, her eyes glittering. "Witches are especially delicious."

"*Enough!*" Bacchus yelled through Sera's mouth in his deep voice before she could throw herself at Danae in fury. Bacchae in Sera's periphery took a step back in surprise. Perhaps they had not encountered the god before.

Danae leaned back into the chair, a satisfied smirk crossing her face. "I wondered what it would take to draw you out."

"Stop toying with this girl. I know what you want, and you know I'm not going to give it to you. Let's be civilized about this," Bacchus demanded, anger lashing out with his booming voice.

Danae's eyes flicked to Julia. "I owe you a thank-you, don't I?" She nodded to two of her guards, who moved forward and grasped the detective under the arms.

Struggling against their hold, Julia's eyes grew wide. "What are you doing? You promised me immortality."

"Your job was to deliver the amulet, not a human wearing the amulet. You are not worthy of an Immortal life." She waved her hand in dismissal, and the guards dragged Julia toward a group of eager-looking Bacchae. Multiple sets of fangs extended as she approached, screaming and kicking her feet out in her attempt to stop what was about to happen.

Her pulse racing and mouth as dry as a desert, Sera could only watch from where she knelt, trying not to think about what they would do to *her* next.

Three Bacchae descended upon the detective, their fangs tearing deep into the flesh at her throat and wrists. Blood spilled like wine down Julia's body from each of the gaping wounds. Within a matter of moments, her flailing lessened until she stopped moving altogether.

Sera shuddered and closed her eyes, but she couldn't rid herself of the sucking and slurping sounds as the Bacchae drained Julia of life.

"Where were we?" she heard Danae ask as if nothing had happened.

Sera opened her eyes to glare at the inhuman girl, fury rippling through her—her own and also Bacchus's.

"That was unnecessary," Bacchus spoke first.

Danae arched an eyebrow. "Was it? I promised my children food, and I always deliver on my promises."

"Do your 'children' know that you intend to destroy the human race?"

"That's hardly the truth," she said. "I intend to reveal humans' true purpose in life—to be livestock to the superior beings." Murmured assent and soft clapping rolled through the hall.

Bacchus's full-throated laughter rang out from Sera's body. The murmurs ceased as he continued to laugh. Danae narrowed her eyes.

"Have you told them? Have you told them why you haven't created any new Bacchae in over twenty years? Why Alexander was the last?" Bacchus asked when he finished laughing.

Danae's eyes flicked to someone behind Sera. Before she could react, a hand shoved a gag in Sera's mouth and tied it behind her head. She reached up to snatch it, but another pair of hands grabbed hers and roughly tied them together against her back. She winced as the rope cut into her wrists.

"I do not like what you are trying to insinuate," Danae said with a raised chin. Her eyes scanned over the assembly of Bacchae. "You all know as well as I do that the High Council is selective in our gift of immortality. Twenty years is nothing to us if it means finding the perfect candidates."

What a bunch of bullshit. Sera snorted over the gag.

Danae turned her frosty stare back to her. "Bring in our guest," she announced with a quick raise of her hand.

Hearing the creak of a door behind her, Sera struggled to turn around on her knees with her arms bound behind her back. Two Bacchae dragged a hooded figure down the middle of the hall toward her. They continued to half carry the figure past Sera and dropped him at Danae's feet, his hands tied together in front of him.

Icicles formed in Sera's veins and time seemed to slow as she recognized his sneakers. A Bacchae removed the hood from Hiro's head. He blinked a few times at the sudden return to light and adjusted his glasses with his bound hands.

No, no, no, no, no! Sera screamed inside her head, her blood pumping wildly. Hiro's eyes met hers in complete confusion and fear. Strong hands pressed down on her shoulders from behind as she tried to leap to her feet.

Danae's lips curled up into a vicious smile. "It seems we may have found the right...*motivation* to help persuade you. How fortunate he was only protected by that paltry defensive ward." She stood from the throne and crouched down in front of Hiro, her heels holding her weight as if she were as light as a feather. A small finger lifted his chin toward her face.

"I'm not sure what she sees in you. I feel as though I would be doing her a favor by getting rid of you." Danae drew a line down his face with her fingertip.

We need to do something! Sera yelled at Bacchus, her heart trying to hammer its way out of her chest.

I'm thinking, Bacchus replied, his tone harsh.

Think faster!

Danae stood again and walked in a circle around Hiro before stopping behind him, her eyes meeting Sera's once again.

"What will it be, darling? Him or the amulet?"

But she didn't wait for an answer. In the blink of an eye, Danae was at Hiro's throat, her fangs sunk deep into the side of his neck. Crimson dripped down the front of Hiro's shirt as it escaped her mouth, and his eyes opened wide from shock and pain. He struggled against Danae's hold, his hands gripping her wrist at his throat, but her unnatural strength held him in place as she drank. Her blue eyes never left Sera's.

Tears poured down Sera's face as she watched the love of her life slump to his knees, losing the fight to live. Danae pulled back before draining him, smacking her lips together as Hiro wobbled in front of her.

"Oh, now I see the attraction. His blood tastes like wedding bells, a few offspring, and a long retirement together." Danae smiled at Sera, lips red with his blood. "Give me the amulet, and he's yours. You can go back to your lives and forget any of this ever happened. I can erase the memory of it all."

She lies, Serafina, Bacchus warned her. *She won't let either one of you walk out of here alive.*

Sera knew it was true, but the thought of watching Hiro die before her was too much to bear. Hanging her head in submission, tears fell to the floor in front of her as she forfeited her life. She would rather die with him.

The girl's laughter filled her ears. Stilettos tapped on the stone floor as she approached. Danae reached forward toward the amulet with a gloved hand.

The gemstone burst into life, a beam of red light pinpointing onto Danae like a spotlight. She hissed as if in pain and drew back. A pulse of energy rushed through Sera and up to the gag, which fell from her mouth as the ties came undone.

"*No.*" Bacchus's powerful voice spoke through Sera once again. "I will not let you kill her."

Stop, Sera thought to the god, ready to die. *I'm not made for this.*

Danae's eyes glittered with hate. "As you wish."

Storming back over to Hiro, she slashed across his throat with her nails. A second later, blood spurted wildly from the wound, a gurgling sound coming from his throat. His hands reached up to try to stop the flow, but he had lost too much already. His eyes met Sera's as the light within them snuffed out.

As his lifeless body fell to the floor, a small jewelry box tumbled from his jacket pocket, rolling to a stop between them.

Life itself stopped as shock ran through Sera like a lightning bolt. She shook her head in denial. This couldn't be happening. He would stand up again, and they would walk out together. He was going to propose! They would laugh at all of the craziness after tucking their kids in for bed, then they would slowly forget any of this had ever happened as they grew old together. That was the plan. That was *their* plan.

"Isn't that just heartbreaking?" The girl bent to pick up the box, opening it for Sera to see. An antique diamond ring glittered back at her.

Her breath grew short and her vision blurry as she waited for him to stand back up, to adjust his glasses, and let her know it would be okay. That *they* would be okay. Together.

She heard Danae speaking again, but she couldn't focus on what she was saying. All she could hear was the blood pounding in her ears as she stared at the lifeless form of the man she loved on the floor. He wasn't getting up. Bile rose in her throat, burning like fire.

Hands yanked her to her feet. Sera looked up at Danae, wondering why she hadn't been killed yet. Why weren't they letting her join Hiro in death?

"As I said before, I will not let you kill this girl," Bacchus spoke through her. "If you do, I will use all of my energy to destroy the amulet."

Let them kill me, she pleaded, tears blurring her vision.

Danae smirked. The snap of the ring box shutting echoed in the hall. "That would destroy you as well."

"Yes, and also you. If my essence leaves this world, your kind will start to wither and die," Bacchus informed her.

"You're bluffing." Danae's eyes narrowed, something like fear flickering through the icy depths.

"Only one way to find out," he replied coolly.

The girl continued to stare, her eyes calculating the risk until she flicked her hand in dismissal. "Take her away until I know what to do with her."

Not yet. I can't leave him! The words wouldn't form in her mouth.

A slight movement behind Danae caught Sera's eye as she was pulled backward, a wail catching in her throat. She noticed Solomon for the first time since she had arrived. He was frowning as if he didn't approve of what was occurring. But it was because of him that most of this had happened. Digging in her heels, she tried to stop the Bacchae dragging her from the room. Fury melted the ice in her veins as she glared at Solomon, but her human strength was no match for the Bacchae holding her.

Help me! she demanded of Bacchus. *They must pay for what they've done.*

There are far too many for us to handle alone, his sad voice replied.

Then we will die in the attempt!

No, he said simply.

Sera screamed and raged at Bacchus inside her head and out as she was half dragged, half carried through the house and down several dark flights of stairs. Her yelling only ceased when she was thrown onto a cold, damp floor. She lifted her head and saw she was in a wine cellar turned jail cell.

The Bacchae who had dragged her untied her arms and legs before securing her hands and feet to the wall with heavy iron chains. They turned and left the room, closing the thick wooden door behind them. Metal slid across metal as they locked the door from the outside.

CHAPTER 27

Solomon

As the two guards dragged Serafina out of the hall, Danae whirled around, her long dark hair fanning out behind her. Solomon cleared his face of his frown as soon as she turned toward him. He certainly didn't think it had been necessary to kill the boy, especially if her goal was to get their powers restored. They could have simply wiped Hiro's and Serafina's memories clean. She had enough *influence* left for that, at the very least.

The world Danae proposed was the vampire world the humans made up in their bedtime stories. The Immortal world Solomon knew was better than that, more prestigious and godlike, and that was the way he liked it. They didn't kill unless necessary, but as their lineage got farther and farther away from the Eternals, that concept seemed to become diluted. So, why did Danae, an Eternal, want to rule over the mortals? Did she want to become a god to the humans?

After dropping the ring box in the growing pool of blood, Danae stalked back to the throne and sat, her nails gouging holes into the wood of the arms as she gripped them.

Walking to the front of the dais where Hiro's body grew cold, Lorenzo spread his hands toward the gathered Immortals and humans that made up the local Council. "Amici! Friends! Thank you for coming to today's event. I hope you found it as enjoyable as I did." His lips pulled back into a grin, displaying his fangs. The crowd tittered with agreement. "If you will follow my associate to the drawing room, we have some dessert to finish the evening."

He gestured to the opposite end of the room where a servant bowed and led the group out the double doors. When the room had cleared of the guests, Lorenzo approached Danae and knelt at her feet. "My queen, rejoice. The amulet is here." He reached toward her hand, but she snatched it away, her lip snarling in revulsion.

"That means nothing to me if we can't use it. I should never have waited. I should have seized the god as soon as he surfaced." She glared at Hiro's body. "I should have seized *him* from the very beginning. Forced Bacchus's hand."

"Alexander has graciously volunteered to administer to our…*guest* in the cellar. Come, watch. It will do you good to see the girl bleed." Lorenzo held out his hand to Danae.

A guard entered the hall, hauling a resisting Leif by the arm. Solomon held in a groan. Did this guy never get the hint?

The guard released him near the dais, and the witch's hands landed in the blood. "Your Majesty, we caught this one trying to sneak onto the premises. How would you like us to handle it?"

Danae narrowed her eyes at the witch, her pupils constricting vertically and burning red in her fury. "You have chosen a very poor time to interfere."

Leif chuckled as he stood, wiping the tacky liquid from his hands onto Hiro's sweater. Solomon had to catch himself from stepping forward to dismember the man for his disrespect at showing his face. Regardless of his opinion of her end goal, she was an Immortal and an Eternal.

"Or maybe the perfect time?" Leif grinned at her as he pushed his glasses back up his nose, his blood-spattered hands leaving a scarlet trail on his cheek.

"Do not waste my time. What do you want?"

"You have the amulet nearly within your grasp, but let me guess, you can't convince *him* of your cause." Leif cackled to himself. "I can help with that."

"I doubt that," Danae said, her eyes returning to their natural blue.

"It'll require a great sacrifice, but the spell will allow you to seal *all* of Bacchus's magic within the amulet so that he can't use his power. With or without a human companion."

Danae stared at the witch, her face expressionless. He stared back with a smirk on his lips.

After a moment, she gave a flick of her fingers. "Give us the room."

Solomon couldn't believe she was going to give the deranged human the time of day. She knew his history just as well as he did. But who was he to argue? He could feel Lorenzo fuming beside him.

Crossing the hall with the others, Solomon noted that her private bodyguard was the only one staying behind. He looked back before he closed the door. Leif sat at Danae's feet, a hand outstretched toward her.

The hair on the back of Solomon's neck stood on end as he watched a black shadowy figure rise from the center of the witch's palm, a human-shaped figurine made of mist. Danae's eyes flicked up and glared at Solomon.

He pulled the door shut.

CHAPTER 28

Serafina

Metal groaned as the bolt on the other side of the door slid back. Sera lifted her head, wincing at the stiffness. Puffy and burning, her eyes focused on the two Bacchae who entered the cell.

Alexander smirked as he crossed to a stone table in the front corner of the room. "You have no idea how long I've been wanting to do this. Although, I'd prefer your pretty blonde friend. What was her name?"

He spread out a folding case on the table, a soft tinkling coming from the items he displayed. Scalpels, wrenches, knives, and some other items she didn't recognize, including what looked like a small blowtorch.

Well, fuck.

"Nora?" He nodded. "That's right. But stupid Solomon—sullen, broody, *annoying* Solomon—had to go and take her from me. He'll make quick work of her once we're done with you, though."

A flash of anger rose through her grief. "You leave her out of this."

The other Bacchae laughed as he leaned against the wall near a skeleton she hadn't noticed before. That was to be her fate as well she was sure. Hanging on this wall forever as she rotted away to bones.

Alexander snorted. "As if." Removing a scalpel from the case, he held it up to the light, inspecting it like it was a prize.

You're going to stop this *at least, right?* She couldn't help the contempt in her thoughts as she pulled at the chains. They didn't budge. Her eyes darted around the cold cell, looking for anything she and Bacchus could use as a weapon.

Silence.

...Bacchus?

Alexander's face darkened as he stepped toward her, his pupils changing into fiery, catlike ovals. Fangs extended from his grinning mouth.

Despite Sera's efforts to suppress her fear, her chin trembled as he approached and Bacchus remained silent. She pulled back against the wall, shaking her head in terror as he closed in.

His hot, rank breath blew the hair back from her face, and she closed her eyes, praying to a god, any god, to save her.

"Let's begin."

Bacchus!

* * *

Alexander walked away from her, blood dripping off the small crescent-shaped blade he held.

Her whole body shook, from pain, exhaustion, and terror. Mostly from pain. Sera hadn't known her body could endure so much for so long, and her clothes were ripped and shredded in more places than she could count. If she was even lucid enough to count. The metallic scent she had come to know as her spilled blood filled the air and mixed with the dankness of the room.

Hold on, Serafina. You're stronger than you know.

She almost laughed, but her body wouldn't cooperate. *I don't really care what you think.*

You need to know what fate awaits humanity. Your father, Nora, everyone you know and love in life will feel this pain if she wins.

You already let her win. Anger stirred deep within her.

Neither one of us would have survived that fight. Not yet.

"Why don't you just take the necklace from her now? She's out again."

Through swollen eyelids she saw boots approach and a blurry hand lifted toward her. A burst of crimson light flared out from the amulet and the hand drew back.

"That's why," Alexander said.

I won't let them kill you, Serafina.

Go to hell.

* * *

Drip…drip…drip…

Her head was heavy, too heavy to lift, and her skull threatened to split itself open. Her arms—where were her arms? She cracked a bruised and swollen eyelid open and slid her eye to the left, the right, and then closed again. Her arms were still there, but they must have gone numb from the weight of her body pulling on the chains that bound her to the wall.

Chains. The haze that filled her head began to lift as she remembered the details of her imprisonment. But as the haze dissipated, the pain settled in, and she let out a deep, guttural groan, the links clinking together as she attempted to stir her stiff limbs.

Drip…drip…drip…

The dripping sound boomed in her head. That insidious sound had woken her to this misery. She managed to pull both eyelids up this time and looked around the cell. There was the door, bolted shut from the outside, there was the previous occupant hanging from his own set of chains, his stomach now a home to the rats infesting the cell, and over there was the work table that held the instruments of torture.

Ah. That's right. She looked down to her feet and found the puddle beneath her, collecting drops of her blood from the gashes that raked her torso and legs through her shredded clothes.

She didn't even know why they used man-made tools. They had fangs and claws that would have done the same damage, if not more when she considered the tearing. A vestige from their human days she guessed. Maybe to keep their existence secret when her remains would be found. Violent waves tore through her arms, her body shuddering as sharp pains threatened to rip her apart. Her cries echoed around the cell in cruel reply as she sank back down into a state of semi-consciousness, willing her body to die.

I'm here with you… The softest of whispers interrupted her pain-induced reverie of death. She opened her eyes again, wincing as new bruises announced their presence. She didn't see anyone. At least, no one except the skeleton. It would make sense that losing one's mind came with the territory of torture and dying. She lifted the corners of her dry, cracked lips in the direction of the skeleton in a wordless greeting.

A deep chuckle, a man's voice, filled her mind.

No, Serafina, my darling. Not him. Me. The amulet, which still hung from her neck, flashed in a brilliance of red and gold, and a warmth radiated across her body. The pain lifted for a brief moment.

"Oh, now you show yourself again," she tried to say out loud, but her swollen tongue stuck to the roof of her mouth, preventing any words from escaping.

Let me show you what we're truly capable of…

Sera was ready to die, ready to join Hiro on the other side, wherever or whatever that may be. All-encompassing grief crashed like a wave through her mind as she remembered his death. She didn't want to finish anything except dying.

I thought I told you to go to hell.

Vengeance. Hiro deserves vengeance for his death. Let me show you what we can do together.

You should have helped me before they killed him, she thought back, but too exhausted to really care anymore.

We cannot take on an entire army at once, but we can pick them off one by one. I am not all-powerful, but I'm still more powerful than

Danae. We needed to let her think she was winning to let her guard down to escape this prison. Say yes, and we will avenge your mother and Hiro together.

Dreaming. She must be dreaming. Or maybe she'd lost her mind. Had she made the entire amulet debacle up to liven up her life? It didn't make any sense that she was talking to a god in her head. An ancient god who hadn't been worshipped in thousands of years. Sera studied mythology as a career. Of course she had to be imagining his voice in her head. She could just tell the crazy lady holding her hostage that it was all a lie, hand over the pretty necklace, and be on her way.

Another pain shot through Sera's arms, reminding her that she may die before the girl ever came back. She was done, done with life, done with dying, done with pain, and done with losing her mind.

"Yes," she whispered, if only to end this last bit of torture courtesy of her mind.

Only the end didn't come. The amulet began to glow, slowly but steadily, building up to a crescendo of blinding light, forcing Sera to close her eyes and turn her head away. As the light grew brighter, a warmth permeated her body and limbs, slow, like honey pouring from a jar. The pain in her muscles relaxed, the open wounds on her torso, back, and legs closed and disappeared, and the exhaustion, which had threatened to overwhelm her, simply vanished.

Her arms lifted away from the wall, and her feet steadied beneath her. A force within her pulled hard against the chains, an unnatural strength now existing within her muscles. The chains strained, then snapped. She was free. A delirious giggle bubbled up and escaped her mouth as she lowered her arms, tingling as the blood returned.

Sera didn't let herself stop to think about what had just happened. Whether she had lost her mind and still hung on chains, or whether the god's energy coursed through her blood making her escape possible, she didn't care. She strode across to the door, broken chains still hanging from the manacles confining her wrists, confident in her walk despite the torture she endured over the last…however long it had been. She had no concept of time in the windowless cell. The lock gave way easily as she pushed against the door, and the metal barricade clattered to the stone floor.

The two men—no, *Bacchae*—who'd tortured her, turned in surprise as she faced them in the stone corridor.

Alexander.

"Hello, gentlemen." Their look of surprise and alarm was short-lived but exhilarating.

"How—" the closer Bacchae started to ask but never got to finish. Sera's hand shot out and grabbed him by the neck, her nails digging into his flesh until it all gave way and his vocal cords and esophagus ripped from his body. She stood holding his throat in her hand, staring at it in equal parts amazement and horror. Time seemed to stop as they all stood transfixed on the gore she held.

Sera slowly looked up to meet his mutilated gaze, a smile pulling her lips up. Vengeance would indeed be sweet. Falling to his knees, the Bacchae's hands reached up to feel his missing throat. Her foot met his chest, pushing him back to collapse in a heap. He may be a Bacchae with the ability to heal, but a wound like that would take anyone down for at least a few hours.

Snapping out of his shock, Alexander reached for her. Sera grabbed his arm as he lunged, and swung him around to collide with the rough stone wall, a loud crack resounding in the hall as his skull collapsed on one side. He stumbled, and she grabbed a chunk of his curly hair in her fist and slammed his head against the wall, watching his face become unrecognizable. She didn't stop until his weight dragged him down to the floor.

Sera stood above them both, watching the blood drain from their wounds. But it wasn't blood, not like a human's. It wasn't full of life and opportunity, but only death and decay, despite its resemblance. Sera knew the true terror of their existence firsthand. She couldn't possibly let them fulfill Danae's sick fantasy.

Alexander twitched slightly, and the sound of metal against stone she had become all too familiar with in her cell met her ears.

Seeing the knife belt at his side, Sera bent over him to retrieve the blade he was trying to grasp. His hand gripped her wrist as she did so, but he couldn't stop her in his weakened state. She straddled his stomach, the knife pressed against his chest.

"You're all going to die. Every last one of you. I won't stop until that's true."

Alexander coughed up black mucus as he tried to respond. Pressing down, the knife began to sink through his skin, to the muscles and ribs beneath. He trembled violently beneath her, his hands reaching up to grip her arms, but she didn't stop until the blade struck the stone beneath him and his body stopped moving. He exploded into glittering dust.

Sera turned her gaze to the other Bacchae, fear and anger resonating from his eyes, blood still pouring from his destroyed throat. Staring back at him, she put her hands on her knees and stood, letting blood drip from the knife in her hand. He raised his hands in a surrendering gesture.

The corners of her lips turned up again. "Oh, you're going to live. For now. I need someone to explain to the others what happened, don't I?"

Relief passed over his face as she wiped the bloodied blade on her torn pants.

"When I do finally kill you," she said, looking straight into his eyes, "it will be a very long and extremely painful death. You'll be my last, and I'll relish my last kill for as long as I can."

Sera stood and kicked him hard in the face which made a satisfying crunch. She walked down the hallway, leaving the confines of what had been her own personal hell. As she neared the last door at the end of the hall, the door she knew led to her freedom, her legs began to feel sluggish, her heart heavy.

"No, not yet. Please don't leave me," she said.

I will never leave you, Bacchus's voice whispered back.

The sluggishness continued as Sera opened the door and stepped out into the fresh air. Dark silhouettes of trees greeted her, but the sky lightened as the sun began its ascent from behind the distant hills. She closed her eyes and inhaled. The cool, crisp air filled and cleared her lungs.

Then her legs buckled, and she blacked out.

CHAPTER 29

Solomon

Solomon turned his head on the pillow, watching Danae's face as she slept, the dim light of evening sun peeking through the curtains. Normally, she kicked him out immediately after a few rounds of copulation, but her anger over Bacchus's threat to destroy himself and their kind had added fuel to the fire—more like inferno. It wouldn't have surprised him if they had broken the bed, or a chair, or the dresser on more than one occasion that night.

She was beautiful, that certainly couldn't be denied. But Solomon couldn't stop thinking of Nora every time Danae called him to fulfill her needs. He didn't even know why she had picked him; there were plenty of other Immortals who could satisfy her animalistic desires. Maybe she had already gone through the lot and was trying out fresh meat.

Nora. Damn, she had such a strong hold on him. He hadn't meant to develop feelings for the blonde beauty, but her charismatic personality was like an electric shock, and he was addicted to the thrill of touching the live wire. He hadn't even talked to her in almost two weeks, but he still couldn't get her out of his mind.

After rolling out of the bed as quietly as he could, he pulled on his pants. A light knock at the door made him groan internally. He looked back at Danae, who was looking at him with her cold blue eyes.

"Why are you still here?" She slipped her legs out from beneath the sheets, her feet landing on the floor without a sound. The red silk robe hanging from the headboard found its way around her shoulders.

"I—"

"I shouldn't have to remind you to leave. Don't make this mistake again." She glided over to the door and opened it.

"Your Majesty, I must regretfully inform you that the girl has escaped," the Immortal said bluntly, his life on the line with such a statement.

Solomon could see the side of Danae's face from where he stood. Her expression hadn't changed, but the hand gripping the door handle tightened. It was highly possible she would rip the handle off and use it to impale the Immortal.

"How?"

"Based on the state of the cell door and the one guard who survived, the god helped."

"Do you have anything else to tell me?"

The Immortal shook his head.

Danae's hand shot out and struck him in the gut, causing him to bend over as the air whooshed out of him. His face now level with her own, she dug her nails into the skin behind his chin, tearing through to hold his jaw like one would hold a bowling ball. If she had never played the game, Lorenzo could probably give her a few tips.

She dragged him down until he knelt in front of her, gurgling sounds coming from his throat as he stared wide-eyed at her, his hands gripping her wrist. The tips of her bloody fingers were visible inside the Immortal's mouth. "*This* is the proper position for you to address me in. I am your queen. Do you understand?"

The man tried to respond but pink, frothy bubbles dribbled out of his mouth instead. He nodded, wincing from the movement.

Danae released him, her hand covered in gore, then kicked him in the chest. The force of her kick sent him flying back into the hallway.

She turned to Solomon, her eyes blazing red with her rage, pupils constricted like a cat's. "Out."

He picked up his shoes and shirt and obeyed. The sound of wood splintering apart and slamming against the walls followed him down the hall, but he never heard her make a sound. Her Majesty's was a silent fury.

Solomon dressed quickly in the hallway, ignoring the groaning coming from the injured messenger, who was slowly crawling away. He turned and sought out Lorenzo in the mansion. His maker sat in the throne room, sitting on the throne and glaring at Hiro's cold, blue body in front of it. The ring box still lay where it had landed.

"You heard, sì?" Lorenzo asked, rapping his fingers on the arm of the chair. He didn't bother to look up when Solomon approached.

"Yes. Has a team tracked them down?"

"To the witch's house, of course. The god must think it is checkmate, but he has underestimated our queen in the past." Lorenzo finally looked at Solomon, tears rolling down his cheeks. "They killed Alexander."

* * *

Despite being excused of his duties to keep tabs on the girl and god, Solomon felt a responsibility to ensure she was, in fact, at the witch's house and being closely watched. It was partly his fault things had escalated to the point they had.

Without Alexander's incessant chatter, the drive to Capitol Hill was as silent as a grave. Glorious.

He found the newly assigned Immortals in a sedan parked in front of the house, both of them looking at cell phones rather than the house or the street. Solomon opened one of the back doors and slid in, startling the two Immortals in the front seat.

"You should have seen, heard, and smelled me coming long before now. If I see you looking at anything but your surroundings again, I'll take your eyes to Danae." Solomon didn't wait for their agreement before getting back out of the car.

His gaze lifted to the row house's door as it opened. *Nora.* She was bundled up against the chilly night air, but her naturally light blonde curls, almost white in the moonlight, poked out from beneath her hat. He leaned back against the sedan and watched her come down the front steps, unaware of his presence.

"Nora," he said quietly, trying not to scare her. She jumped anyway.

The glare she threw in his direction would make most mortal men quiver in their shoes. Solomon reveled in it. Her fiery personality called to him like a moth to a flame. Only he didn't mind the burn.

"If you think you can scare me into helping you in any way, you're sorely mistaken."

She spoke the truth. He couldn't smell an ounce of fear coming from her, only anger and a dash of excitement.

"I'm not here to scare you. I didn't know you'd be here."

She harrumphed at him and walked toward her car, parked at the end of the street. Disappointment flashed across her face for a brief moment. Despite everything that had happened, Solomon could tell she still desired him. He fell into step next to her.

"I'm sorry about what happened. I don't agree with all of it." He didn't have to lie to her anymore.

"But you agree with some of it by that statement." Her reply was as frosty as the air, but at least she was talking to him.

He shrugged. "It's my job to follow orders."

"Well, your *orders* almost got my best friend killed." She stopped walking and looked up at him, eyes narrowed. He could see the green in them despite the limited light of the streetlamps. "What did you do to Sera? She hasn't woken up yet."

Solomon considered his words carefully, not sure how much she knew at this point. "I wasn't involved in anything that happened to her."

Nora rolled her eyes and kept walking. "Why are you here? Are you going to kill her to get to the amulet?" She pressed the button on her keys to unlock the door of her coupe as she reached it. "Good luck with that."

"I'm not going to kill her," he said, hoping he spoke the truth. Following her around to the driver's side door, he held it open while she climbed in.

"But you might try." Her eyes met his as she reached for the interior handle. "I'm really disappointed in you." She pulled the door shut.

Solomon watched as she drove away, his heart and mind conflicted in a way he had never experienced before. Her last words had driven an ice pick through to his core. He wanted to be the kind of man to make Nora proud but to go against his maker would be a fatal mistake. Possibly for both of them.

CHAPTER 30

Serafina

"I think she's waking up."

Faint voices floated around her and warm hands, human hands, touched her arm. Sera shot straight up and looked around. She was in a bed, and two women looked at her anxiously. It took a few tense moments for her to recognize Nora and Renee.

"What happened?" Sera asked, her voice cracking.

"You tell us. Two days ago you walked in the house covered in blood, clothes in shreds, but no injuries that I could see. You didn't say a word and locked yourself in this room. We finally got the door open, but you've been mostly asleep ever since. Not even a peep from Bacchus. We were about to take you to the hospital…" Nora's voice trailed off.

"The only reason you're not already is because I was able to magically diagnose you, and everything seemed okay. Physically." Renee's furrowed brows said she may have thought otherwise.

Closing her eyes, agony flooded through Sera as the memories surfaced, her stomach clenching. So, she hadn't lost her mind after all.

Hiro…

"What—" Nora started to ask.

"I need to be alone."

"No way, you need to explain what happened. Whose blood is that? Where were you?"

Sera opened her eyes, letting tears slide down her cheeks. "Please, I just need a little time. I'll tell you everything, I promise. But I need to be alone right now."

Nora stayed put for another moment, looking at her with a worried expression, before nodding. She kissed Sera's forehead and walked to the door.

"If you don't come out by this evening, I'm coming back in," Nora said as she closed the door behind her and Renee.

Sera rolled over onto her side and curled into a fetal position. Repressed sobs threatened to tear her body apart as she gave in and let the full pain of his death hit her over and over again. Grief ripped through her, anguished tears wetting the pillow beneath her cheek.

"Why did you let him die?" she asked, her voice cracking.

Ah, my darling, even I am not powerful enough to have protected both you and him from that many Bacchae, not in my current form, Bacchus replied in her head. *You would have died from exhaustion even in the unlikely event I had succeeded. I made a choice to protect you.*

"I would've rather died by his side."

I know. Heat rushed through her body, replacing her grief with the comforting buzz she got after a few glasses of wine. Her anger dissolved as invisible arms wrapped themselves around her in an ethereal embrace. Visions of revenge for her mom's and Hiro's deaths played in her mind.

"I wanted to at least try to save him," she said, wiping her face with the sheets.

You both would have died, and I would have either died as well or been captured and used to bring about the destruction of the human race. Bacchus's tone was blunt.

"*Why* did you let them do that to me?" Nausea rolled through her like a wave at the memories, bile threatening to rise.

You're not going to like my answer.

"Nothing new there."

I needed you to know what we are up against. The cruelty my creations are capable of inflicting upon humankind. Up until now, you've only seen the fun side to working with a god—the supernatural strength and magic. To truly be ready for this path, you needed to know what despair awaited the world.

His brutal response sucked the air from her lungs and she gasped for breath. "You don't think I felt despair when I watched Hiro die? Or when I learned my mom was killed by that monster?"

And yet, his response made sense to her. Sera propped herself up into a sitting position, leaning back against the headboard. The horror she experienced in that cell would be inflicted on all humankind if Danae got her way, and there was no way she could let that happen. Letting out a deep sigh, she rubbed her face and accepted his words as truth.

"Okay, so we lived. And we escaped. Now, she needs to die."

She gripped the sheets tightly in her fists, her body tensing, as she thought about the loss of her mother and Hiro and all that her future would no longer hold because of that girl. She had long since come to terms with a future without her mom, but her body flushed with anger at the idea of not getting to live out the years she had envisioned with Hiro. Danae had stolen not only Hiro's life, but also their life together and their future children. Determined to not let his death be in vain, she would do whatever was needed to stop the bitch from succeeding.

An image of Hiro's dead body flashed before Sera's eyes, blood pouring from his gaping throat. She thrust the heels of her hands into her eyes as sobs erupted from her once again.

"I want you to numb me, remove my feelings, whatever. I don't want to feel this pain anymore," she choked out, tears soaking the sheet beneath her hands.

Feeling is what makes you human. His sympathy was palpable.

"I don't care. This police are going to look for him eventually, and I can't focus with this constantly lingering over me and threatening to crush me. You have to make it stop. I'm not strong enough. Please. *Please.*" Her lip quivered as she pleaded with him.

I'm not in favor of this...

But a moment later, the tears ceased to spill, her heart returned to its normal pace, and she could breathe. Really breathe. Serenity settled around her shoulders like a warm blanket. She relaxed her grip on the sheet, relishing the lack of emotion.

"Okay, where do we start?"

We start with you getting dressed.

Sera pushed herself off the bed, her legs swaying beneath her for a moment before she caught herself. Two days of sleep and a night of torture before that had done a number on her muscles. She would need to get food in her soon if she was going to plot out the murder of an evil Bacchae witch.

A bag of her clothes lay at the foot of the bed. Nora must have gotten some of her things while Sera was comatose. She threw on some clean clothes, grabbed the bag, and headed downstairs to the kitchen.

Renee and Nora sat at the small kitchen table, talking softly over their steaming cups. They fell silent when she walked in. She poured herself a cup of coffee.

I'll be here if you need me, Bacchus whispered in her mind.

Sera took a deep breath and released it before turning back to face them.

"Hiro's dead," she said bluntly. There was no way to sugarcoat it. She watched their faces move through confusion then shock as the realization of her words struck home.

She told them everything. From Hiro's capture and death to Danae's sadistic plot to take over the world. It came out monotone, without feeling, and Sera was grateful.

"That's just brutal," Nora said. Pain and anger flashed in her eyes as she must have thought about what Sera had witnessed. "Are you okay, babe? For real?"

Sera took a few sips of coffee before answering. "I don't know. Honestly. Physically, yes. I slept off the exhaustion that came from Bacchus's power to help us escape. But emotionally?" Sera shook her head. "I'm going after Danae. *We* are going after Danae." She tapped the amulet to indicate Bacchus.

Nora's mouth dropped open. "Sera, you can't possibly be thinking of that after what she did to you and to Hiro."

"She's right. I know that was Bacchus's original plan, but she's proven herself ruthless time and time again," Renee said in a firm tone. "It's not a game, and it is far too dangerous, even with a god's help."

"She's going to continue to come after me as long as I have the amulet," Sera said.

"Then you need to ask Bacchus to find someone else." Nora narrowed her eyes as she glanced at the amulet around Sera's neck.

"*No.*" Sera pushed herself off of the counter. "I appreciate you looking out for me, I really do. But I'm tired of being weak. I'm tired of letting things happen to me and not standing up for myself. I'm tired of the bad guys getting away with shit. Something inside of me broke watching Hiro die. And knowing that my mom died at the hands of this monster?" She shook her head. "I am going after Danae, and I'm going to kill her."

The note of finality in her voice hung in the air.

May I? Bacchus asked.

She silently assented, and the tingling sensation she had come to know as Bacchus controlling her body washed over her.

"Ladies," Bacchus's booming voice spoke through her mouth. "You are correct that it will be dangerous, very dangerous, for both Serafina and myself. But Serafina is strong and has talents I don't think she, herself, knows she possesses."

Sera raised an eyebrow at that, wondering what the god saw in her that she didn't.

"I would not lead Serafina on this quest if I did not think she was capable. But I have more good news. There are others like me out there. Other gods who have encased their energies within a sacred object. And other humans who have been chosen to wield that power."

All three jaws hit the floor.

Renee composed herself first. "Well, that certainly changes things. Why didn't you tell us this before?"

No shit. Seriously, Bacchus.

Sera's shoulders shrugged. "I didn't want to trouble any others if we didn't need their assistance. But at this point we should acquire all the help we can get. Do you have any wine? I'm getting quite thirsty."

"We're not getting drunk." Sera took control of her body back. "We need to plan. But first and foremost, I need to head home, take a shower, and get some of my things." She set the empty coffee cup down on the counter.

"I'll drive you," Nora said as she stood.

"Come back here tonight," Renee said. "It's still the safest place for you to be."

* * *

The drive back to her building was silent. Sera would talk when she was ready, and her best friend seemed to know it. When they parked, Nora gripped Sera's hand in hers and gave it a squeeze.

"Are you going to head home?" Sera asked after they entered the apartment.

Nora shook her head emphatically. "There's no way in hell I'm leaving you alone after what just happened. I'll be right here." She plopped down on the couch and flipped on the TV.

Sera's cheeks warmed as she regarded her best friend, loving her protective nature, even though Sera also had the protection of a god. She trudged down the short hall to her room.

A few minutes later, she stepped into the steaming shower, her clothes a tattered pile on the bathroom floor. The nearly scalding water fell over her hair and down her body, washing away the final traces of the night Hiro died. She closed her eyes and breathed in the sauna-like air.

Life had changed in the blink of an eye. Sera hadn't been fully convinced she was cut out for avenging her mother's death, which had happened so long ago. The truth didn't fuel her with the anger she would expect she'd need to purposefully take another's life, even a Bacchae's life. That is until she met Danae and saw the evil within those cruel blue eyes as she took Hiro away forever. Now, she couldn't imagine doing anything else with her life. How could she possibly go back to a "normal" life?

Sera no longer saw a happy, love-filled future ahead of her. Instead, the path was dark, bleak, and unknown. The only thing she could see for sure was killing Danae. After that...

Stepping out of the shower, she wrapped up in a towel and rubbed the condensation off of the mirror in front of her. Unfamiliar cold grey eyes stared back at her. The hardness she saw within them surprised her, but as she stared back, her resolve strengthened. She could do this.

After getting dressed, Sera packed her duffel bag full of clothes and left her bedroom behind her.

HER
MAJESTY'S
FURY

IMMORTAL RELICS: BOOK 2

CHAPTER 1

Serafina

A s she turned to close her bedroom door behind her, a flash of red and blue caught Sera's eye. She crossed the room, choking back a sob as she grabbed the Spiderman comic from her bedside table. The wall-crawler superhero was Hiro's favorite, and her boyfriend had saved the newest release to enjoy when he got back from Seattle. She had almost forgotten it.

Guilt gripped at Sera's raw throat, making it difficult to breathe. She held the book to her chest as tears spilled down her cheeks once again. Because of her, he would never have the chance to know what happened next to Peter Parker. A silly thought, perhaps, but after seeing his body growing cold on the floor at Danae's feet? Not so much.

We need to kill her, Bacchus. Fast, she thought to the god as she tucked the comic inside the duffel bag she carried.

We will. The pinecone-shaped amulet pulsed as Bacchus replied. A moment later Sera's tears ceased when his calming energy took hold. But the guilt remained.

Just over a week ago, Sera had wondered how she would ever get used to an ancient god speaking in her mind. A god who lived in an amulet around her neck. An amulet considered stolen from a national museum and hunted by vampire-like creatures called Bacchae. Minor details.

Now she couldn't imagine getting through this ordeal without his help, even if he did let Danae's Bacchae followers torture her so she would know firsthand what future was in store for humans if Danae won. It wasn't pretty. She understood his reasoning and forgave him… mostly, but she didn't have to like it. Soon she would let the pain in; soon she would need it to drive her plan for vengeance to fruition. But she wasn't ready for that. Not yet, but soon.

A knock at her apartment door stopped Sera as she walked back toward the living room where her best friend Nora waited to drive them back to the safe house. The hairs on the back of her neck stood on end and a chill ran up her spine.

Surely Danae's Bacchae guards hadn't come to attack her already. And besides, they wouldn't knock. Right? She took her chances, and a deep breath, confident that they couldn't come in unless she invited them inside. Or at least semi-confident.

You are correct, Bacchus said, amusement in his tone.

"I need your help," Ms. Patton said when Sera opened the door. Her next-door neighbor's normally grim expression shaped her wrinkled face, but her eyes had an odd glossiness to them.

"Are you okay?" Sera could count the number of times Ms. Patton had spoken more than two words to her on one hand, usually after Sera had pissed her off somehow.

"Please. I need help in my apartment," the woman said and turned away. She hobbled toward her own door down the narrow hall, beckoning to Sera with a hand. Blood stained the back of the woman's shirt as it dripped from a gash in the back of her head.

Sera gasped.

Serafina, wait—

Without a second thought, she dropped her duffel bag and rushed out of her apartment, hoping to catch Ms. Patton if she fell. The woman was obviously hurt and needed to go to the hospital. Sera had known it was only a matter of time before the old woman injured herself; she just hadn't realized she would be the one to help her.

Strong arms wrapped around Sera from behind, cinching her arms to her sides. Her heart leaped to her throat, and the memory of Hiro doing the same thing at the mall only a few weeks prior flashed through her mind. Only this was most definitely not Hiro.

As she turned her head to face her attacker, a stranger stood where Hiro once had. An unknown man—no, a Bacchae—with long, greasy black hair and ghostly white skin grinned at her with fangs extended. The scent of his unwashed hair, thick with cigarette smoke, wafted beneath her nose, and bile roiled in her stomach. She swallowed hard.

"Happy to see me?" the creature asked, his grip tightening. Three other Bacchae appeared out of the shadowy stairwell next to Sera's door, their irises red and pupils dilated like cats'.

Shit, Sera thought as dismay settled in the pit of her stomach.

Thanks for reading!
Please consider adding a short review on Amazon and Goodreads
and let me know what you thought.

I love to get to know my readers. You can reach me on Facebook, Instagram, or Twitter **@stephaniemirro**. Sign up for my mailing list to get new release information, special deals, giveaways, become a part of my ARC team, and more. I look forward to hearing from you!

www.stephaniemirro.com

ACKNOWLEDGEMENTS

This book started as a dream while I was in college, over fifteen years ago now, and it's hard to put into words just how amazing it feels to *finally* put this story out into the world. The people in my life who helped turn my dream into a reality deserve so much more than I can offer in return, but I'll start with this.

To my parents, who always pushed me to follow my dreams no matter how difficult, *thank you*. To my husband, who did more than his fair share of chores and parenting while I wrote, edited, and marketed, *thank you*. To my kids, who tried their hardest to let me work even though work is a foreign concept to them still, *thank you*.

To my editors, Natasha Raulerson and Lisa Gilliam; my critique partners, authors Savannah J. Goins and V.M. Darkangelo; and all the members of my local writing group, the Hourlings, who provided invaluable guidance, support, and critique, *thank you*.

To my mentor, author Martin Wilsey, and my new friend, author C.J. Ellisson, for helping me with the final magic touches, *thank you*.

To Hampton Lamoureux of TS95 Studios, who managed to create a cover that literally took my breath away, *thank you*. To lauralidesigns on Etsy, who allowed us to use an image of one of her items for the pinecone-shaped amulet, *thank you*.

To all my family and friends, who showed their support in so many ways—asking how writing was going, becoming Patrons on Patreon, and following me on all things social media—*thank you*.

To you, my dear reader, for picking up this book and making it through to the end, *thank you*.

I couldn't have done it without each and every one of you.

ABOUT THE AUTHOR

Stephanie Mirro's lifetime love of ancient mythology led to her majoring in the Classics in college, which wasn't quite as much fun as writing her own mythology stories as she did growing up. But that education, combined with an overactive imagination, being an active fantasy reader, and having a vampire obsession, resulted in the *Immortal Relics* series.

Born and raised in Southern Arizona, Stephanie now resides in Northern Virginia with her husband, two kids, and two furbabies. This thing called "seasons" is still magical.